THE TIGER-HEADED HORSEMAN

THE TIGER-HEADED HORSEMAN

The first book in the Nomadic Sky series

Chris Walker

Book Guild Publishing
Sussex, England

First published in Great Britain in 2013 by
The Book Guild Ltd
The Werks
45 Church Road
Hove, BN3 2BE

Typesetting in Fiesole by
Norman Tilley Graphics Ltd, Northampton

Printed and bound in Great Britain by
CPI Group (UK) Ltd, Croydon, CRO 4YY

A catalogue record for this book is available from
The British Library.

ISBN 978 1 84624 937 2

To Grace, Sam and Alice.

Acknowledgements

Sarah, Grace and Hugh; Peter and Nicola Bell; Bridget and Richard Storrie; Year 6 of 2013 at Saltwood Primary School and Mrs Selby; Enkh-Undram Bayartogtokh; employees of Oyu Tolgoi and Rio Tinto Mongolia; Glenn Bowman and Elizabeth Cowie; Peter Clayton; Jill and Alan North; Chaucer; Book Guild Publishing; Grant and Annalisa Hopkins; Pascale and Bruno Rodriguez; Mum and Dad; Rebecca and Ewen Angus; my very wonderful Granny.

Special thanks to Sharon Whyte for her cover design.

Prologue

As Chinggis Khaan rode out to save his friends, he felt uneasy. It wasn't that he had ventured out of his camp alone without his private guard. Something more sinister was afoot. He could sense it in the chill air shrouding him as he galloped across the Steppe. Ahead of him lay a barren herder encampment. Four round thickly-felted tents – gers – stood stiffly against the freezing wind. A dozen Mongolian ponies sheltered in their wake, anxiously seeking out any protection from the storm. Mountains rose up around the camp keeping a keen watch over the petrified site. Chinggis called out but only the sub-zero weather answered. The wind snapped at his enormous sheep-skin coat and he pulled his fox-fur hat down tight over his ears. It may have been August but the winter of 1227 remained stuck fast across the southern Gobi Desert. Chinggis's shaman advisors had been sure it portended evil but he had ignored them. He was, after all, the Mongol emperor; ruler of the largest empire ever known to mankind. His lands stretched from what we now know as the Pacific to the Mediterranean; he wasn't going to be afraid of a bit of cold weather. Jumping from his steed, he raced to the largest ger. A dusting of snow betrayed the otherwise steely blue sky. There was no sign of his friend's insignia but he was too frantic to notice such details.

Throwing open the wooden door of the ger, Chinggis peered into its murky interior. There was no sound from within. He stepped over the threshold and closed the door behind him. As

1

his eyes grew accustomed to the gloom, he made out shapes and shadows standing around the walls but noticed too late the dozen shards of sparkling steel that were now suddenly thrust in unison towards him. The moment he drew his sabre, his life departed him. A dozen foreign swords continued to stab and slash at him repeatedly as his eyes began to freeze. Given Chinggis's reputation, his enemies wanted to make sure he was well and truly dead.

During his lifetime, Chinggis Khaan had never been a man who had ever tired of fighting. It had been expected of him. It was what emperors did. However, since his assassination that summer long ago, he had been trapped in a steely afterlife; incarcerated, seemingly for eternity, by his evil cousin Khad. It was Chinggis's blood relative who, jealous of his cousin, had orchestrated his murder. For his part the malevolent Khad had, upon his own earthly demise, joined his cousin in the same frozen eternal state of limbo. The pair had continued to fight one another each day for almost eight hundred years and Chinggis was wearying of it. There was never any question about him losing the fight; sometimes he even appeared to enjoy it. Secretly, though, all he really wanted was a truce, followed by a hot bath, a generous massage and a nice glass of chilled, fermented yaks' milk. Khad, though, would never yield.

Khad despised Chinggis. The younger cousin hated the fact that, despite everything, people still adored Chinggis. Although he had brought about the downfall of Chinggis's empire and created his own, he was still neither respected nor loved. To make matters worse, being forced to confront his cousin every day in the afterlife reminded Khad why it was that Chinggis was more popular. Khad could not accept this fate and vowed to vanquish him for ever. He would never give up. His hatred was deeply rooted and losing was not an option. The more he saw of Chinggis, the deeper his rage took hold. Khad would never win,

2

could never win. Chinggis was as supremely strong as Khad was weak; as virile and masculine as Khad was churlish and self-important. The cousins were locked in immortal, eternal combat.

Had Khad simply been willing to sit down and talk with his cousin, each could have agreed to differ and moved to their ultimate sanctuary. Chinggis would gladly have helped Khad by calling a truce but his cousin would not listen. Khad failed to understand that peace was the only way for them both to escape the indeterminate state in which they had been trapped for centuries. Both longed to escape their limbo but Khad's rage would not allow him to see how easy it would be to move on. Neither did he appreciate that their final destinations would be in very different places.

1

Nineteen-year-old Tengis frequently thought about Chinggis Khaan and his evil cousin Khad. They had both played out their eternal struggle in Tengis's dream world every night since he had been born. It was Tengis's private joy. The two most famous, most infamous men Tengis had ever read about were somehow linked to him. It was only as he grew older that Tengis began to question why.

Tengis shook the recurring dream from his mind and crept out of bed. Stretching to his full five foot ten inches, Tengis stood proudly in front of the mirror and stared at the moonlit reflection facing him.

'You're the man,' he said, pulling his stomach muscles taut and adopting a weightlifter pose. He didn't have much muscle but that didn't stop him loving his appearance. He looked deep into the eyes that stared back at him and knew without any shadow of a doubt that he was Chinggis Khaan. He had to be. It all made sense.

Tengis was taller than any of the other boys his age. He could beat anyone in a fight – mostly by foul means. He could debate more directly, if less diplomatically, than anybody else. He had always been top of his class in every subject. He looked just like the pictures and statues that lined the city avenues . . . or so his mother said. She'd even given him the same surname. He had an unhealthy level of ambition of which everybody was wary. More importantly, his dreams confirmed it. Night after night, between glimpses of the fighting cousins, Tengis dreamed about leading armies across the wide-open Steppe that ran through the heart of Ongolium. He dreamed of taking his armies towards victory through the mountains; about frenetic bloody battles where he was always the victor; about ruling the vastest empire the earth would ever know; about being revered and loved by a billion loyal and fearful subjects. There was also the voice that whispered to him.

Tengis had been born in the centre of the bustling disjointed Baatarulaan (formerly known as Ulaanbaatar), capital city of Ongolium (the country that had once been known as Mongolia). His father had joined the army and set forth on a very important campaign when Tengis had still been a youngster, or so his mother had said. Tengis was still waiting for his father's return fourteen years later and couldn't understand what was keeping him away. As far as he was aware, Ongolium hadn't quarrelled with any other country since the infamous sacking of Baatarulaan eight centuries previously. Why Ongolium even needed an army was beyond Tengis, although he knew it was only proper that it had one. Ongolium had resolutely determined its own course and Outsiders were not wanted in any shape or form.

The voice that whispered was what really confirmed his belief. Before any dream got underway, and after every enemy had been vanquished, the voice of a man spoke quietly to him. It told him to look for his greatness; to remember who he was; to forget all others and be true to himself. Despite being born several hundred years after Chinggis had died, Tengis had all the proof he needed. He was the true Mongol emperor. He just couldn't quite figure out how this could be possible. What Tengis did know was that he was Chinggis and that it surely meant change was coming; though he didn't know exactly what it would look like.

As far as Tengis was concerned, Ongolium had only one truly famous son and one infamous legend.

Chinggis Khaan was that son, although he was now widely known as Genghis Khan much to the chagrin of purist historians. Chinggis had lived at the turn of the thirteenth century and during his sixty-six long years had successfully built an empire stretching from the Strait of Anian, between Asia and North America, to Italy, and from the Arctic Circle to Siam. At the centre of Chinggis's domain was his beloved Mongolia: the land of the eternal blue sky; land of the horse; land of his fathers and their fathers and their fathers and so forth. From Mongolia he ruled his empire with ruthless determination. Key to his success had been the natural abundance of horses in his homeland and the innate ability of his countrymen as expert horsemen. He established the largest, most highly skilled and utterly fearsome cavalry to gallop the globe. As Chinggis was wont to say: 'Spare the horse, spare the enemy!' He killed bountifully and showed mercy sparingly but, contrary to many history books, he wasn't all about anger and tempestuousness. He was one of the very first people to see the vast benefits that could be found if one embraced cultural and religious diversity. He allowed his subjects to worship who, or what, they chose and to continue the traditions of their choice so long as they paid him a tax for the privilege. Indeed, Chinggis and his people revelled in the new-found wealth of knowledge that their exploits uncovered. Theirs was a civilisation that surpassed all that had gone before in terms of intellectual accomplishment and was responsible for inventing many of the aspects of life we take for granted today.

The thick fur hats that kept Chinggis's warriors warm on the Steppe were later adapted into portable food stores, with horsemen keeping their meats warm for longer atop their bonces. This invention was later also adapted to keep infused hot water warm. Chinggis's excellent archers all had second jobs as messengers. They would wrap notes and military orders around their arrows and fire them to a post some 200 metres away, where another archer would do likewise until the desired recipient was reached. Chinggis was responsible for inventing many modern sports as well. After beheading his enemies, his men would often throw the vanquished heads to one another and endeavour to wrestle one another to reach a distant line – rugby was born in Mongolia long before any snotty schoolboy picked up a football. When his army were bored of tossing the heads to one another, or when the heads started to go a bit mangy, the soldiers would pitch them to a chosen soldier with a big stick who would try and hit it as high as he could into the air. In one fell swoop baseball, rounders, cricket and, ultimately, racquet sports came about. Eyeballs became golf balls. Teeth became dice.

Fearsome, intelligent warriors they may have been, but Chinggis and his fellows also knew how best to kick up their heels at the end of each campaign. They were often to be seen singing boisterously at the end of battle about the good old days when things were in order, goats were plentiful and there was enough peace and quiet to enjoy a good book with a cup of boiling hot water infused by herbs. It was a delicately balanced dictatorship with a faint aroma of jasmine, but it worked. No one had managed to come anywhere near achieving this feat during the intervening centuries. Mongolia cradled the world in its hands and nurtured its billion or so subjects. Peace held throughout and although there were those who were jealous of Chinggis and did their best to deride him, most people loved him and lived in harmony and happiness.

Chinggis only kept counsel with his three closest allies. His army general Bold ruled the western empire from Italy to Kazakhstan. His childhood friend Khasar ruled the southern

Asian region covering China and the spice routes. The northern reaches covering Russia were the domain of his young cousin Khad. Chinggis lived in his beloved Ulaanbaatar in the heart of Mongolia, a city overflowing with tradition, learning and virtue. He had been so forthrightly downright aggressive and angry with those he had encountered as he built his empire that they remained in fear and awe of him for years afterwards. As a result, he could rest happily in his city and idle away his days having fun with his beloved Tsara, a princess from eastern Europe whom he had met in a bar in Budapest. These were happy days for Chinggis, though he tried not to be smug.

Khad, however, wasn't happy; he wasn't happy at all. He didn't like the cold and as a keen gardener Siberia proved useless to him. He was jealous of Bold and Khasar who retained warm, fertile and rich lands. Khad was also an ambitious young man, very ambitious. Full of mischief he arranged a supper with Bold and Khasar under the guise of discussing a surprise birthday present for Chinggis. Shortly after the onion soup had been served he had his friends beheaded. Rather than own up to his wrongdoing he ran to Chinggis declaring that he had uncovered a vile plot to ambush and murder his closest friends as they slept in camp. Khad knew that such news would enrage Chinggis. He knew his cousin would undoubtedly depart immediately to try and save his friends. Khad knew Chinggis would act rashly and set off to wreak revenge without waiting for support from his personal bodyguards. The moment Chinggis had entered Bold and Khasar's ger he was slain instantly. So came to an end the world's greatest emperor, hastily undone by a greedy cousin who didn't like the cold.

2

The reign of Khad had been very different from his cousin's. He wrote complicated processes and procedures and governed by bureaucracy. He also involved himself in complex negotiations with surrounding countries whereby he sold off vast swathes of the Mongol empire. In return, Khad received vast riches and an eternally guaranteed assurance that none of the neighbouring countries would ever again set foot in Mongolia. He assured them that if they broke this accord then the angry spirit of his beloved Chinggis would rise and the empire would be bloodily reborn. This had proved more than enough warning. Blood-letting had always tended to remain long in the cultural psyche and this warning, which was no different, came to be known by Outsiders as the 'Legend of Khad'.

Retreating to Chinggis's beloved capital city, Khad quickly made his mark. So resentful was Khad at having had to spend several years catching colds in the northern territories his cousin had given him that he endeavoured to turn upside down everything that Chinggis had fought so hard to establish. He changed the name of both city and country: Baatarulaan and Ongolium were thus born. Rather than the music, art and democracy that had been hallmarks of Chinggis's reign Khad promoted gambling, prostitution, greed and all other manner of vice. Those loyal to Chinggis were forced into hard labour or expelled from the new republic. Those who had lived in fear of Chinggis, and there were many, flocked to Khad's side and spoke in the honeyed voices he had longed to hear. A large police presence was established with a primary objective of making people enjoy themselves. They were called the 'Fun Brigade'. Dressed in long red cloaks, they used big sticks to encourage people to have fun. Khad believed that if people were having fun they would remain loyal, even if this fun was forced on them upon pain of death. The people were fickle enough to embrace this forced fun and it enjoyed enormous success when it was instigated. Khad also established a very large walled vegetable allotment but he didn't tell anyone about it. In it he grew marrows, pumpkins, turnips and a wide variety of melons.

The neighbouring countries remembered and recounted the 'Legend of Khad'. However, as the centuries passed and Khad's new kind of cultural identity seeped deep into the psyche of the people, few if any of the neighbouring countries wanted to communicate with Ongolium, let alone set foot there. The Ongolians believed they were special and referred to themselves as the 'Chosen Million', never more, never less. To Outsiders, the Ongolians were an example of everything that is wrong with humanity. By the time Tengis was born the world had mostly forgotten about his country and Ongolium had mostly forgotten about the rest of the world. It was an equilibrium that worked for all parties concerned. The Ongolian legend remained and its most devout followers did their best to erase the memory of its greatest son.

'How's my little emperor,' said Mrs Khaan as she admired her son preening himself in the mirror. She had always thought of him as an emperor and, despite his encroaching manhood, still treated him as an infant.

'Morning, Mother,' replied an embarrassed Tengis. He hated being mothered but was too lazy to do anything for himself. 'What's for breakfast?'

'Whatever my little soldier wants,' said his mother. She made her way over to him and tried to pinch his cheeks.

'Get off, Mum!' shouted Tengis. 'You're so . . . embarrassing. I'm nineteen now, almost a man.'

'I know,' said Mrs Khaan. 'I'm so proud of my little Tengis.'

She made to embrace her son. He stormed out of his bedroom and locked himself in the bathroom. 'Sausages!' he shouted through the closed door.

Mrs Khaan smiled dreamily and made her way to the kitchen. Her son was growing up far faster than she would ever have allowed herself to believe. Still, he did like sausages and that was something. Mrs Khaan walked into the garden and pulled a string of five sausages out of a box. It was late January and the outdoor temperature never rose above freezing before mid-April. Winter was Mrs Khaan's favourite season because she was able to keep fresh food fresh longer and prepare too much too often for her son. She wanted to see him nice and round – just like Chinggis had been in his later days after the yakburgers had got hold of him and he'd taken to wearing one-piece fur suits and crooning.

Mrs Khaan – 'Choogi' to her friends – had always secretly been a big fan of Chinggis, even though she knew this was a dangerous pastime. Since the time of Khad the cult of Chinggism had been all but outlawed. She had a copy of every poster that had ever been printed of him. She had mugs where his cheeky face smiled into her coffee. Every bill she paid or letter she wrote was done so with a pen bearing Chinggis's name. She had a small room in her small ground-floor apartment set aside for Chinggis. She served up Chinggis porridge on particularly cold mornings and heaped platefuls of Chinggis-branded ice cream in front of Tengis on balmy summer nights. She called her larder her Chinggiserator. She wore colourful Chinggis pyjamas to bed and equally exuberant Chinggis gowns to work. She worked in the Chinggis post office where she wore a Chinggis-branded helmet and facemask and adorned brown leather Chinggis gloves. She was a Chinggis messenger. She manned, or rather womanned, post 3276a and caught arrows from post 3277a as they sped out of Baatarulaan.

Most of Mrs Khaan's friends were Khadists. They would poke fun at her and say she was old school but Mrs Khaan didn't care. She loved her Chinggis, she did. So did many other Ongolians. Chinggis and Khad were big business. Most businesses were called Chinggis this or Chinggis that. Those that weren't called Chinggis were called Khad this or Khad that. For every factory making Chinggis golf clubs (complete with eyeball motif) there was a Khad factory doing likewise. It forged an unhealthy consumer competition, although the resulting angry capitalist tribalism helped the Fun Brigade keep the peace. Although Chinggis had been a very bad word during the time of Khad, recent centuries had seen him re-emerge as a viable contender to the self-anointed usurper. It was seen as a guerrilla brand whereas Khad was seen as the public service staple.

Choogi had been unfortunate during her life but liked to think that overall she had done quite well. She was annoyingly forgettable. Annoyingly, because she was just so nice to everybody and always thought the best of everyone and every situation, but she was simply one of those people whose name and face would evaporate as she left the room. Everyone could remember there was someone who was much lovelier and had a bigger heart than anyone else; they just couldn't remember exactly who that was. Born without much, Choogi had pursued and fallen in love with a junior bureaucrat who worked for the Fun Brigade in an administrative capacity. Although his job might have implied fun, Batbold was anything but. He took his role very seriously. He was in charge of procuring the large pieces of wood that the Fun Brigade used to 'encourage' fun among the good people of Baatarulaan. In his view, all other people were revolting and he didn't like revolution, even if it amounted to little more than a heated discussion in the media about what length fur should be worn this season.

It had taken more than a little persuasion for him to even agree to meet Choogi. Procuring large knobbly pieces of wood was a growing and important business. When Choogi suggest they move in together it had taken him weeks to calculate the extent to which cohabitation would affect his efficiency and effectiveness. When marriage was mooted, the computer said 'no'. Choogi resigned herself to living in sin, which was after all very much the rage in Baatarulaan (as was anything remotely related to sin). The Khaan–Khaant household (for those were their names) was not a happy one but it worked. It worked well, really well. Barely a moment, morsel or movement were wasted, so robust were Batbold's calculations.

Choogi had been a free-spirited young woman when she met Batbold; after six months living under the same roof she seemed to barely register with him anymore. Yet Choogi loved Batbold and she knew from all the books she had read that love conquered all. She hadn't realised that love was a two-way arrangement or, if she had, she ignored it. Her Batbold was her man. Nevertheless, the headiness of bedtime frolics over Ycel spread sheets were not the gymnastics Choogi had envisaged when she bought such a large bed. It soon became apparent that Batbold had conceded to the purchase of a double-super-dooper-emperor bred not for the space it offered for night-time shenanigans but because it enabled space for solitary slumber.

When Choogi discovered she was pregnant she seriously wondered whether immaculate conception was indeed a possibility. When Batbold discovered Choogi was pregnant his computer blew up. This was something which no number of variables could model but Batbold knew from experience that a child, let alone a baby, would have an irrevocably detrimental impact on his professional effectiveness. That was something he could never entertain. Instead, Batbold simply never came home from the office – never ever.

Choogi had known in her heart that this would be Batbold's reaction. Some part of her had prepared her for the eventuality. When it came she barely shed a tear. Her heart had still not melted after the ice of winter. It was July. She simply took herself to live nearer to those few relatives she knew about, fully realising that, while there was little prospect of them being hospitable, at least they would have faces she knew. Living alone, she promised herself that her son would not have the life she had led. He would have love, lots and lots of love. She would look after and mother him. She would make sure he had whatever he wanted whenever he wanted. She would teach him to believe in himself, to not accept criticism or second best. When Tengis was born she lived up to every one of her promises. Perhaps too much.

3

Chinggis had modelled Ulaanbaatar on everything he deemed to be good in the new world he had found himself governing. He respected the cultures of the nations he conquered; he adopted the spiritual knowledge of the many faiths he led; he devised a language that was recognisable across the many tongues of his realm and he encouraged freedom of thought. His city attracted the greatest minds of that time. Architects helped build magnificent palaces and temples. Artists painted enormous wall paintings that depicted the landscapes of his vast empire and he erected gargantuan statues of himself in all major cities to remind any potentially dissenting rebels that he was still watching over them. Poets and playwrights would work tirelessly to convey their love and admiration of their fine leader. In reality, the people were so proud of Chinggis that they had no real need for the bronze and marble statues or the epics or plays. Chinggis was in their soul. He had built a utopian society where everybody had a place and everybody had a chance. Certainly, there were detractors but they were few and far between. All of this had changed overnight as the result of a very spoiled little cousin with a penchant for gardening.

Ulaanbaatar had been a fine city based on principled thought and a successful society. Baatarulaan was anything but. If Ulaanbaatar had pristine avenues and ornately carved temples, then Baatarulaan had dingy alleyways and red light districts. Khad had, in a very short time, turned inside out everything that was good about the city. Khad had been a man with a small, very small, teenie-weenie, absolutely miniscule amount of sense but a whopping great humungous, monstrously large sense of self-importance. In his day he had demanded to be known as the 'Right Honourable Younger Cousin of the Emperor of Emperors, Grand Deity of the Northern Territories and King of Kings Amongst Those Who Grow Exquisite Tulips But Don't Like People Finding Out About It', which was quite a mouthful especially if you were playing a team sport and wanted your ruler to pass the ball to you. Normally, the opposition had dispossessed him and scored by the time anyone got to 'Exquisite'. If Khad had been born the same year as Tengis, he would simply have been known as a prat. He wouldn't have been alone – there were lots of prats around. Back in the day Khad had been mightily able at surrounding himself with prats who thought that of all the prats Khad was clearly the best prat and that prats were in fact seriously superior to non-prats if only because non-prats were 'non' and prats had nothing 'non' about them whatsoever. Prats were everywhere; scientists estimated that over 90 per cent of men were prats. Chinggis had been successful, despite the fact that lots of prats worked for him. He knew they were fickle and easily intimidated. Unlike non-prats, prats were easily assuaged if they were paid well and given a job title that fulfilled some sense of self-importance.

Upon taking control of Ulaanbaatar, or Baatarulaan as he immediately renamed it, Khad had sought to eradicate any means of tracing his vindictiveness back to him. Anyone who had been at the camp with Bold and Khasar was beheaded, as were their horses just in case they could retrace footsteps or pick up certain smells (Khad was sure he had read somewhere that horses were able to follow scents for hundreds of miles). Wiping the slate clean of his crime against Chinggis was more straightforward. He had employed Vaandals from the far north-eastern borders of his empire. After they had toppled the true emperor the Vaandals had been ordered to take his body to a secret place known only by Khad buried deep within the Ongolian mountains. Once there, they were commanded to entomb Chinggis's body in ice and bury him deep inside a glacier. It was Khad's way of returning a favour to his cousin. If Chinggis had been happy to make Khad spend time in the icy north, then Khad would gladly help his cousin spend all eternity enjoying the same hospitality. After the Vaandals had disposed of Chinggis's body they had set off to return home. Khad had sent his closest men after them, pursuing them secretly across the plains to the ice bridge that separated Khad's domain from that of the Vaandals. As the hired executioners had ridden halfway across, Khad's men started a fire at their side of the ice bridge and fired a barrage of flaming tar-covered arrows to the other. The Vaandals' breath simply melted away with the bridge into the icy Strait of Anian.

A prat Khad may have been but he was far from stupid. Having been, in his eyes, duped by his aggressively peace-making older cousin, his mind was bent on ensuring he and his legend lasted for all times. When Khad assumed his role as emperor, Ulaanbaatar still held Chinggis close to its bosom. Not a bad word could be said against Chinggis; there simply were no bad words to say against Chinggis. He had been a great man who had made a great city and an even greater empire out of little more than dust and a healthy herd of overzealous horses (he would always hold that it was the horses themselves and not their riders that had won him his empire). Changing names was not going to be enough for Khad to convince the people to forget about his cousin. Khad had to be more cunning. Fortunately, Khad had been born with plentiful amounts of cunning and at which he excelled. A lesser man might have pulled down all the statues, paintings and billboards that exalted their enemy. Not so Khad. He had something far more ugly in mind. He wanted to help his people turn and truly hate their beloved Chinggis. He wanted them to spit every time they said his name. He wanted children to call the ugly weird kids Chinggis in the playground. He wanted Chinggis's name to become synonymous with bad things so that people in the future would say 'Don't be a complete-and-utter Chinggis' whenever they wanted to be rude.

In order to attain the badness he craved, Khad would employ his preferred weapons of choice – bureaucracy and fear. He had already created the Fun Brigade, who were not having nearly enough fun in his view. Khad wanted to encourage them to have more enjoyment by having them force anyone over-heard saying anything nice about Chinggis to dance in circles on one leg for an hour while reciting all of the procreative thoughts they had had over the previous week. This was sure to provide the citizens of Ulaanbaatar, or Baatarulaan, with copious amounts of hilarity. Mongolians, or Ongolians, were exceedingly wanton in the bedroom department and enjoyed days on end of frolicking pleasure with their partners. They were also adventurous, so upon hearing the threat made by the Fun Brigade they suddenly fell silent. Not only did they stop saying how fine a fellow Chinggis had been, they stopped saying just about anything. Having to recite the details of their parlour panderings was not a task to be taken lightly. They didn't mind being forced to dance – that would be real fun – but having to let their mother-in-law know exactly what they'd been doing with their son or daughter (or both) was enough to fill even the toughest Mongol, or Ongol, with abject terror.

With the Fun Brigade patrolling the streets, Khad set about installing various practices and processes that would help further his cause. He drew up a list of 'Chinggis crimes' that included not only mention of his name but all things that were deemed to have been fit and proper during the rule of Chinggis. These included virtue, charity, pleasantry and gallantry. Offenders would eventually find themselves in the newly built House of Fun. The House of Fun was a large four-storey building constructed at the highest point in Baatarulaan. It could be seen from most corners of the city and, just in case anyone couldn't see it, large red neon bulbs flashed its name into the night sky accompanied by barrel-organ music. There wasn't a whole lot of fun to be had at the House of Fun other than by the wardens. The wardens, who wore brightly garish clown costumes, were handpicked for their sickly psycho-pathic tendencies and relished every opportunity to correct the behaviour of their guests. By the time Khad's rule came to an end no guest who had been entertained at the House of Fun had ever wanted to leave because they were 'having so much fun', or at least that was what was written in the letters received by the families of 'guests'.

Khad secretly admired the city his cousin had constructed. He privately adored wonderful architecture. He harboured feelings of adoration for open public parklands, particularly the flower beds. He even felt inwardly positive about the wide avenues that were lined by busy shops and businesses; even the statues of his deceased cousin were in his view sculpted magnificently. He refused to have any of the buildings that had been constructed during the time of Chinggis destroyed. After all, good builders were hard to come by when you needed them and there was no guarantee they would do the job you wanted even if you did find them. Instead, Khad determined to change the meaning of Chinggis's city. All schools and places of study were closed; when they reopened the interiors had been ripped out and replaced by enormous vodka and karaoke bars com-plete with a labyrinth of 'private rooms'. History and geography went out the window and teachers were instructed to teach people a set of altogether more carnal lessons instead.

Indeed, Khad completely overhauled the education system. Libraries were emptied of the classic texts and theological tomes to be replaced by thinner, more photographically oriented publications that had until then been kept under the counter or on the top shelves of less savoury shopping establishments. He pardoned all of the non-dangerous prisoners that Chinggis had put away. Mostly they were burglars, bank robbers and fraudsters, just the sort of people who would be loyal to him and help him re-educate his people. Given their understanding of how to get from A to B with minimal effort and without attracting attention, burglars were appointed as neogeography teachers, bank robbers were selected to instruct their pupils in arithmetic and business studies. Courses in faith, drama and politics were to be given by the fraudsters. Khad knew that, within a generation, two at the most, he would rule people so ruthlessly mercenary that everything his goodie-two-shoes cousin had stood for would be rendered despicable.

The number of bureaucratic buildings quadrupled. They absorbed all of the splendid palaces built by Chinggis and many of the larger private homes. The wealthy families who had lived there were deemed not to have laughed enough and sent to the House of Fun accordingly. The number of bureaucrats employed by Khad increased six-fold. Khad knew the surest way to slow a system down and make it far more ineffective was to employ more bureaucrats. There were now three people employed to check every application made for anything by anybody. Three times as many checks were made for anyone applying to start a business to ensure that they were credit-unworthy enough. It took three years to apply for a passport so as to discourage any cross-border movement. Khad instigated monthly censuses so that he could keep tabs on exactly what everyone was doing at any particular time. The results were inscribed on hefty stone tablets and kept in a cave that was guarded by fifty burly Fun Brigade members. Khad had inadvertently invented the world's first database. He would later lose various versions of the database as they were transported between the secret cave and his office in Baatarulaan. Although the lost tablets showed exactly how much money the city's inhabitants had in savings, and where it was stored, he was able to ensure that his incompetence was soon forgotten; in a large part due to threats made to anyone who mentioned it. Khad was an insecure little man. His view was that this knowledge he was creating would lead to power. Observers wondered how he had any time to do his day job what with all this silly and pointless bureaucratic posturing.

Faith was not outlawed. Instead, Khad set about altering what it was that his people had faith in. He made it illegal not to laugh at designated times during the day. During laughing time people were instructed to think of nothing other than how wonderful their new country was and how much of a jolly good chap their new emperor was. All other acts of faith or worship were strictly forbidden. The decree read: 'Every day people must laugh at exactly 0500, 0730, 1200, 1700 and 2100 without exception.' Chinggis's temples were reformatted as 'Laughter Houses' where the people of Baatarulaan could gather together and laugh. The Laughter Houses were manned by the Fun Brigade. The Fun Brigade had a list of everyone who lived in Baatarulaan. If somebody missed a laughing session, a member of the brigade would pay them a visit and, unless a very convincing excuse was offered, or a large amount of money, the missing somebody would go missing on a more permanent basis in the House of Fun. Laughing was one thing; people enjoyed laughing. What people didn't enjoy was being told *when* and *where* to laugh. Managing one laughter session a day was

22

enough of a chore. Laughing five times a day upon command was nigh on impossible. Yet Khad persisted. Failure was not an option. Failure would not be tolerated. A whole industry had developed around this law. It offered any number of means to induce laughter from clowns and puppets, tickling sticks and feather dusters to gas and other chemical intoxications.

For most, the chemical solutions usually ended up being the medicine of choice, although they were exceedingly expensive. Khad's nephew's cousin's best friend's girlfriend, Khazza, ran a chemical cartel that produced, packaged and distributed chemical solutions throughout Ongolium. Khazza was a heartless wench with few friends, but she was a big lass and could pack a punch. Even her boyfriend was afraid of her. She seized the business opportunity that the Laughter Law presented. There was no law against chemical consumption, even though everybody knew it was bad for you. Khazza created an ingredient that made her special brand of laughter absolutely addictive. Within a matter of months the streets of Baatarulaan were literally littered with the less salubrious of the city's inhabitants lolling about horizontally on pavements laughing uncontrollably at some secret joke only their minds were able to fathom. Khem, as the chemical became known, was freely available and its price moved inexorably upwards.

Groups of Khazza's employees would persuade Baatarulaan residents to purchase their wares. They were generally very large men with intimidating faces and amazing powers of persuasion. Had the cartel worked on a commission-only basis, they would most certainly have received a far healthier salary than that fixed by their miserly, ambitious employer. Those residents who did decide against using Khem were reminded of their virtue by having their windows smashed and their pet dogs set alight; it was a sign of honour to be seen promenading with a charred poodle. Khazza's cartel set up Khem houses where people could freely indulge in as much laughter as they were able before passing out (and being robbed). The chemical enhancement changed people's view of faith. New types of festivals emerged that involved pulsating rhythms and flashing lights. Khem users would sway in time with the beat and throw their arms in the air as if in praise of their new spiritual incarceration. The festivals attracted new users and grew as Khem usage spiralled. Khad rubbed his hands in glee and Khazza counted her pennies. Khazza's cartel forged an alliance with the Fun Brigade and between them they ruled Baatarulaan. What need did Khad have for democracy when he had a far more effective tool with which to reap immediate reward? Martial law became a permanent shadow. Very soon the loyal and virtuous subjects of Chinggis were slowly being turned into fearful zombies intoxicated by the greedy and self-important Khad. Baatarulaan was changing. Khad felt decidedly smug. He had created a city of vice and corruption that, while almost universally despised, had been emulated in many other desert regions throughout the world. 'Oh, how I wish the golden child Chinggis could have seen this!' mused Khad.

Khad saved his most devilish activities for Chinggis's beloved Tsara. Khad disliked women. He was a simple fellow and could not begin to understand the finer workings of the female mind. Instead, he undermined it whenever the opportunity arose. Many of the things he said and did he would never have done to a man; he saw women as weak and to be dominated. He was a very silly man in this respect. To Khad, Tsara represented the life of his nemesis. However, despite Khad's affected hatred, Tsara was as loved by the people as Chinggis had been while he had ruled. The people saw Chinggis's love for his lady as true romance. It had long been the talk of the bathhouses. When it was announced that Chinggis was dead, the people mourned as much for the grief they knew Tsara would be experiencing as for the loss of their illustrious emperor. It infuriated Khad. 'Why should this silly little woman who was born in a distant and barbarian country hold the affections of his people?' he wondered. Khad thought long and hard, plotting for far longer than most people would deem sane. He had to bring her down. He couldn't kill her as he had her husband, his cousin. Khad needed to be more cunning. He knew that, although Tsara was immensely popular, and although the people of Baatarulaan were progressive as a result of Chinggis's advanced policies, were he able to humiliate and destroy Tsara's character then as a woman her reputation would be forever sullied and would never recover.

Finding means for such humiliation took Khad to places his imagination had never sought to dwell. He was not by nature a man personally interested in physical love and lust but knew that it was a pastime enjoyed greatly by his subjects (in thought if not in action). Khad determined that, if he could somehow implicate Tsara as having been unfaithful to Chinggis, then this would produce a tarnish suitably tainted to irrevocably ruin her. Searching the nether regions of his city, Khad met a lowly Khem addict who would willingly be interviewed by Khad's media people and testify that for many years he and Tsara had been enjoying illicit Khem-fuelled rumpy-pumpy. It wouldn't matter that Tsara denied the accusations vehemently. What mattered was that doubt would be cast in the mind of Tsara's supporters. After all, these were minds that were becoming increasingly addled and reliant on Khem. They would be easily moved against Tsara.

Khad's plan worked brilliantly. Within a year of killing Chinggis, Tsara had taken her own life. So it was that Khad managed to eradicate the remaining loyalty to Chinggis and in so doing wipe away the memory of Ulaanbaatar and replace it with his own visionary Baatarulaan. Khad lived far longer than anybody could have dreamed or wanted. One day he simply disappeared while out tending to his water geraniums. Rumours spread that he had drowned mysteriously in a bizarre gardening accident. Khad's body was never recovered.

4

Despite Khad having sold vast swathes of the country, Ongolium was still a large country by modern standards. There were far smaller countries, geographically, that punched far above their tectonic weight. Ongolium didn't pack a punch at all. Outside of Baatarulaan there were no towns as such. During the Terror of Khad people living outside the city had been forced to give up their way of life and move towards the centre. Khad had wanted to control everything and everyone. However, over the years those who had become disenfranchised by Baatarulaan and who longed for the old ways sneaked out of the city and into the mountains. The modern Fun Brigade still patrolled the countryside. They searched for anyone leaving the city while simultaneously ensuring that no Outsiders entered Ongolium. In order to evade the Fun Brigade small groups of escapees lived a nomadic life as herders, forever in search of peace and forever in search of solace. Living in white, round, canvassed gers, they were able to survive the harsh terrain and life on the Steppe. The gers were thickly quilted with felts and all aspects of family life took place within. Being some ten metres in diameter and with families usually being a minimum of six, people became very close and tolerant of one another very quickly. Central to the ger was the stove, a metallic fireplace with a flat top and a long chimney that snaked up two metres to the hole in the roof of the ger. Clothing, bedding, heirlooms and people clustered around the stove. The gers were very portable. They could be taken down and packed on to the back of a camel within an hour. As such, every family had at least one camel in addition to their numerous horses. Ongolium had fifty-five horses per person. Given that most people lived in Baatarulaan, that left an awful lot of horses running wild in the countryside. Winters were harsh and summers stifling in Ongolium. People worked hard to keep things going. Meals were one of the few times that people gathered together, mostly for warmth. In summer they ate the few vegetables and fruits they were able to gather. Meat was exclusively the reserve of winter when it was cold enough to keep it fresh outside the ger. Life in the herder communities was not easy. There was little time for fun but when it was had it was intense. Song and vodka filled the air, as it had in the time of Chinggis.

In one such herder population lived a young lady called Lily. Lily was fifteenth-generation nomad. Her fathers had led their group for centuries. Lily and her people had wholly rejected the ways of Baatarulaan. Stories of Chinggis had been kept alive by word of mouth passing from generation to generation. Lily knew of the faith and knowledge that had been the bedrock of Ulaanbaatar. Knowledge was kept alive through the stories told. Faith was kept alive through shamanism. Within the group one person was born with the gift of shamanism each generation. Lily was that person. Her father had been worried for her. He knew of the power such a gift held. He also knew that other people would always be slightly afraid of her.

Despite this, when Lily's father was captured during a foraging expedition in the city, everyone in the group agreed that Lily was the right person to take over leadership of the group; at least until her father got back. Reluctantly, Lily agreed. She now found herself in the rare position of being the spiritual and political leader to her group of a hundred herders. A leader needed to produce an heir (or heiress). At the age of twenty-two, Lily had no intention of finding herself a partner. The thought of pregnancy and childbirth filled her with abject dread. Her mother had died giving birth to her and Lily had carried the emotional scar with her all her life. However, she knew she wouldn't have long before her people started making demands of her and sending eligible young men with fruit baskets to ask her to step out. However, she also knew that most men in the group were too scared to come anywhere near her with any romantic intention.

Twenty-two years had not been long enough for Lily yet to come to terms with being a shaman (or shawoman). It was not as though she had asked for the 'gift' to be thrust upon her. Much as she enjoyed helping other people resolve issues and thwart illness, there were only so many drum sessions and psychological vacations that she could cope with. Visiting the spirit world on a daily basis was exhausting. It also made other people rather sceptical of Lily. Although everyone in her group had always been nice to Lily, she didn't have any real friends to speak of. People were simply too intimidated by her ability to 'see things' to allow themselves to get close to her. Even Lily's family felt uncomfortable spending any time with her.

When Lily was about to find her gift upon her she would start to tingle all over. It was always the same. The tingling would start in her hands and work up her arms. She would begin to feel warmth flowing upwards from the pit of her stomach. Although she never felt faint, a reeling sense of parting from her body swept across her. This would be followed by a lull, before suddenly her eyes shot into extreme focus and she was able to call herself into the spirit world. In the early days she had no choice but to be pulled into the spirit world but as she matured so did her ability to control the portal between worlds through breathing, chanting and mental focus.

While she was able to hide preliminary symptoms, as the portal opened her inner feelings became apparent to those around her. It must have petrified her parents. It most definitely petrified Lily.

By the time she was ten years old Lily had learned that taking meals sitting away from the central table on her own was a nicer experience than eating in silence while everybody else stared at you, waiting for the chanting to begin. She also enjoyed simply observing her family and hearing what real people did day by day. Having no mother she had to find her own way. Lily never felt she had been intended, she felt alone; she had no siblings and there was no one to help her understand the world around her or begin to understand, or believe in, her gift. Her father was simply too busy being the leader to have much time for her, though she craved his affection.

Being a shaman she was excused any of the many manual tasks necessary to group survival. By fifteen she had schooled herself. Sitting out of sight behind the round canvas gers where the group elders lived, Lily soon realised that by listening to them telling, and retelling, their stories to one another year after year she learned pretty much all she would ever need to know. She learned that invisible eagles soared far above over-head watching out for her people. If enemies came close, the eagles would let the group know. Of course this had never happened. The group had no enemies. The elders also spoke about cats as their enemies. Lily couldn't quite understand this – she loved cats. Stories were told about bad duplicitous people who were reborn as cats. She had to confess that there weren't any cats in her camp and that any that ventured too close were soon chased away.

Having few people close to her, Lily spent much of her time alone on the Steppe. Although the group was slightly afraid of her they did empathise with her solitude. Every birthday she would be given an animal, something with which she could spend her days: camels, marmots, hares . . . even birds of prey. For her fifth birthday Lily had received her first horse. Everybody in the group knew how to ride even before they took to a saddle. Lily was no exception. She loved to ride. The horses in Ongolium were far shorter and more hardy than their European cousins. The horses often only reached a man's chest but their size belied their ability. Whereas a European horse waited for its owner to dictate a course of action, the Ongolium horse knew what its master wanted the moment the two touched. The bond between Ongolian rider and their horse was almost as inexplicable as the spirit world where Lily was spending an increasing amount of her time.

Lily's forays into the Steppe became longer and more distant. She was at home in the vast open spaces the Steppe offered and always yearned to be riding out beneath the eternal blue sky that was the hallmark of her country. She could not imagine any other place could offer such striking natural enormity. What had begun as the odd hour or so turned into whole days out on the Steppe or exploring nearby mountains. As she got older, her endurance levels grew and she was able to ride harder and further. By the time of her twentieth birthday she was spending several days at a time on horseback, by night sleeping nestled on her steed. The two became inseparable yet never more than horse and rider. The old Ongolian ways forbade people to name or become overly attached to their horses. One never knew, after all, when it would have to become dinner during a harsh winter. Secretly, Lily called her horse Lucky; it had saved her life on too many occasions not to be. Days spent away from the ger camp enabled Lily to come to terms with herself – who she was, what she wanted, how to fulfil herself.

Lily was a robust girl and even more so now that she was maturing. Robust mentally from having to live in solitude and deal with her gift. Robust physically from the nomadic life her parents had chosen for her. Having spent so much time riding out on the Steppe she was naturally athletic. As tall as any man in the group, Lily knew that, if any of the boys in the group were brave enough to overstep the mark and make untoward romantic overtures, they would find themselves wiping a bloodied nose. Being the newest in a long line of herders of the Steppe, Lily had far darker skin than her compatriots living in Baatarulaan. Though a young woman, her muscles were more finely tuned and her stamina far greater than most men in that city, too. The outdoor life had heightened her senses. She could clearly identify a bird from over three kilometres away. She could sense when it was that rains were going to break periods of drought. At night, as the group rested around their stoves, Lily was always the first to hear a horse in distress or any other noise out of the ordinary. If a group elder was nearing the end of their time, Lily would be the first to take their hand to ease them through the process. Hers was a blurred world of perception, empathy and just a little confusion.

In her childhood Lily had enjoyed playing with her gift. She thought it was all a big game. Jumping into another world and speaking to people who weren't in the physical world felt exhilarating. As she became a young woman, the game ceased. She could begin to understand what it was people in both worlds were saying to her. She could understand how desperate both sets of people were for Lily to help them. It was a lot to ask of a girl who was only just coming to terms with being a young woman. The more time Lily spent in her other world, the more comfortable it became. There she met people who had long passed from her world but who were still forced to resolve, or were willing to resolve, issues and mysteries that existed in the physical world. Before long, Lily had befriended a young woman about the same age as herself. Lily's friend was also lonely and the two soon became as sisters. Lily's friend also had the gift, though she was more accomplished in wielding its power. She began to teach Lily how to manage and control the gift.

The young Lily was finding herself spending more time in the spirit world than the physical. Had a stranger come across Lily's camp they would have been bemused. Sitting cross-legged beside a dying fire would be a young woman deep in meditation. Lily was so deep in meditation that she was not present to the physical world in any guise other than bodily. Nearby, Lucky stood guard, ever attentive and watchful for danger, protecting his human ward. Lucky cared for his mistress as much as she did for him. In Lucky's world Lily was known as 'Dream Light'.

Led by her friend, Lily's skill as a shaman became ever sharper. As her skill became sharper, she was able to help her group more readily. As she was able to help her group more readily, she was accepted more willingly. By the time her father gave her a twenty-second animal to add to her menagerie Lily was a thoroughbred shaman. She even had a cloak, knobbly stick and small drum. That's how serious a shaman she was. It was as a serious shaman that her group accepted her as interim leader. Without her cloak and stick they would have been forced to draw lots.

Lily had no qualms about accepting the call to be leader. From her sideline position in the ger she had spent many winters watching her father preside intelligently over group meetings. She had learned from him the resources necessary to maintain the health and well-being of the group. Watching him on the Steppe she had learned how to walk with aplomb and act with honourable authority. She knew how many camels the group needed. She could sense the Fun Brigade coming two hours before they came into sight, and an hour after the group had decamped elsewhere. It was deep winter in Ongolium and the herder communities tended to remain camped in the same sheltered spot for the duration. Most returned to the same winter campsite year after year, some built permanent walls to ward off the plummeting temperatures. It made things easier for Lily; she wouldn't have to think about where to move to next. It also comforted her that her father would know where to find her as and when he escaped. Until he returned, the graves of her mother and dead sister would keep her company. She had no one else with whom she could speak frankly, at least not in that world.

Aged twenty-two Lily had the diplomacy and tact to manage intergroup wrangling, know whether two star-struck lovers would make a lasting couple and what the weather was likely to do for the coming week. Lily did find herself using her gift on certain occasions just to confirm that she was making the right decision, although invariably she found that she was. Being separate from the group gave her the distance a leader requires from their people while her blood bond ensured loyalty and acceptance. Becoming leader should have been a simple process and a simple task. What Lily hadn't bargained for was the extra secret knowledge that only a leader could know. Upon taking up the mantle the group elders handed her an ornate box with a golden key.

'Inside there be secrets,' said the elders as one. 'Read and ye shall discover what it is that we are and what it is that we are doing.'

'Do you have to talk so strangely?' asked Lily.

'No, not really,' said the elder who was known as Chuluun. 'We always thought it added more . . . more gravitas.'

'It sounds a little bit mad, if you don't mind me saying,' said Lily.

'Oh!' said Chuluun. 'Sorry about that. Must try harder – what with you being the new leader and everything. Ho-hum, I guess everything changes with each generation but doesn't really vary. Anyhow, toodle-pip.' He waved her goodbye and wandered slowly away to where his elder friends were discussing what voice they should adopt next. Lily had always found conversations with the elders to be ambiguous at best. Chuluun in particular had a special ability to be enigmatic, vague and peculiar.

Lily took the box, packed it on to Lucky's back and rode off to one of her favourite haunts out on the Steppe. Lily had always thought they were merely a small band of slightly rebellious outcasts who wanted to live on their own terms and according to the old ways. Apparently, it wasn't as simple as that.

5

Although the sun shone pretty much every day in Ongolium, the weather was rarely nice in Baatarulaan. City dwellers didn't really have a sense of environment. It was more important that they kept themselves warm, were able to power their super-casinos and ensured that the red lights along certain designated streets were kept bright enough for the many human moths attracted to them. It was midday but could easily have been dusk. Thick smog sat smugly over the city. Barely any natural light filtered through to street level. Baatarulaan was not a city where you were likely to catch skin cancer; other, more cruel cancers were far more prolific.

Lunchtime was Tengis's favourite part of the school day. He found school particularly dull. There was little that the teachers were able to teach him. The libraries contained little reading material; it was mostly picture books containing images of women photographed to please men who were spending some time alone. Tengis had found that the many statues and paint-ings that existed in Baatarulaan held texts engraved or painted into them. From these he was able to educate himself far beyond the levels his school was ever likely to achieve. From these readings he had learned the history of his country, the stories about Baatarulaan's son and legend. He could see many positives in the world Chinggis had created, although secretly he doubted whether running such an enormous empire was truly efficient or the best use of funds. He also saw the benefits of what Khad had set out to build. Tengis had always enjoyed having a strict sense of order and the Fun Brigade offered an identity with which he could relate. If only he had known his father – perhaps he would have been of a different opinion. Lunchtime was when Tengis learned what he really wanted to know and undertook his true schooling.

Today Tengis was walking towards Trouble Bridge with his close and only friend, Odval. The bridge spanned the river Fuul that flowed north–south across Ongolium, starting and ending beyond its borders. None of Ongolium's frontiers met the sea. The river Fuul was the only source of water in the entire country. Thankfully, it was a big river. Nobody knew where it came from or even if Fuul was its correct name, but Khad had come up with it so it had stuck. No records existed to show what it had been called before Khad took over from Chinggis.

Odval came from a wealthy family who owned the largest of the super-casinos in Baatarulaan as well as a number of Khem distribution outlets for users of that particular laughing narcotic. Odval's family was respected, as much as respect was ever given in that city, and most definitely feared. Tengis thought they were charming people and was particularly fond of Odval's father with whom he had begun to grow close. Although an intelligent young woman, Odval would only ever be second best in her school class so long as Tengis was in the same class. It didn't bother her, though. She marvelled in her friend's ability to absorb information, create order amid the chaos of Baatarulaan, and eke out real education when for most there was none.

'What's so special about Trouble Bridge?' asked Odval.

'Trouble Bridge was not always named so,' said Tengis, assuming a professorial stance as they walked across the stone slabs, thumbs tucked neatly into his waistcoat pocket. Tengis had an unusually mature sense of fashion. He spurned the leather-and-link chainmail that was all the rage among others his age. Instead, he preferred to wear camel-hair trousers, waistcoat and matching jacket. He thought this made him look clever but others thought he looked like a children's toy.

'How so?' asked Odval. 'Father says that absolutely nothing has changed since the Fun Brigade started.'

'That may be so,' remarked Tengis, 'but before then there was a world, too – though few dare admit it. It was originally known as Peace Bridge. The bridge carried Chinggis Khaan and his Mongol hordes back to his capital after they had secured the empire. From that day on Chinggis made all who entered the city wait and pay respect to those who had fought to win the empire. Sometimes the wait lasted hours.

'When Khad was elected to run the country' – it was always believed that this must have been the case so democratic was Baatarulaan, so long as you were from the right family and could afford to pay for the privilege – 'When Khad was elected,' continued Tengis, 'he declared that the empire his beloved cousin had created was simply too big, cumbersome and unwieldy to be in the best of interests of his subjects, the Ogoliumns, as they had come to be known. I have to say, I agree with that sentiment – it was ridiculously large. Anyway, because of the land sale Khad initiated, getting rid of large swathes of the country in return for peace, he gave himself several migraine headaches. He didn't like feeling so bad so he renamed the bridge Trouble Bridge because it had given him anything other than peace. Though Trouble Bridge had changed a great deal since the time of Chinggis, Khad's followers unwittingly allowed the inscriptions to remain. Waiting on the bridge had become legendary.' They looked around them. Several dozen carts, wagons and motorised vehicles were stuck one behind the other as they made their way towards Baatarulaan. Some people appeared to be quite irate and were banging on tambours and honking makeshift horns.

'That makes sense,' replied Odval. 'Everything Khad did made sense and I hate the thought of anything having troubled him.' Odval's family were strong Khadists. 'So, why have we come to this bridge? There is another one which is far newer and cleaner – why this one?'

'It's to do with the pillars that line both sides of the bridge,' said Tengis. 'They have barely changed since they were built and a man with a dog I met when I was on my last little learning mission said that they were worth inspecting closely.'

'I can't see anything special about these,' said Odval. 'They all look the same. All the same height. All made from the same boring stone. No sparkly lights or tinsel. They have images of people on them but what can you learn from that? They look like the work of Outsiders, if you ask me.'

'Well, I'm not asking you,' said Tengis gruffly. 'You need to look at the detail. See, these people here?' Tengis pointed to some images towards the rear of the pillars. 'They are holding scrolls.'

'How on earth are you going to read that?' asked Odval. 'The writing is so tiny.'

'Aha!' said Tengis. He fished a magnifying glass out from his jacket pocket. Odval leaned over his shoulder as he moved closer to the sculpted scroll.

As she and Tengis had grown older together, she had begun to have different sorts of feelings for him. When she was up close to him a moments like these she felt different; it was more than just friendship. She had known that boys smelled funny but Tengis had a natural aroma which Odval relished. She had once borrowed a sweater from him to keep herself warm. For many nights afterwards she had held it close to her face breathing in Tengis's scent. When he had asked for it back, she had pretended to have lost it. She wasn't sure why but she wanted to keep that part of him close to her while she slept. Admitting this to Tengis was impossible. She knew that men and women thought differently and hadn't had enough experience to second-guess what his reaction might have been. For the time being moments such as these when she was kneeling close to Tengis would have to suffice. It was a small pleasure but taken gladly.

Unbeknown to Odval, Tengis felt similarly excited when she was close to him. He had first noticed the shine of her hair and softness of her skin. She was far more confident than he was, especially in public. The strength of her family background offered Odval a degree of security Tengis could only dream of. He was not jealous. He cared too fondly for Odval. In the same way that Odval was impressed with his knowledge, Tengis was proud of her natural exuberance. More recently he had started to watch closely for a stolen glimpse of her body. The curves that were emerging from beneath her jacket filled him with a keen sense of desire he had never experienced before. The feelings filled his fantasies and riddled his private emotions. They were private, though; never to be shared, particularly with Odval. He would not be able to take the humiliation or rejection if she had laughed at his declaration. He had always held his emotions tightly wound up inside. He had his father to thank for that. He hoped that one day he would be able to ask him why.

'See that scroll there,' said Tengis. Odval leaned in closer, but not too close, so that she could see more clearly what it was that Tengis was pointing at. Tengis thought she sensed Odval turn her face towards him and breathe in deeply through her nose. He ignored it. 'This scroll is talking about the original group of four that ran the first ever empire. Here, see that – that lion brandishing a shield marked K denotes Khasar. Khasar was said to be the bravest man to have been born. His fearlessness and leadership endeared him to his long-standing friend Chinggis. They grew up together fighting, feuding and frequenting houses of ill-repute, whatever that means. The dolphin marked T relates to Bold. He was a keen sailor, not a natural skill for us Ongolians given that we are landlocked and the nearest sea is over a thousand kilometres away. His ability to undertake successful military campaigns by boat, ship and, on one occasion, a school of porpoise gave him the nickname Dolphin. They say he could speak to the aquatic mammals and even teach them to do his underwater bidding.'

'Wow!' replied Odval. 'I would love to meet a man like that.' Her face lit up as she thought of Bold talking freely with the animals in their clipped clicking language.

'Personally,' added Tengis, 'I think it was just a flimsy technique he adopted to chat up girls. They say he was a terrible womaniser.'

Odval's face dropped and she refocused on the task at hand. 'What about that one?' she asked. She was pointing at a snake that formed a circle and appeared to be eating its own tail. 'It looks particularly odd.'

'Ah!' said Tengis. 'You'll like this one. The serpent represents Khad. He was known to be silent, cunning and deadly by those closest to him. It was a description he derived great pleasure from.'

'Why does he look like he's eating his tail?' asked Odval.

'Well,' answered Tengis, 'it is said that Khad is so powerful that he lives for ever. The complete circle represents infinity. He is said to live around us, in us and between us. Though not in our world, he sees and hears all that we do. People believe that if the strong values and sense of community that Khad fought so bravely to create are forgotten or even changed too much then he will return to our world.'

41

'How can that be?' asked Odval. 'The Laughter Laws dictate that there is nothing after we die. They say that the life we have is our only one, which is why it is so important to do whatever we want regardless of what others might say or think. If that's the case, how can Khad possibly still be around? He died so long ago.'

'I don't think that normal rules apply to Khad,' said Tengis. 'He seems to have seen himself as above all others.'

'We know that,' said Odval. 'He *was* emperor after all.'

'Yes,' said Tengis, 'but it was more than that; he seems to have considered himself as some sort of ethereal entity. He named himself as lifelong executive officer of every bureaucratic body he established. By "lifelong" he meant for all time. It is written into their mission statements: "The Fun Brigade",' Tengis quoted verbatim, '"will make sure everybody has fun as and when it decides they should have fun and this fun will be presided over for all time with strictest humour by the chief fun-maker Khad." It's a bit of a strange thing to do, but then again Khad was, and perhaps still is, all powerful.'

'OK,' said Odval, who didn't really understand what it was that Tengis had been talking about. 'What about that one?' She pointed at a simple-looking yet proud horse. It had no rider but wore a somewhat more elaborate saddle. The horse was facing to the left. 'That doesn't look very significant.'

'You're joking, right?' asked Tengis. 'Everyone knows what the horse represents, don't they?'

Odval looked at him blankly. 'The horse stands for Chinggis, obviously.' Tengis wondered about his friend. Although she was special to him, he had to question her intelligence sometimes, even if he knew that measuring anyone against his own superior knowledge was more than a little unfair. 'Chinggis conquered the world from horseback. He was not a proud or showy man. Unlike others of his time, he didn't drape himself in golden robes and walk about wearing a crown. He dressed like his people did, although he did eat slightly better dinners.'

Domestic produce in Ongolium, or Mongolia, had always been more than a little thin on the ground. Most people lived off mutton, dumplings and fat-based stews. The weather forbade all bar a few vegetables or fruits from being grown and these were normally given to the more well-to-do families. Given the diet and harsh weather conditions, a person's fortieth birthday was greeted with enormous festivity and a considerable measure of thankfulness. If someone lived till they were fifty, even the Fun Brigade were impressed and stopped using their sticks on them. It was felt by the age of fifty people didn't need to be encouraged to have fun; it simply happened. On reaching sixty people were deemed witches and most were normally burned to death on a barbecue.

'Why would he act like the common people?' asked Odval. 'If I were empress, I would wear only the finest finery, eat only the tastiest foods and wouldn't look at the common people, let alone speak to them, if I could possibly help it.'

This annoyed Tengis who had always considered himself high-minded. It annoyed him because, although he, and his mother, loved Chinggis to the point of worship, he actually felt the same way as Odval. He couldn't understand why someone with power wouldn't wield their will and lord it over others. He banished this thought. He was Chinggis; he just needed to find out how.

'Don't be petty,' said Tengis. 'Chinggis was the greatest man ever to walk this land.'

Odval looked at him aghast. 'How can you say that? You'd better not let anyone else hear you saying things like this. Khad is our beloved emperor, no other has ever lived that is as good, kind or wise as he.'

Tengis could tell from her tone that Odval didn't really

believe this. She was of the same opinion as he. Eventually they started to giggle.

'House of Fun!' said Tengis through his laughter. 'Who would come up with something quite so ridiculous!' Odval and he laughed hard until tears rolled down their faces and they crumpled next to one another on the dusty bridge. They looked at one another through dampened faces and for a second there was more than friendship.

'We,' said Tengis, suddenly standing up, 'had better get back. School will be starting soon and we don't want to be late; people might become suspicious.' He closed the door on his emotions, locked it, put the key in a padlocked box and threw it into the river. He helped Odval to her feet and the pair walked back towards school as though nothing had happened.

So it was that Tengis and Odval spent their time together. Neither had or needed any other friend. Their relationship was based on intellect, or at least mostly, and they deemed themselves to be above the other pupils at their school. The other pupils in turn didn't want anything to do with the kids that they referred to as 'weirdos' either. Tengis and Odval were a closed unit. They didn't blanch or react when their peers shouted insults at them. 'Chinggishites' was not an insult in their opinion. They knew better. It made them stronger.

6

Lily dismounted Lucky and pulled the bags and boxes from his back. It was nearly night-time and she needed to set up camp. She lit a small campfire and sat down with the box the group elders had given in front of her. She ignored it; instead she prised open a tin of beans and poured them into a pot, balancing them near the fire to heat them through. The box shone and sparkled in the firelight. Lily delicately placed a blanket over the top of it. Moving away from the fire, she left her illuminated sanctuary and walked out into the darkness.

Staring at the vast starry expanse, Lily immediately felt claustrophobic. Something about the fire was drawing her back towards it. Not being near the fire felt stiflingly uncomfortable. Lily knew what it was. It was the box the group elders had given her but something about it forced her to stay away from it. The box felt as though it carried a weighty responsibility with it. Lily was used to responsibility. All of her life she had been responsible for helping her group overcome adversity. When she had accepted the role of group leader she had not expected it to carry the additional burden she now felt.

She moved back towards the fire and circled the box warily, never getting too close to it. Lucky watched on intently and gave an equine snort that sounded more of a chortle to Lily. She knew she was being stupid but there was something about this box that would change her life. Once it had been opened, Lily sensed that a chain of events would begin that would forever change the world, if not the worlds, she had known. She backed away from the box and sat at the other side of the fire from it. As she ate her beans she stared through the flames towards it. Even though it was covered by a blanket it shone brightly in her mind. Lucky snorted again. Lily finished her beans and threw the used pot aside. Standing erect, she breathed deeply. Her eyes never once left the box. Lucky snorted twice. Striding around the fire Lily pulled away the blanket that had been keeping the box warm. Kneeling down beside it, she fumbled in her pocket for the key. Having placed it in the lavishly designed lock, she hesitated. Was she really sure that she wanted to do this?

It was a fairly ordinary-looking box by Baatarulaan standards. For the nomadic people, though, it was a marvel. Carved ornately in the ancient Ongolian style, it was covered in a shiny metallic leaf and studded with jewels of a kind she had never seen before. The lid rose towards the middle giving the box the look of a Buddhist temple. The lavish lock to the front of the box mimicked a front door. The panels on either side and to the rear depicted gardens long since overgrown and birds long since caged.

Lily held the box up in the firelight to examine it more clearly. She turned it over and over in her hands; even the bottom of the box with its four corner feet was more elaborate than anything she had seen before. She mused that the box must have been in her camp since before she was born. The elders had certainly implied as much. She wondered how such a possession could have been in her camp without her knowing about it. Her father had been leader until his capture, which meant it had probably been in her ger every day of her life. She had never seen it, though she had often helped her father pack up the family ger before moving on. She had spent too many icy-cold winter days cooped up in the ger examining every inch of it, yet somehow the box had evaded her. It must have been there!

As she gazed more intently upon it, she was reminded of her father. She hadn't wondered about him very much since his capture. He wasn't much more than simply another man in the camp other than the fact that he was leader. Affections were hard to come by in such a harsh environment, and even harder to come by in her family. But now she found herself fearful for him. She could sense that he was still alive. He had to be – she would have felt something if he had been killed, surely? She hoped that he was being treated favourably wherever he was, although she doubted this as quickly as the thought had entered her head. A sense of injustice began to sew itself into her thoughts. What had her father, her leader, done to deserve capture? Why were the city dwellers so quick to feel hatred towards the nomadic groups? All of the stories she had heard from the group elders talked about the city dwellers as a group larger than any other on the Steppe; more disgusting, more un-law-abiding and more disrespectful than any Ongolium had ever given sanctuary to; so sickeningly riddled with greed and self-interest that even the infamous Khad would have taken time to approve of them; and ever closer to destroying the old ways of life for ever. Lily knew that this also meant destroying her group. While she had always harboured a degree of fear towards the city dwellers since her father had been taken, these feelings had been replaced by anger, repulsion and an over-whelming urge for justice. Why should her people live in fear of those lesser than they? Why should the city dwellers have so much power over Ongolium? She didn't know the answers but felt sure that whatever was in the box she was holding would certainly lead her to them.

Carefully she turned the key ninety degrees clockwise. A soft click announced that the box was now open. As she slowly began to lift the lid all sense of place disappeared. Lily felt a rush of cold air flow from the box and drift through her hair. The light from the fire had dwindled almost to nothing but Lily could see better than she had been able to earlier. There was no sound. Even Lucky remained silently motionless.

Inside the box was a piece of old and dusty material folded over on itself. Lily took the package out and carefully placed the box on the ground. She eyed the shroud suspiciously. She was embarrassed to admit it to herself but Lily felt it was a bit of a let-down after the elaborate casing. She carefully unwrapped the material. She could feel something deep inside it. As she unravelled the material she noticed worn and faded markings on it. It also held remnants of colour embedded in its fading threads. Reaching inside the material, Lily grasped the object it contained. It was a cylinder of sorts. Like the box it was carefully crafted and ornately decorated.

Lily examined it further and noted representations of the herder life she knew fashioned on to the tube. A representation of a ger complete with the familial stove. Images of horsemen riding across the Steppe. Herder families sitting taking a meal and laughing with their friends. An eagle soaring overhead protecting the group. Lily felt an odd affinity with this pictorial portrayal of the life she had lived. It both calmed and soothed the confusion and trepidation that had begun to take root deep within her. Larger than the other images, a Mongolian horse stood proudly, its head turned leftwards. She held the cylinder to her ear and shook it gently. Something moved softly inside. Lily looked for a means to open the container. She ran her nail under the ornamental ends of the tube. Nothing obvious presented itself. She held the cylinder tightly and tried to turn one end. Nothing moved. She turned her attention to the other end. Again there was nothing. She let out a frustrated sigh. Lucky came closer and gently brushed his head against her hair. Lily had always been able to rely on her beloved steed. She returned her attention to the cylinder. Exerting a little more pressure Lily gasped quietly as one end began to slowly ease and turn. Delicately, she turned the cylinder until she loosed the stopper. She removed it completely and placed it next to the loosened material. Peering inside, she could see a parchment of dry paper. She turned the tube slowly upside down to allow the paper to present itself. Lily cautiously removed the paper and placed the cylinder on the ground. She was bemused. What on earth can this be? she thought.

Lily laid the paper next to its container. With both hands she removed any stones and smoothed out an area of earth to be used as a workspace. Returning to the paper, she nervously began to unravel the scroll. It was so dry that it felt it would surely crumble at any moment but Lily simply had to know what it contained. At full length it measured the same distance as between her wrist and elbow. It was roughly half as wide as it was long. Although it was weathered and dirty, she could make out some writing ingrained into the paper. Despite her youth she still needed to peer hard in the fading firelight to make out what the words were saying:

'A tiger wearing a bell will starve and a cat that likes to eat fresh fish will not go into the water; however, the distance between Heaven and Earth is no greater than one thought.'

'Well, that's a lot of blinking use,' said Lily to Lucky. 'What on earth is that supposed to mean?' Lucky neighed softly in response. She sat down haughtily on the dirt. She knew that the stories warned humans never to trust cats. That was obvious. She had been scratched ferociously each time she had spent too long stroking a cat, particularly if she went too close to its stomach. This was annoyingly cryptic, though. Lily did not know what to make of it. As for the second part, she knew from her time in the spirit world that she could jump between them as she desired.

'So,' said Lily to Lucky, 'cats are silly untrustworthy creatures and the real and spirit worlds are joined together by people like me. Duh. I so didn't need some overly luxurious cryptic box to tell me that.'

Lily was grumpy and disappointed. She regretted being so excited in anticipation of what the box contained. She should have known better. What on earth could the old people in her group know, let alone teach her? Lily was angry; she felt she deserved something more magical than something she already knew. She cast the items aside.

Lucky approached her again and nudged her shoulder.

'Go away, will you,' said Lily.

Lucky again pushed his hairy head into her armpit, this time with a little more gusto. Lily was momentarily unbalanced. Lucky licked her face with his massive tongue as she sought to steady herself.

'You silly beast!' cried Lily, although she didn't mean it. She knew better than to be angry with her horse; that was just silly. Lily took a deep breath and collected herself before returning to the items scattered around her.

She scanned the parchment for any clues or further pearls of wisdom. She could see none. Turning the page over she glimpsed what looked like a smudge at the foot of the sheet. She drew her face closer to try and decipher what the smudge was. It appeared to be what looked like writing but it was far too small to be legible. Lily put a couple of logs on the fire and stoked it up. She needed all the light she could muster. Returning to the page, she kneeled and bent over it, her face merely centimetres from the smudged writing. She squinted her eyes, trying desperately to see what the tiny words on the page said. She hooked her fingers under the page and drew it closer.

It took her several attempts before she was finally able to make out what the miniscule text read:

'Chinggis Khaan, Ulaanbaatar – capital city of my beloved Mongolia.'

Lily dropped the parchment on to the ground and backed away aghast. She had heard about Chinggis Khaan. Everybody had. Reports of his life had been mixed. Depictions of him ranged from saviour to executioner, glorious to infamous. Ever since Lily had become a young woman she had secretly harboured a special love and adoration of him. She would think of Chinggis while she was riding out on the Steppe. She would wonder what the world would be like if Chinggis had not been killed by Khad. She had even dreamed of Chinggis at night. Lily blushed and pulled her clothing tight around her. She tried to push all thoughts of Chinggis from her mind.

In so doing, another thought came to her that caused her to blush even more. She wondered if Chinggis had any relatives who were alive somewhere in Ongolium and whether they might be about the same age as she was. She stood up and ran from the firelight hiding her face from Lucky as she fought back her embarrassment. She took several deep breaths and began to compose herself. She was horrified that she was even able to entertain such melodramatic, improper and outlandish thoughts. She had always been a sensible, if slightly abnormal, girl. Although she hadn't attended class, she would almost certainly have been top of it in every subject. It was this damned womanhood thing that was changing the way she thought about life. It made her think about things differently...

Where a man used to be merely someone who could carry heavier things than her or run faster than her, he was now more besides. Rather than watch the heavy boxes he was carry-ing, she would admire his muscle definition. Rather than be annoyed that the man had overtaken her running, she would now marvel at the tone of his thighs and other . . . parts. All the stories had said that Chinggis was more manly than any other. It set her imagination alight. Lily turned red again. She turned her head and looked back at the fire. Lucky was staring at her. She was sure he was mocking her. She returned to her deep breathing exercises – they usually worked.

Presently she had calmed herself enough to return to the fire. Sitting beside the items that now no longer seemed so silly, she shook the dirt from them and delicately placed them in some semblance of order. She examined each in turn repeatedly. Each examination ended with Lily staring longingly at the name Chinggis. She fought back her reddening cheeks. There was something in these items that Lily was not getting. Perhaps she did understand a little about what the words meant. There had to be a deeper meaning that Lily was as yet unable to comprehend. Why had Chinggis written them, though? Had Chinggis even written them at all? It could easily have been someone else – who could possibly know otherwise? The words had been written so long ago, there was no possible record to verify their authenticity. There was no proof and Lily knew that people liked proof. However, somehow Lily *knew* they were Chinggis's words. They had to be. When she had read his name, something had stirred in the depths of her belly. When she had run her fingers across the writing, her entire body had shaken with anticipation. There was something more to the words that the group elders had directed her towards and she needed to know what it was. Chinggis was speaking to her directly, and she, Lily, had a duty to listen. She knew that it was easier to catch an escaped horse than to pluck back an escaped word, but for the time being Chinggis's word had slipped away into the night air.

7

'Tengis and Odval up a tree,' chanted their classmates. 'C-H-I-N-G-I-N-G. First comes love, then baby Ching, then comes the worship of a fallen king!'

The children blew raspberries at Tengis and Odval before running off into the playground. The school day often began like this for Tengis and Odval. It didn't bother either of them. They knew they were far better than the rest of their school mates. Odval, simply because she was; her family was among the wealthiest in Baatarulaan. Tengis because he knew he was Chinggis Khaan; he just hadn't been able to prove it yet. He knew that eventually he would, though, and that then the other children would be sorry, or so he hoped. A small part of him feared that when he did discover the reason he was Chinggis Khaan, he might be wholly ostracised or even banished from the city he knew was rightly his. He was a very confused young man. Still, he was in his final year of school. He would soon be free.

The allure of university didn't appeal. He had little interest in the various sham courses on offer at Baatarulaan University for Khadists and Other Future Reprobates. Tengis could not ascertain what advantage he could gleam from studying for a degree in 'Banking Irregularities and Financial Fraud', 'Home Economics and the Art of Effective Burglary' or 'Anthropological Gambling'. Even he, a mere high school pupil, pulled his hair out at the way education in Baatarulaan was heading. The traditional courses were being overrun by too many students of poor ability. Access to university was a norm, no longer for the exceptional few. The number of people electing to go to university had risen dramatically in recent years. The Khadist bureaucrats supported the rising numbers, since it meant there was less scope for free spirit or entrepreneurism and they could maintain full control over people for longer. The proliferation of new-fangled courses made Tengis nauseous. Surely there was no place for degrees in 'Celebrity Worship', 'Junk Food Cuisine' or 'Immoral Politics'. A university education was no longer necessarily a good thing. Tengis wanted to stand out from the crowd not be part of it.

By the time he was sixteen Tengis had already determined that he wanted to make a difference with his life. He was smarter, better-looking, wittier and quicker-witted than any of his peers. He wanted to instigate change. He was not happy with the status quo in his home city. He was appalled that the select few could gorge while the remainder fought over scraps and were reduced to Khem to escape their sorrows. He knew the person closest to him in the world, apart from his mother, was part of that select few. Odval understood him, though. Their relationship transcended class or wealth. The pair had talked long and often about how best to harness his talents. Many a good night's sleep had been lost trying to single-mindedly unstitch Tengis's abilities and weave them into a pattern that would unleash his potential.

During one such discourse they arrived at a conclusion. To make a difference Tengis would have to enter politics. He might abhor the political parties currently at work in his country but he could implement his will once he was *inside*. As for Odval, she had spent the last ten years trying to keep up with Tengis's intellect. She was keen to stay by his side, purely on a platonic basis. Tengis's mother was equally exuberant about her son's ambition to move into politics. Tengis was a driven young man. He had a vision. He would see Chinggis's power reinstated and he might even throw in a few twists of his own.

Without a university education, however, he would need another means of getting himself into a position whereby he would be deemed credible to work with, for and, secretly, against the Khadists. That means was simple and straight-forward. He was Chinggis Khaan – once he could prove that, what more would matter?

Tengis had been learning applied arithmetic all morning. There were only three pupils in the class – Tengis, Odval and Bankher. Bankher paid little attention to the teacher, pupils or just about anything. His parents ran the Khem plant in Baatarulaan. He had a swagger and aplomb unbecoming to a lad almost twenty years old. He also wore clothes beyond his years. Whereas Tengis wore professorial garb, Bankher wore tight black trousers pulled down so hard around his waist that they barely left his modesty intact. He wore colourful canvas shoes, a white T-shirt under a black sleeveless woollen jumper and a hat that would have suited an aged crooning singer had it been properly proportioned; Bankher's version was as small and tight around his head as his trousers were around his bottom. On his fingers Bankher wore a variety of outlandishly gaudy and oafishly expensive rings. No matter how silly he looked – though he thought he was the very model of a modern major-general layabout, he did have an uncanny ability to add, subtract, multiply and divide. This skill was particularly adept when the problems posed related to weights and measures cross-referenced with going market rates, client desperation and causing unhappiness. Despite detesting his classmate, Tengis found it astonishing to watch his mind in action.

Today Bankher was exceedingly addled from a party the previous night; he sat slumped in the corner at the back of the classroom. Their teacher, Mr Clumphod, was only too painfully aware that his wards had far superior mental agility than he. When the three arrived at class most of the time there would be a note pinned to the blackboard stating that Mr Clumphod had been called away on urgent business to see Principal Ahgresor. The note would ask them to open their books where they had left off last time and continue to work until the class was over. The book in question was over a thousand pages long. They had all finished it long ago, so afraid was Mr Clumphod of attending his own class. It didn't matter to them. Bankher liked to catch up on sleep and it gave Tengis and Odval an opportunity to continue career-counselling one another.

'I have got to find the link between me and Chinggis,' said Tengis.

'Are you sure there is an actual link?' said Odval. She knew she was stepping into dangerous territory doubting Tengis on matters relating to Chinggis. 'Do you really *need* there to be a link? You have such a brilliant mind; you will succeed no matter what.'

'It's not as simple as that,' said Tengis, ignoring his friend's cynicism about his link to Chinggis. 'It's not just about me, it's about how other people see me. At the moment they see me as a weirdo. Sure, they see me as a smart guy but I'm not from a well-connected family. I don't have money and influence like you and your family. If I don't have a degree, how am I going to be perceived as professional – even though in my view the degrees they hand out these days aren't worth the paper they're written on. It's degrees that people in business and politics look for. I'm better than their stupid education system. I need another angle. I know how things work. I know what people blindly value. But I am nothing at the moment. No matter how book-smart I am, they'll only ever see some boffin kid. They will never see my potential.'

'Look,' said Odval, 'don't look for bad things in the good that you do.'

'That's the problem,' replied Tengis, 'you're the *only* person who sees, let alone understands, the good I do now and could do for the whole of Ongolium. I need to prove that I am linked to Chinggis.'

'Forgive me,' said Odval, 'but are you really sure that is the wisest thing to do? What makes you so certain there is a connection?'

'You have to trust me on this,' said Tengis, trying hard not to get annoyed. 'There have been too many signs, too many dreams, too many coincidences! It started as an occasional vision where I would be embroiled in some fantastic situation whereby the country depended on my courage and ability. The dreams became more frequent and a voice started to guide me through the dreams, explaining things . . .'

'This is what I mean,' Odval interrupted. 'You have no real evidence.'

'Let me finish!' snapped Tengis. 'The voice visits me more often now. Almost every night I hear him and sometimes even during the day when I am thinking hard. It is encouraging me to follow my instinct and unleash myself on the world. It says that I have the ability to become emperor.'

'Tengis!' shouted Odval. 'That's crazy talk.'

'It's so easy for you,' said Tengis sarcastically, 'you were born privileged. I have had nothing and now that I have an opportunity to do something good, something big, you try and take away my hopes and aspirations. How very typical of *your lot*.' Tengis waved his hand dismissively in Odval's general direction.

'How can you say that?' said Odval. She was deeply offended. 'I have always been here for you. I have always been devoted to you and admired your confidence and capacity for thought.'

Tengis calmed himself. 'I will find evidence.' He pulled some documents from his bag. Bankher stirred in the corner, then returned to snoring. 'Here, help me with these.'

Odval helped him open several large sheets of paper. They spread them out over their desks.

'What on earth is this?' asked Odval.

'I have been doing some digging,' said Tengis. 'This here is my family tree going back in time. This paper here shows Chinggis's family tree down through the generations. I drew it up myself.'

'It is so complicated,' said Odval.

'Chinggis had many children,' said Tengis. 'By my reckoning he fathered thousands as he built his empire across the world. That is why I must be related to him. Some of the children must have been in Ongolium. One of them must have had a child who had children and grandchildren of whom one was my great-great-great-great-great-great-great-great grandfather. I just have to find the link.'

Tengis stared hard at the papers in front of him. The family tree for Chinggis measured four metres wide, and Tengis's writing was so small as to be barely legible. He pored through the names, sporadically shifting focus to his own more modest tree.

'Have you found anything?' asked Odval. She was a little concerned that Tengis was taking his link with Chinggis too seriously. She knew that the chances of finding a link were slim at best; she knew that finding proof that he was a reincarnation of Chinggis was utterly impossible, wasn't it?

'There is nothing on my mother's side,' said Tengis. He excitedly explained the maternal family history. It dated back to the correct epoch but there was little grandiose about it. 'The voice insists that the connection is on my father's side.' Tengis had not even met his father, yet he ardently awaited his return. Until then there would be no means of finding any information that could shed any light on his claim. Tengis frantically searched the papers looking for clues, his hands moving from entry to entry on the page.

'Tengis,' said Odval, 'are you sure about this? Have you been working too hard or something? I'm a little concerned – shall we go back to your mother?'

'Shut up!' barked Tengis, suddenly losing his cool. 'Stupid little rich girl. I have never been more sure of anything in my life. It is plain and simple. I am Chinggis Khaan. The voice in my head has told me so. *I am Chinggis!*'

'I want to help,' said Odval. Tears began to fill her eyes. She had never had reason to doubt her friend. She knew that he was not being logical and he had always been logical. Tengis's actions and apparent delusion bore no logic whatsoever. Odval wanted him to stop. 'Please, let me take you home and we can talk about it there.'

'What do you know?' ranted Tengis. 'You have always been spying on me, trying to steal my ideas, my thoughts. You're jealous of me. You might have all the wealth and riches that make you popular in this hellish place but secretly you have only ever been my friend so that you could rob me of my philosophy and ideology. Well, you can't! I'm glad I've had a chance to finally see you for who you truly are. I am Chinggis Khaan and *you* are my enemy.'

A chair scraped gently behind them. Turning, Tengis and Odval saw Bankher craning forward to look at the papers, a wide smirk upon his face.

'Very interesting,' said Bankher calmly. 'Voices in your head? And you think you're Chinggis, do you? That *is* interesting.'

'I am!' yelled Tengis, squaring up to Bankher across the desk. 'I am and you will come to regret your doubt. Both of you.' He stood rooted to the spot, staring madly at them both. He was ready to attack either or both of them.

'Good,' replied Bankher. He casually flipped a coin and put it in his pocket. 'Very good. Let's see what the good people of Baatarulaan think about your claims. I'm sure the Fun Brigade would love to hear about this heresy, too. I think you'd best contact the Post Office. You're going to need to get your mail redirected to the House of Fun. Have a nice day now, freak.'

'You wouldn't?' said Odval.

It was too late. Bankher had speedily crossed the floor and flown through the classroom doorway. Odval stared pityingly into her friend's eyes. Tengis was seething with rage and ready to fight.

8

By the time Tengis had run home from school his mother already knew. He knew that she knew because she was standing outside the front door looking very cross. He had never been in trouble before and had certainly never had his mother give him a hard time. Unbeknown to Tengis the school, informed by Bankher, had called to complain that her son had been inciting civil unrest. Unrest the school and Baatarulaan could cope with but not if it was civil.

Mrs Khaan had also been contacted by Clown Oldortar, nominal leader of the Fun Brigade. Clown Oldortar was a large round man who, had things turned out differently, would have been naturally kind but whose job dictated that he be anything but and so he wasn't. He was concerned that her son had been being far too serious and not paying enough attention to humour and Khadism. He made it clear to her that they were very keen to meet such a morose fellow in order to teach him how to have more exuberance and embrace life more wholeheartedly.

Odval had contacted Tengis's mother, too, in order to explain her concerns, tell her what it was her son had done and how he had behaved, particularly towards her. Mrs Khaan was a very worried and angry woman. None of this concerned Tengis; he was still furious about what he saw as Odval's betrayal.

'Where have you been?' asked Mrs Khaan.

'I have been at school obviously,' replied Tengis. 'Where else would I normally be on a weekday morning?'

61

'Less of your cheek, young man,' said Mrs Khaan. 'Why aren't you there now in that case and what is this I have been hearing about you? I brought you up better than to go about inciting hatred. Do you have any idea how much trouble you are in? Principal Ahgresor wants to expel you. Clown Oldortar wants to introduce you to his Clown School. You know that is only one step away from the House of Fun, don't you? As for Odval, how dare you speak like that to such a charming young lady. Where on earth are your manners?'

'Mother,' said Tengis. He drew himself together. It was about time she heard how he really felt about life and what he thought about her. 'Do you honestly think I give a flying fig what school says? Do you think they have actually taught me anything during my entire time there? I have had to educate myself entirely on my own. They don't have any books, let alone teachers, that can help me. They focus on passing exams and fitting into society, a society I think is rotten. I am far wiser than they are!' Tengis scarcely paused for breath before continuing his rant.

'Clown Oldortar is nothing more than a thug with a badge and a big stick. Those Khadists don't have an original thought between them. They run Baatarulaan as they believe Khad would have wanted. Who could possibly have wanted the filth and debauchery they peddle? They take our money in taxes and spend it on bureaucrats and drug development. Have you any idea how addictive the new Khem is? Almost 60 per cent of the city's population is hooked on that stuff. It's just a way of us giving them even more money. They think they are so smart. I have ideas for the city. I could make this city a great place once more. I am far more intellectual than any Khadist. As for Odval, she betrayed me. She is rich and looks down on me. She thinks I am just an ordinary man but I tell you I am not an ordinary man, I am Chinggis Khaan.'

'How can you say such things?' implored Mrs Khaan. 'Wise men talk about ideas, intellectuals about facts; the ordinary man talks about what he eats. You will soon starve if you carry on with this nonsense. What has got into you? Have I raised you badly? Is it because your father left?'

'Leave him out of this!' yelled Tengis. 'He is a good man. What's more he will come back, I tell you!'

'He's gone,' said Mrs Khaan. 'He left when you were still a child. He just couldn't cope with the responsibility of father-hood, he disappeared, and not with the Fun Brigade. Your father disappeared because he never really wanted us, or if he did he was more concerned with what he wanted for himself. I did, though. I have raised you, fed you and loved you as only a mother can, and yet you treat me this way?'

'You!' screamed Tengis. 'Why is everything always about you? Have you not heard what I have been saying? This whole place is putrid. We are being treated like idiots. Somebody has to make a stand and do something before we degenerate any further. I am going to be that person. You'll see. One day you'll remember what I've said and maybe then you'll understand me. Until you do I cannot live under the same roof as you. So long as you put up with this way of life your home is as putrid as the gutters of Baatarulaan.'

'Tengis!' said Mrs Khaan. She had begun to cry. 'My son, what are you saying?'

'I'm leaving, Mother,' said Tengis. He had started to calm himself. 'I have a life to find. That life is certainly not here, not at the moment anyway. Don't cry for me. I will survive; I know how to stay alive. You will hold your head high once I have made things better. You will be proud of me.'

'I *am* proud of you,' sobbed Mrs Khaan. 'Please, Tengis, please don't go. What will I do without you here? You might be able to survive but I don't know if I will.'

'You have survived worse than this,' said Tengis. He took his mother in his arms. 'This is something I need to do. I am sorry if I have hurt you. I have to leave, I have to be what I am meant to be, I am destined for great things.'

'What about Clown Oldortar?' said Mrs Khaan. She knew that her son had his mind set. 'He will be looking for you. He controls everything. How will you keep safe? Odval, you must contact Odval. You can't leave or go anywhere without speaking to her. Where are you going to go?'

'I cannot tell you, Mother,' said Tengis. 'The less you know the easier it will be when you speak to Clown Oldortar. He won't hurt you. Odval will have to wait. Perhaps the passing of time will help her see that I am being logical, that I am Chinggis Khaan, that I am the great person she once believed me to be. Perhaps she will come to love me, even – perhaps not! My purpose transcends friendship. For the time being it transcends family, too.'

9

Lily had spent several days at her makeshift camp trying in vain to understand what it was that Chinggis had meant when he wrote: 'A tiger wearing a bell will starve and a cat that likes to eat fresh fish will not go into the water; however, the distance between Heaven and Earth is no greater than one thought.'

Her first task was to identify who it was that Chinggis was referring to. There were only city dwellers, herders and Outsiders.

She surmised that the feline references related in some way to Baatarulaan. She had heard the elders often refer to the city's inhabitants as 'fat cats'. That made sense – who else could it mean? Lily knew that city dwellers were far more showy and extravagant than her nomadic group. In Lily's opinion, the people who lived in the city were too lazy to fend for themselves. Her father had warned her against the corruption and base nature of those within Baatarulaan's walls. Still, he had also inferred that they did have riches far beyond anything any mere herder could ever expect. Lily's father and the elders actually shunned riches; so long as they had enough they knew that was enough. More led to more problems. But riches were riches and would never lose their real appeal so long as humans breathed.

However, Lily knew that the appeal of riches was greed and that, no matter how many riches she accumulated, greed would have kept her poor for ever; even the abundance of this world would not make her rich. It was an odd conundrum but Lily knew that living as a herder she was living on the side of the equation she preferred. City dwellers were welcome to the other and from what she had heard they wallowed and waddled in it each and every day. They certainly acted like the furry fat felines that occasionally took up with the nomadic group, always expecting to be lifted into carts when it came time to move on rather than walking anywhere! Fat cats of all kinds had an easy life.

As for Outsiders, Lily had only ever heard of them in stories told by the elders to frighten the group's children. No one from the group had actually ever seen an Outsider or been further than a day or two's ride by horse from wherever the camp was based. That had never resulted in crossing or coming close to any borders. People knew better than to stray too far from Baatarulaan, no matter how much they disliked the urban sprawl. Indeed, no one had been outside Ongolium, let alone met an Outsider, for over a dozen generations.

At least, that was the case in the real world. In the spirit world Lily had encountered many oddly dressed people who had strange customs. However, she knew that the words of Chinggis had to refer to the real world. As far as Lily was aware, Chinggis had never had the shamanic gift. No Outsiders existed in Lily's experience of the real world.

Lily couldn't understand the Heaven and Earth reference. Although she spent an increasing amount of time in the spirit world, she had never thought of it as Heaven. She often wondered whether Heaven even existed; it did seem a far-fetched idea. Her time in her other world was interesting, wonderful even, but certainly not heavenly. It was full of challenges and surprises, and not always pleasant ones. There were people in that place that were anything but ethereal beings.

By the time of Lily's fourth night of camping, Lucky was

becoming agitated. The horses in Ongolium are not like those found elsewhere. They are shorter, sturdier and more single-minded than their cousins in other lands. When an Ongolian horse is agitated everybody knows about it. Lucky had started stamping his front legs that afternoon. By the time evening had fallen into darkness he was listlessly jumping up and down on the spot. He whinnied loudly and snorted messily.

'Shhh!' said Lily. 'Please, Lucky, we will go home soon, I promise. I just need a little more time trying to think about this.' She stroked the nose of her faithful steed and nuzzled her face against his.

Her actions appeared to appease Lucky, at least for the time being. He stopped being restless and relaxed back into his usual sensible, if slightly grumpy, self.

Lily, as leader, had the pick of her group's horses. There were many fine stallions among the herd. Generally each person had at least two beasts to do their bidding. One horse was rarely sufficient if undertaking a longer journey. While Lucky was not the runt of the herd, neither was he among the equine in-crowd. For a breed of short horses he was one of the shortest. For a breed of single-minded horses he was most definitely one of the most bloody-minded. Lily could have chosen any of the horses, but she didn't. No matter how grumpy, stubborn or obstinate Lucky was, he more than made up for with his sense and sensibility. For Lily he had a charm that none of the more flighty fancy horses could ever attain. As Lily would reply to her steed's various detractors: 'A donkey that carries me is worth more than a horse that kicks me.' She was very sensible like that, and so was Lucky. Both lived on the periphery of their respective communities; they made perfect life partners.

Having settled Lucky, Lily returned to her thinking. She decided that, since the answer wasn't readily coming to her around the campfire, then she would explore for it in the spirit world. She placed some logs on the fire to make sure she stayed warm during her visit. Sitting cross-legged next to the warmth, she glanced at Lucky knowingly. He nodded back to affirm that he would keep his eyes open. Returning to the fire, Lily gazed long and deep into its bright dancing flow. She sank into herself and began to slow her breathing. Her eyes remained open, staring at the glowing embers. Lily began to emit a strange noise. It was far from her usual voice and came from much deeper inside her. She began a slow chant. Lucky snorted casually as he watched his mistress fall into her trance. Lily chanted more loudly and slower: 'Ooohhhhhhhhhhhhmmmmmmmm . . .'

Her body resonated to the sound. She could sense her spine tingling and senses buzzing. Natural electricity began to pulse, rising from her tail bone, spreading its power throughout her abdomen and up through her neck. As the electricity increased, a force began to build inside her. It grew with each pulse, welling upwards. Extending through her limbs, it focused on her diaphragm. Breathing became more difficult but she forcefully expelled the air from her lungs. The pressure mounted. It snaked its way up her body towards her head. It targeted her forehead. Once there it exploded from the centre just above her eyes. Lily remained motionless, breathing deeply with her eyes fixed upon the fire. Lily blinked her eyes and departed.

10

When Tengis had walked away from everything he had ever known, he had not really figured out where it was he was going to go or how he would face the inevitable consequences, particularly from Clown Oldortar. Planning ahead in life had never been one of Tengis's strongest traits. He was confident that his advanced intellect more than negated the need for planning. He believed things would simply happen as they were supposed to. After all, he thought of himself as beyond mere mortal humanity; he was special. The normal rules of life did not matter to him and really didn't concern him very much. Tengis was an exceedingly empathic young man. The only problem was he was only capable of empathy with himself. However, he really did know every corner and recess of his mind and that gave him a great sense of comfort. He viewed truly knowing oneself as another means of transcending the norms of the world.

Smart as Tengis might have been, he had to confess that on occasion he wished he had thought things through a little more robustly. Nightfall was going to arrive soon and he had no ready means of shelter – or food or warmth or water. He may have been top of his class but at that moment he would gladly have traded place for fourth or fifth place – no lower, though. His stomach groaned. It had been hours since breakfast. His throat was rasping and hoarse. The atmosphere that breathed across the Steppe was blisteringly dry.

As he walked away from Baatarulaan, he cast a last look back at the vast cluster of shimmering buildings that stood out so starkly against the enormity of the Steppe. He *had* to go. Today had been what he had long needed to push him towards starting his real life. He knew that things would never again be the same. He had no doubt that he didn't want them to be.

Tengis made a mock salute to his home city, turned and walked towards the wilderness. He didn't know where he was going but he knew he would get there. He turned his mind towards more meaningful matters. If he was to change Baatarulaan, he had to be clear how he was going to achieve this. For the first time he admitted to himself that he did in fact need a plan. Before long his mind was lost in a myriad of complex calculations, ornate philosophies, extravagant religions and perplexing politics. He had a good deal to think about. Fortunately, he now had a good deal of time to think.

Tengis walked on into and through the night. The Steppe stretched out before him and the stars watched overhead. He didn't pay them any attention. He was busy.

The Steppe was immense. Its slowly undulating terrain was broken only by sporadic boulders, bushes or groups of huddling goats. By moonlight the terrain seemed hauntingly ethereal. A carpet of light blue covered the ground as far as the eye could see. A chilly air contributed further to the other-worldliness of the scene. Nothing stirred. Tengis continued with his thoughts as he moved slowly across the landscape. He no longer felt either cold nor hunger, so intense were his thoughts. His face was lined with a frown of concentration. A hare ran across his path desperate to find some shelter from the cold. Its rapid movement was in stark contrast to the stillness of its surroundings, but Tengis didn't notice it. Onwards he walked into unknown places and unchartered thinking.

As the sun rose the following morning, Tengis was almost two days' normal walk away from Baatarulaan. The terrain had not changed even slightly since he had set foot on the Steppe but now the distance was fringed by advancing mountains. Tengis continued to stride out in body and mind. The mountains moved closer with each step. Tengis had transcended thirst and sleep.

By the time the sun was overhead, had he focused his gaze or shifted his thinking, Tengis would have started to make out the valleys and hillsides that lay ahead of him . . . but he didn't. He had too many things to work out. Fortunately, the voice in his head was keeping him company throughout all of his contemplations.

'Change is inevitable,' said the voice. 'The people of Baatarulaan have grown fat and lazy. They need to be reminded of who they are and who it is that truly leads them.'

'But the Khadists still control them,' said Tengis. 'The Fun Brigade makes sure that people do as they should.'

'People have lost their faith,' said the voice. 'The Fun Brigade is not as strong as it used to be. People do not show one another the respect they should. They have turned Baatarulaan into a joke. They live merely to entertain themselves. It is not as it should be.'

'That is Khad's fault,' said Tengis, 'not the people's. It was Khad who invented all that crazy stuff about laughter. It was Khad who changed the way the people were educated. It was Khad who ensured the people were driven to drugs and debauchery so that he could reap the rewards from the sale of Khem. If anyone is to blame, it is Khad, not the people.'

'But why do you think that Khad formulated all of these things?' asked the voice.

'That's obvious,' said Tengis, 'he just wanted to break the spirit and memory of his cousin Chinggis whom he had hated so much.'

'Do you really think that was the reason?' asked the voice.

71

'Could it not be that Khad *knew* the people. Perhaps he knew what they *really* wanted. Perhaps he knew that they lacked the natural intelligence to be able to think for themselves. Perhaps he knew the best way to ensure the progress and survival of the Ongolian race. Perhaps he didn't really hate his cousin. Perhaps he just found a different way to govern than Chinggis. Perhaps Chinggis had something dreadful planned for the people and Khad saved them by destroying Chinggis.'

'You watch what you're saying!' shouted Tengis.

His voice echoed across the Steppe. An eagle flying overheard suddenly changed direction, startled by the solitary human's outburst far below. It ruffled its feathers against the cold, wondered whom the human was talking to and flew on towards its mountain-top nest. 'Chinggis is the reason why any of us are here. He was the one true emperor and I will see his vision reinstated.'

'Are you sure that's wise?' asked the voice.

'What on earth do you mean?' replied Tengis. 'How could it *not* be wise? Chinggis was the greatest man to have walked the Earth.'

'Tell me,' asked the voice, 'what do you really know about Chinggis? I mean really, truly know about him as a man; about his real desires; what he really wanted to achieve?'

'He brought peace and prosperity to our country,' said Tengis. 'He united a thousand tribes across his empire. He permitted many faiths to coexist in harmony. He was our true leader.'

'But,' said the voice, 'why do you really think he did those things?'

'What do you mean?' yelled Tengis.

A group of goats looked on in bewilderment at the human marching past talking to himself.

'Could there not have been some other reason?' said the

voice. 'Could it not have been that Chinggis had motivations other than to be a good and just emperor? Could it not have been that Chinggis wanted something else, something altogether more sinister?'

'You're mad!' screamed Tengis. 'Stop talking like this. Get out of my head!'

'You know there is possibly some truth in what I'm saying,' continued the voice. 'You have spent your life believing only the best of Chinggis. But remember, he was merely a man and men are weak . . . even Chinggis.'

'Chinggis was never weak!' shouted Tengis. 'He united the known world. He was the greatest ruler ever to have walked the Earth.' In his desperation, he was repeating himself now.

'He was an incredible man,' said the voice, 'there's no deny-ing that, but he *was* a man. Men all have their weaknesses; men all have their price. Look at the people of Baatarulaan. Even among the good there is corruption. Even among the faithful there is depravity.'

'That is the fault of the Khadists,' said Tengis. 'I believe that all men are good; I have to believe that. It is the Khadists that have polluted the minds of Baatarulaan. I have to have faith that they can be good again. I want to be the man that helps them get there. I want to lead the people in revolt. I want to help the people help themselves no matter what it takes.'

'*No matter what it takes?*' asked the voice. 'You sound like Khad.'

'I am nothing like him,' said Tengis. 'He killed out of spite and jealousy. All I'm saying is that I would be prepared to be strong, tough even, if required.'

'So,' said the voice, 'you'd consider killing so long as it wasn't out of spite or jealousy?'

'I'm not saying that,' said Tengis. 'I know that control is important and that you can't have people doing what they want if their intentions are impure or if it is going to damage the way things need to be.'

'But if things got out of hand?' said the voice. 'What then? You'd consider using some stronger force, say death?'

'I would never let things get out of hand,' said Tengis, 'but if they did, then yes, it would only be logical to consider capital punishment if it was deemed to be for the greater good. Even Chinggis would have endorsed that and all I am trying to do is reinstate his idealism.'

'Khad was always fond of death, too,' said the voice. 'He would say that even foul water will put out a fire. Are you sure you understand what Chinggis's cousin was trying to do? It sounds as though you're not sure. He was only trying to do good by the people in his view.'

'All Khad ever wanted was power,' said Tengis. 'He didn't want change. He didn't like it when people rocked the boat. He polluted his people's minds and encouraged Khem addiction. I want to help people break free.'

'No matter what it takes, I know!' said the voice. 'You've already told me, I believe.'

'The people need assistance to help them see the error of their ways,' said Tengis. 'Chinggis would have never let his country go into decline the way it has. I can't even believe that Khad would have allowed it. That city is close to anarchy. Only the Fun Brigade and the power of Khem keep people from killing one another, and even that doesn't always work. It needs a strong leader. It needs someone its people can believe in. I am Chinggis, am I not? Have you not told me many times that I am an emperor?'

'Indeed that is true,' replied the voice. 'You will be emperor, in time, if you listen to me. At the moment you are just a very clever man with good ideas – *great* ideas. You have the potential to be as great as Chinggis. You have the promise to be wealthier than Khad. We need to see what we can do to help you take the right path. For the time being, keep thinking and keep walking towards the highest mountain.'

'Who are you?' asked Tengis. 'Why are you so keen to help me?'

The voice remained silent.

Tengis walked on into the evening light. For the first time since leaving his mother he became vividly aware of his surroundings. He was no longer in Baatarulaan; he was a long way from home. His stomach noticed that Tengis was paying attention and reminded him loudly that it needed some attention, too. Tengis was approaching the foothills to the mountains and set about looking for some shelter and provisions.

Close by was a small grassy bank laid out invitingly next to a small stream. Tengis gathered together some twigs, leaves and larger branches. He had read in a survival handbook that if he rubbed two sticks together the right way he could start a fire. Just in time before darkness fell he succeeded. Exhaustion began to claw at him but he knew he needed to eat. Scouring some nearby rocks he sought out birds' nests. He also foraged for some berries, fungi and roots. He found a thinly layered concave stone that acted perfectly as a skillet of sorts. He was glad he had read about herbology and botany. He was even more glad once he had finished cooking a mushroom omelette.

After his meal Tengis was soon fast asleep. It had been a long two days. He had learned a great deal about himself and his potential. The voice in his head had confirmed his path towards greatness. Tengis had understood most of what had been said and he knew now more than ever that he was Chinggis Khaan; he had to be, didn't he?

Waking the next morning, Tengis found himself disappointed that the voice had not come to him during the night nor led his dreams off to glorious battles. Instead, all he had dreamed about was wealth. Lots and lots and lots of wealth. As his dream returned to him, Tengis recalled that in it he had lived in a cave. The cave lay deep in the mountains. In its depths lay piles upon piles of a yellow-orange shining metal. Tengis dreamed that he languished on top of the piles of sunny metal, playfully letting pieces slip between his fingers. He had bathed in the metal. He had slept upon it. Outside the cave a million people waited, all kneeling with their head turned towards its entrance as if entranced – entranced by Tengis. He had dreamed that these were his people and that they all had absolute faith and confidence in him. It had felt good, really good. It was an even better dream than usual.

Even though the voice hadn't come to him during the night Tengis knew that he needed to head towards the biggest mountain. Behind him lay the Steppe, and beyond that lay his home and Baatarulaan. Ahead of him lay a range of mountains that stretched upwards, left and right far out of sight, further than the horizon in any direction.

Following the stream he had drunk from the previous night Tengis now began to clamber across the rocky foothills and. within an hour he was walking through a narrowing valley. Rocky outcrops rose high around him with cliffs and large birds of prey circled overhead. Strange goat-like animals with long curved horns stood on vertical precipices peering down at him intently as they chewed whatever it was they were eating. Tengis walked onwards..

The valley walls became steeper and steeper, though curiously the floor began to slope downwards. Tengis knew he was walking further into the mountains and couldn't understand why the stream that earlier had been flowing away from the mountains was now flowing towards the very middle of them. The valley turned into a gorge and he walked on in a state of slight trepidation. Icicles began to decorate the stream and rocks around him. The sun had not shone here for thousands of years. Dank chilly darkness began to pervade everything.

'Don't be afraid,' said the voice in Tengis's head. 'There is nothing here that can harm you.'

'Stop creeping up on me like that,' said Tengis. 'Try and give me notice that you are about to arrive, will you?'

'What?' said the voice sarcastically. 'Like moaning and wailing or something? No, no, that wouldn't do at all.'

'I guess not,' said Tengis, 'but it's not at all polite. What is this place? It's absolutely freezing here.'

'This place has no name,' said the voice. 'No one ever comes here. In fact, no one has *ever* been here. That's what's so special about it. There are things here that nobody has ever found, things that nobody has ever dreamed of. Well, *almost* nobody...'

'If there's nothing here, though,' said Tengis, 'what am I supposed to do?'

But his question remained unanswered; the voice had disappeared again. Tengis determined to carry on into the darkening gorge. What little light remained came from far above. Natural ice sculptures loomed down overhead from long-frozen waterfalls. The gorge narrowed and narrowed and began to descend more steeply to the point that the only way to walk was in the icy stream itself. Tengis continued onwards, both hands feeling their way along the side of the icy gorge. Several hundred metres ahead of him Tengis could see that a bright light was shining from the middle of the gorge. He picked up his pace. He had no sense of danger; he just wanted to be nearer to the light and away from this murky and desolate prison.

As he neared the light, Tengis saw that it marked the end of the gorge. His pace quickened. Beyond the corridor the ground opened up into a large open wasteland. The area was wide enough to allow in enough sunlight to grow sparse vegetation but was otherwise surrounded by steep cliff faces that rose up into the mountains. At the opposite side of the opening from the gorge Tengis noticed that the ground rose slightly. He was unable to see what was there. He finally exited the gorge and hopped across several large rocks that formed a path across a forbidding-looking pool that seemed to mark the destination of the backwards-flowing stream.

Climbing up the small rise, Tengis froze mid-step. Further ahead, at the far end of the clearing, the cliff landed sheer into the ground. Tengis stared at the stone, his mouth drying and his heart racing; in front of him stood a natural chasm hewn into the rock face. It was a cave entrance exactly like he had seen in his dream. It penetrated into abject darkness and was just large enough for a young man to walk through.

Excitedly, Tengis hurriedly searched for wood to make a torch. He pulled up dried or dying vegetation that surrounded the water's edge and tied the lengths of grasses around a larger stick. He had kept some of the sticks he had used to create fire the previous night and was glad for having done so. He prayed that this would work. He was apparently in favour with the gods and within minutes he had himself a large flaming torch. There was no telling how long he would need the torch to last, so Tengis had made it especially large. He stuffed the remaining dried grasses into his pockets and lifted the torch with both hands. Blinking slowly, he moved towards the darkness.

It took Tengis several long seconds before his eyes became accustomed to the gloom, but his torch looked as though it would serve him well. Holding it out in front of him, he walked forwards into the unknown.

'This is it!' whispered a voice. It wasn't quite the voice in his head. Somehow the noise seemed further inside him.

Tengis ignored it and crept onwards. Inside the cave entrance the roof rose upwards into unseen darkness. He found himself standing in what seemed to be an enormous hollow cavern. As he moved forwards, the light from his torch began to glow brighter and brighter. The grotto became more and more apparent to him. Its walls appeared to glow and sway with the torchlight. Tengis moved closer to inspect them. Staring at the rocky walls, Tengis could see that there was another material embedded into the rocks. In some places he could make out dots the size of pinpricks; in other places the material was larger than a plate. Whatever it was, it reflected the torchlight brilliantly. Tengis had no idea what it was but it was definitely the sun-drenched metal he had seen in his dream the night before.

Moving to the centre of the cavern, Tengis fixed his torch into the ground using a few larger stones as buttresses. He ran back outside and found as much wood and grass as he could. He built piles of wood within easy reach and used some to create a substantial fire in the middle of the grotto. He wanted to see the whole space. He wanted to see what it was he had found. It made no sense to him yet but Tengis knew that this was something important. This was something that would help him fulfil his destiny. By stoking the fire, Tengis got the flames to rise high into the cavern and their light licked and flickered at the glowing material all around him.

Tengis sat and waited for the voice inside his head. It would surely come. He wouldn't have to wait long.

'You did it!' said the voice in his head. The voice sounded mildly surprised. 'I *am* impressed. You really are as good as we thought you were.'

'What on earth is it?' asked Tengis. 'It's beautiful.'

'It's power!' said the voice.

'What do you mean?' asked Tengis. 'It looks like rock or metal or something. How can that be power?'

'As you said, it's beautiful,' said the voice. 'People will find it more beautiful than you can possibly imagine. People will kill to possess even a small amount of this. You have it all. That means people will do exactly as you say. You can . . . how did you put it? . . . you can help people to help themselves. You have power over men. They will worship you.'

'But,' said Tengis, 'why? We are sitting in a cave filled with shimmering magic in the middle of nowhere about four days' travel from Baatarulaan. How does that give me any power?'

'We will have to figure out how to take some with you when you return to Baatarulaan,' said the voice. 'Just a little will be enough to make people fall in love with its appeal. It will prove more addictive than Khem; it will wield more strength than a dozen Fun Brigades.'

'But it's stuck into the rock,' said Tengis. 'How on earth do I get it out?'

'Not everything in life is easy,' said the voice. 'I suggest a little sweat and toil. You will find the tools you need in the cavern somewhere.'

Tengis walked around the room's lengthy perimeter, as the voice told him: 'I think it was left over there.' Tengis followed the instructions given to him. In one far corner, amid some rocks and rubble, he found a length of material. As he picked it up and moved it aside, heavy dust fell away to reveal a number of metal implements – a pickaxe, a large hammer, a small chisel and a number of buckets and sieves of varying size.

'What do I do with these?' asked Tengis.

'Use your imagination,' replied the voice somewhat tetchily.

Tengis looked at the various implements. He had never attended the construction class at school; it had always seemed to him below somebody of his intellect. Now he regretted that hasty decision.

He tried using the tools in a myriad of ways. After several hours, and at the cost of a fistful of blisters, Tengis succeeded in using the pickaxe and chisel to chip away a significant piece of rock. He put it on the ground and set about smashing it into smaller and smaller pieces using the hammer. He placed the smaller rocks in the sieves of varying size and worked away the pieces he didn't care about. Eventually he was left with small nuggets of the sunny substance. He held a large piece up to the firelight. It truly was beautiful. The fire's reflection glistened from its every edge. Its touch brought Tengis a confidence he had never previously known.

'How did you know about this?' asked Tengis. 'You knew to guide me here. You knew what was here.'

'I haven't been here for hundreds of years,' said the voice. 'I don't think anybody has – in fact, I'm certain of that.'

'But what has this got to do with Chinggis?' said Tengis. 'I am linked to him; in fact, I may well *be* him – you know that. You've hinted often enough. And it was you that brought me here. There has to be some link between this strange metal and Chinggis Khaan.'

'This cave was first uncovered during the age of Chinggis. When it was originally found, the cavern was little more than a hole. The shimmering metal quickly asserted itself as a thing of power and allure. The more that was found, the greater its power grew. Over time, more and more of the precious material was uncovered. The hole became a cave, then the cave became this cavern. The metal became an idol; whoever owned it became a god.'

'Are you saying,' asked Tengis, 'that Chinggis and his people found this metal, dug it out and used it to fund the growth of his empire?'

'Hmm,' said the voice, 'something sort of similar to that, you will find out one day. Everything will reveal itself in time.'

'So,' said Tengis, 'who does it actually belong to?'

'That doesn't matter, does it?' answered the voice.

'Of course it does!' said Tengis. 'If somebody owns it, then taking it would be theft. That much is obvious.'

'Really?' said the voice. 'Look at how beautiful it is. Do you honestly care who it belongs to so long as you possess it? Think about the strength and command it will offer you. There is no man who will be able to stand against you so long as you control the shining metal.'

'I suppose that, so long as I use it for the greater good, then there is no harm in my doing so,' mused Tengis. 'If no one has put a claim on it for hundreds of years, then logically *no one* owns it; finders keepers.'

'That's the spirit,' said the voice, 'but remember, if you are going to steal bells, plug your ears. You will be shocked at the amount of influence you now have in your hands and you'd better be ready to face the consequences. Are you clearer about your purpose yet?'

'I think so,' said Tengis. 'I just have to dot some *i*s and cross some *t*s. On our way here we went through most of it. I should probably write it down though in case there is any confusion.'

Tengis scraped around looking for some slate on which to write. He found several large tablets and sat down to scribe his ideology. He scratched his stubbly chin in contemplation, put stone to slate and began to write.

The Ten Recommendations

by Tengis Khaan

1 You shall have only one belief (and that belief is that the Ten Recommendations are the right and proper thing to believe in and that the owner of the Ten Recommendations tablet is the right and proper person to tell you what to believe in).
2 You shall not worship false idols (unless they help you keep the faith or understand something really important such as the Ten Recommendations).

3 You shall not say bad things about the Ten Recommendations or the keeper of the tablet. (He or she does have feelings, you know, and is only trying to help.)

4 You shall have one day off a week from all work and on that day you shall read and discuss the Ten Recommendations.

5 Respect your elders (and other people of influence or authority, particularly if they might prove useful in the future).

6 You shall not kill people. (It really is not nice no matter how rude someone might be – only the keeper of the tablet can decide to murder someone and even then only if it is really, really for the greater good.)

7 You should only ever have children with people you care for and who care for you. (Moreover, fathers should never ever leave a pregnant woman before the child has been born because that is just plain wrong; as punishment they shall be subject to a penalty equal to that deemed appropriate by the keeper of the Recommendations).

8 Do not take things that are not yours (at least not without asking beforehand, the only exception being if something has lain untouched for several hundred years, in which case it is to be deemed fair game).

9 Do not say bad things about other people (unless you think they really deserve it).

10 Do not be jealous of donkeys, goats or, for that matter, anything because it doesn't get you anywhere. Channel that energy into hard work and maybe one day you will be able to afford a horse. (Important people, however, can be jealous and take what they want by force or other means.)

Once Tengis had finished carving his thoughts into stone, he lifted them high above his head and read them by the firelight. He looked at his shadow flickering against the precious metals in the wall. He breathed in, puffed up his chest and liked what he saw. To him it appeared to be a very imperial profile.

'And so,' shouted Tengis to no one in particular, 'New Chinggism is reborn!'

He tucked the tablets under his arm, put out the fire and headed back towards Baatarulaan with renewed vigour. The voice in his head said nothing but sat with a satisfied grin across its beaming face.

11

Opening her eyes again, Lily was in the familiar territory of the spirit world. Each time she visited the spirit world she seemed to arrive at the same place. She was standing outside a large gate on a road that ran left and right along the side of a river. Behind her a track wound its way up a mountain beyond the gate. It was a serene, silent and solitary place. Lily almost always felt comfortable here. She knew the feel of the air as its freshness blew down the mountainside into her hair. The smell of the freshwater river flowing in front of her filled her nostrils with a soothing familiarity. She also knew that before long her spirit friend would come and find her.

Lily set off walking along the river in a direction that could have been east or west; there were two suns in the spirit world. She knew the route would soon bring her to a bridge that spanned only half the river. It had crumbled in some forgotten age and grass grew through the remaining tarmac. No cars had been here as there were no cars in this world to the best of Lily's knowledge. Balmy winds ran through the surrounding hillsides causing the low-lying trees that lined their flanks to chime mystically. Noises of various pitch soothed the air. Lily knew there was some force greater than the wind at play; it was probably some spirit or other whiling away the hours. This sort of thought had initially caused her concern but she no longer thought about such things; such things were normal in this world.

Little concerned Lily here. She had visited hundreds of times and, despite meeting various untoward characters who had frightened her, her fear had been little more than thrilling; there was no danger for her. This was a world where Lily could explore and expand her horizons with carefree abandon. She had her friend to look over her. From what Lily had experienced so far, her friend was an important spirit. Although she guessed that her friend was only about the same age as she was, perhaps a couple of years older, other spirits, regardless of age, tended to kowtow to her.

Standing upon the bridge, Lily looked across the river to the land beyond. She had never been to that side of the river. Her friend had suggested she stay on this side. Like any young lady, Lily was intrigued by implied danger. Her gaze into the distance was broken by a friendly sound. Three young puppies ran circles between her feet chasing one another. Their mother padded towards her more sedately. There were a great number of stray dogs in the spirit world and mostly they were affable. This family had been here for as long as Lily had visited.

Lily reached into her pocket and pulled out some scraps from the dinner she had prepared for Lucky and herself. The pups and their mother always seemed so grateful for Lily's kindness and generosity. They couldn't offer anything in return but nonetheless Lily was filled with a curious sense of having done something good and worthy each time she visited. The mother dog barked her appreciation as she led the puppies back down under the bridge. Lily smiled and returned her gaze to the land on the other side of the river.

Little stirred over there, but then again little stirred on this side either. A few trees swayed gently and a pillar of smoke rose from a small cluster of houses. There was nothing more or less remarkable than on this side of the river. The eerily echoing tones continued to soothe and reverberate around her ears.

'Lily,' said a quiet voice behind her, 'how lovely to see you again.'

'Hello,' replied Lily. She didn't know her friend's name. Her friend always evaded that question. 'I needed to get away. I wasn't able to think straight and there is so much I need to think about.'

'Well,' said her friend, 'we are good at finding solutions here. Let's take a walk.' She beckoned Lily to follow her.

Lily obliged without hesitation. Presently, they came to a bench beneath a tree. It wasn't particularly hot but it is always nice to sit under a tree canopy. The branches opened out overhead, their arms trailing down almost to the ground. Once the young ladies were seated, other spirits began to stir. People of and from all ages gently milled around beneath the tree's protection.

'Good afternoon, ladies,' said a man who looked like a Roman centurion. He was particularly handsome and Lily could not help admiring the musculature of his bronzed thighs. The Roman appreciated the admiring looks and flexed his muscles accordingly. The ladies laughed nervously. 'Such pretty ladies. I do hope you enjoy the day. Would you mind helping me? Which way is the lighthouse? I must get back to Alexandria and see my dear girl.' The Roman theatrically bent the arm he was pointing with so that his muscles bulged. Droplets of sweat ran out from beneath his armour. He winked and walked off.

'Lovely day for a walk,' said another man who wore a heavy bearskin hat and red military jacket. Lily thought the hat looked funny and began to giggle.

'You must be roasting with that badger on your head!' joked Lily. The man in the red jacket picked up his rifle, vigorously leaned it against his shoulder and marched off into invisibility. Her friend shot her a glance that stopped her humour dead.

'We must be respectful!' said her friend. 'If you drink the

water, follow the custom.' Lily knew that meant something; most of what her friend said did. It was just that sometimes Lily didn't quite understand what it was that was being said. 'When you are in the spirit world, value those in the spirit world. You might learn something about yourself.'

'I apologise,' replied Lily. She knew she was more intelligent than to have acted like the child she used to be. She also wondered what it was that she might learn about herself. That sounded interesting. She was keen to listen to whatever her friend would say next.

'Now,' said her friend more calmly, 'what is it that you want to think about?'

'I . . .' Lily hesitated. She worried that what she was about to say might sound fanciful or downright silly. She needed to know though and curiosity won out. 'I received a golden box from my elders. In the box I found a message secretly hidden away from all but the most prying eyes. That message appears to have come from Chinggis Khaan. Have you heard of him?'

Her friend stood up abruptly. She looked displeased and a little startled.

'What do you mean, you have a message from Chinggis Khaan?' said Lily's friend.

'So you *have* heard about him?' said Lily.

'Of course I have, you stupid child!' replied her friend.

It was the first time that Lily's friend had spoken to her in anything other than a kindly tone. Lily was taken aback. She didn't know how to proceed. She wondered whether she had done something wrong.

Then, more calmly, her friend asked, 'Are you sure it was from Chinggis Khaan?'

'I have no evidence to the contrary,' said Lily, trying to sound more grown up, 'but neither do I have any evidence to confirm it. I just have a feeling that it is from him. It feels right.'

'What do you mean, a feeling?' asked her friend.

Lily's cheeks turned an embarrassed shade of red.

'Well,' said Lily coyly, 'when I read the words I had a strange sensation in the very bottom of my stomach. It was as though Chinggis Khaan had been with me and had whispered the words directly into my ear. I know that sounds weird but I don't know how else to explain it.'

'I have heard he has been known to have that effect on people sometimes,' replied her friend dreamily.

'What do you know about him?' enquired Lily. 'Did you ever, you know, meet him or anything either in this world or in the real one?'

'Which one is real?' said her friend. 'He and I crossed paths but it was so long ago I can barely remember. He has a reputation, though. Many are aware of him but very few hear him. Those that do appear to have been chosen for a reason and are ultimately destined for greater things.'

'Do . . . do you think he really chose me?' asked Lily. She was excited at the prospect.

'Had you thought about him before you received the box from your elders?' asked her friend. 'Did you ever wonder what it would be like to have met him and spent time in his company?'

'Perhaps a little,' said Lily. She wasn't sure where her friend was taking this conversation and, while she had spent a considerable amount of time with her, she didn't feel that she wanted to disclose her more intimate thoughts and feelings.

'I can see by your hesitation that he has been long in your thoughts,' probed her friend. 'Do not be embarrassed. There is no shame in feeling as a woman ought to. I have often thought about him myself. It would appear that Chinggis has indeed identified you for some purpose. They say that he is still around somewhere, waiting for an opportunity to bring about peace to his people. I am less sure. From what I see of your world they have little desire for anything other than carnal pleasure, and certainly not peace. What was it that your message said?'

Lily quoted Chinggis's words to her friend: 'A tiger wearing a bell will starve and a cat that likes to eat fresh fish will not go into the water; however, the distance between Heaven and Earth is no greater than one thought.'

'I think the feline references relate to the city dwellers of Baatarulaan,' said Lily, 'though I'm not certain. I don't know what the stuff about the bell and the starving means or about not going into the water. It's very obscure, isn't it? I'm not sure I even believe in Heaven, so that can't have anything to do with me, can it?'

Her friend looked at her pensively. It took her several minutes before she answered Lily.

'You are correct about the "fat cats" – that much is true,' said Lily's friend. 'They are certainly odd people that live in that city. If only they knew how much more pleasant a culturally rich and honest way of life could be. If they could only see the great cities that stand on the oceans in the west or the river cities to their south. Then they might think about changing. Then they might see that there is a way other than evil, debasement and debauchery.' Lily's friend sighed.

'That's all very well,' said Lily, 'but no one knows anything about anything outside Ongolium. We all know the Legend of Khad. We all know that we have more than we need if only we could make it work. Anyway, what's this got to do with the words on the box? What about the other references?'

'There are some things we can see clearly,' said her friend, 'there are others that we see but do not understand. You are a clever lady: you already know the answers you are seeking; you already have the solution available to you.'

Lily raised her eyebrows. She knew that conversations in the spirit world were rarely straightforward and often unusual, but his one felt particularly silly.

'Please!' pleaded Lily. 'I don't understand what you are saying. Can you please stop speaking in riddles and just tell me what it is that I need to know? If I am set to undertake some sort of challenge, I need your help in understanding what it is I am supposed to do.'

'You already know,' said her friend. 'Are you not the youngest herder group leader of our age? Do you not have control over your shamanic gift? Are you not able to walk in both the physical and spirit worlds? All this and you appear to have some sort of bond with Chinggis Khaan, the greatest emperor of all time!'

'I know,' implored Lily, 'but I am still young and have so much to learn. I need your help. I have never been anywhere other than the Steppe. I have never met anyone other than herders. I have not had dealings with the city dwellers – that was my father's job. I am just a young woman who has been given a special and unusual box she doesn't understand, with words written on it that seem to mean very little. I don't know what it is I am supposed to do. You need to tell me what I have to do. You have always been here for me . . . Please!'

'The more you listen to me, the more you give yourself room for doubt,' said her friend. 'Believe in yourself and act as you feel you should. There is no wrong decision other than not making one. Now, go and fulfil your destiny.'

12

Tengis had been back in Baatarulaan for only a short while but he had already noticed that the city had begun to change more than it had in the previous three hundred years. Tengis was shocked by just how fickle his countrymen were. When he had left a few days previously they had all been ardent supporters of Khadism. They had been people for whom laughter was more than just a way of life. But now it appeared that he had not been alone in wanting regime change. His Ten Recommendations had been an instant success.

People adored new proclamations of this sort. When the proclamations were made in the presence of the lumps of lovely shining sunny metal, people dropped to their knees and venerated them and a whole new faith was born. Tengis truly did believe he was doing the right thing; that his actions were exactly what Chinggis would have done, only with less blood-letting and womanising, which he personally felt was a good thing. It didn't matter to him whether people were in love with the Recommendations or the shiny stuff. What mattered was that they were helping him facilitate positive change. Change was always good in Tengis's mind.

Tengis had adopted a solitary and solemn persona. He decided he could be more effectual if he worked alone, trusted nobody and delegated nothing of importance. He did need help in some areas though. The first people he had visited were the Fun Brigade. The voice in his head had suggested that overly angry militia types would definitely be more impressed by the shimmering metal than by the Ten Recommendations. The voice had been correct.

Despite Jester Oldortar having been excited by the prospect of educating the reprobate Tengis after his schoolroom heresy, he was even more delighted to hold and eventually own a small fragment of the sunny shimmering stuff. Tengis was surprised by the extent to which the material clawed control of the hardman cum jester's mind, and even more so by his exceptional willingness to undertake Tengis's bidding whatever that might be. So keen was Jester Oldortar to help Tengis that within hours of having arrested Tengis he was slapping him on the back, telling him how fond he had always been of him and asking him if there was anyone special whom he would like earmarked for future education by the Fun Brigade or whether he had ever had someone in mind for a lengthy holiday in the House of Fun.

It was all a little bewildering for Tengis but he was enjoying himself thoroughly. He had always been treated as an Outsider. The shimmering sunny substance was winning him much acclaim and even more friends. By the time Tengis left Clown Oldortar, the leader of the Fun Brigade had agreed that he would undertake any bidding that Tengis wished. He had also readily agreed to drop the word 'jester' from his name, so that Tengis's endeavours could not be tainted by Khadism. The two men set in motion a feasibility study of the city's public services, most of which related to discipline in some way or another. They agreed they would meet again soon to decide what to do. The shining metal was more powerful than Tengis could understand; nonetheless he was a little upset that it wasn't his Ten Recommendations that were inciting such excitement.

To Tengis's credit, when he had written the Ten

Recommendations he had been suitably vague in his wording. He was smart enough to know that, if he committed *everything* to slate, then it might be difficult to change things in the future; and change was almost always necessary. However, his vagueness was also down to the fact that Tengis had not really thought things through properly on his two-day trek; he had just known that he would need to retain a flexible approach as he sought to wrestle control from the Khadists he despised so much.

Tengis soon discovered that, as a mass, people didn't so much seem to *read* the words as *feel* what was being said, or what was reported as having been said. Tengis knew the power of a good soundbite. There was no mention of laughter. There were only Ten Recommendations. Each Recommendation was short, concise, easy to talk about and straight to the point (if you read it as such). The Khadist laws of the land were so lengthy and numerous that they filled every floor of a string of eight-storey buildings on both sides of one of the main city boulevards. Ten was a far more manageable number, though for many still too high a number to remember or in some cases count up to. It fitted neatly into posters and was easy to use in zippy advertising: 'The Tengis Ten', 'The Power of Ten', 'Ten-tation', 'Anyone for Ten-gis?' Far better than the opposition's eighty-eight billion, two hundred and seventy-four million, six hundred and forty-three thousand, nine hundred and thirty-two edicts. That really did not work for marketing purposes and gave many Baatarulaan advertising executives no end of sleepless nights. These same executives were among the first to embrace Tengis's proclamations . . . and the shiny metal of course.

Initially, the Khadist bureaucrats' reaction had been to simply ignore Tengis. 'How on earth can one man and ten ideas be any threat to the might of the Khadist regime?' asked Bureaucracy Chief Officer in Charge of Dictating Answers No.

322. Even when it had become clear that Tengis was winning considerable support with his shiny material and abbreviated approach to ideology they refused to change. 'There are men who walk through the woods and see no trees,' said the same Chief Officer to Tengis, 'and there are men who walk through the same woods and dedicate their life to counting and cataloguing every pine needle, bark chipping, squirrel pooh, mouldy mushroom and mosquito, not to mention the trees themselves. We are the latter kind of men – what kind are you?' It was meant as a threat, as much of an overt threat as a bureaucrat was ever able to conjure without contravening their own rules and regulations. Bureaucrats didn't normally need threats; people usually got so bored listening to them that they didn't hear what they were saying and ended up agreeing with whatever it was the bureaucrat wanted so long as they agreed to stop talking.

Within a week of Tengis's return, however, they had started to panic. He flew the Chinggis banner. The advertising executives had worked on Tengis's image and brand proposition. The voice in his head had insisted – against his better judgement – that, after securing the assistance of the Fun Brigade, Tengis make friends with the advertisers and marketers. They were people who knew that image was everything and that substance was insignificant. So long as people said the right things and believed strongly enough in what it was that they were saying, then other people would start to believe them, too. They found the effect of their words was magnified infinitely if they were able to sprinkle a smattering of made-up science and theory over their over-bloated words. Tengis disagreed but had reluctantly made the executives his second port of call.

'Blue has to be the colour,' said one executive. 'Not only does it carefully juxtapose the infinitesimal power of your ideology with the heavens; it also embraces the Ongolian belief in the sky as protector. After numerous focus groups we have knocked up the following – I just *know* you are going to love it.'

Tengis shifted uncomfortably in his chair.

'I suggest setting the blue off against black and white,' the executive continued. 'Not only does it show that you have no favouritism, it looks really nice too, which is very important for future merchandising opportunities. I imagine a blue box framed in white. On the left- and right-hand side there is a thicker black fringe. Can you visualise this? Can you not see it as a flag flying high over the city?'

'What does it really matter?' asked Tengis. 'I mean who cares what colours or images I use. I mean why do I need to use any at all? I would rather people listened to me rather than look at what designs or iconologies I have adopted.'

The executives, for whom iconology was sacrosanct, turned to one another in horror, clasped their hands over their ears, and began to burble loudly, feigning deafness. Tengis got up to leave.

'Tengis, please! Sit down, please,' said the executive who had been talking before. 'I realise that you are young and have perhaps not had as much experience of this city and its people as we have. Please, have faith in what we are peddling . . . umm, I mean *saying*. Marketing is a science if not an art form. Careful consideration and contemplation mixed with a healthy dose of manipulation can truly create a thing of beauty and a thing of beauty is a joy for ever, as someone once said.'

Tengis sat down. 'What do you propose?' He found what was being said entertaining. It was against everything he believed in. He was a man for whom fact and substance carried more kudos than fluff and fancy. He also thought that having a dozen mature advertising executives pandering so willingly to his every whim was utterly amusing.

'Thank you,' said the executive. 'Picture this. You are standing giving one of your amazing speeches. You are standing on a podium. Behind you, draped a hundred feet high, are your insignia. Can you see it?'

The other executives gasped and looked into the air imagining what the insignia might be.

'What on earth would be on this insignia of mine?' asked Tengis. He crossed his arms and raised his eyebrows.

'Focus on the colours!' said the executive. He waved his arms theatrically. 'Blue, white–black. The colours of Tengis and the Ten Recommendations. What's that amid the colours? I hear you ask . . . *I hear you ask.* I can't hear you asking!'

'What's that amid the colours?' gasped the other executives in unison. They all appeared to be considerably more excited than Tengis about what was amid the colours.

'Behold. The proud horse of Chinggis,' said the executive. 'And riding that horse, a young warrior with the head of a tiger; a youthful defender of the people; a rightful leader bedecked in a suit made of the shimmering shining sunny substance. He holds his right hand up in defiance. Grasped in that hand, the tablet of the Ten Recommendations.' The executive began to sob. 'We have Tengis and Chinggis united and uniting our country; the horse representing the past, the tiger signifying the future. Beneath the knight and his steed, read the following words, emblazoned in sparkling letters: "Believe in ideas and ideals not outdated ideology. What counts is what works. The objectives are radical. The means will be modern. Change is good."'

The other executives began to clap zealously. They stood as one and embraced the executive.

Tengis shook his head. The words were not his, although they did give an approximation of what he was trying to achieve. As for the colours and imagery, they really didn't appeal to his sense of logic. However, Tengis did what the voice in his head suggested, even if he didn't understand the wisdom behind it. That would soon change.

During the days following his meeting with the executives Tengis began to notice posters, flags, pendants, T-shirts and flyers appearing around Baatarulaan. It looked as though people didn't really know, or care, what they stood for but there was a frenzied rush to get hold of the merchandise nonetheless. People were queuing outside designated stalls just to get hold of some item or other that would show that they were part of this new political pandemic. Tengis doubted whether any of them could have recalled even one of the Ten Recommendations though he was increasingly sure that they did know they existed.

Later that week Tengis started to see people walking around with shiny paper wrapped around the outside of their clothing. These people would randomly hold aloft a large flat rock and shout: 'Hail the Ten Recommendations!' Everyone within earshot would cheer enthusiastically and offer up three hip-hip-hoorays.

By the end of that first week Tengis had inadvertently created enough people in his own image that several thousand Deggites dressed in the same colour as the shining metal marched through the streets chanting slogans against the Khadist regime as well as no shortage of obscenities: 'What do we want? Khadists out! When do we want it? Now!', 'Come try take some shining material if you think you're hard enough', 'There's only one Chinggis Khaan, one Chinggis Khaan, one Chinggggissss Khaaaaan!', 'Tengis, Tengis, he's our man; if you don't like him we'll chop off your hands!'

Tengis had found that he had a natural aptitude for addressing the mob. His professorial attire made him stand out and people immediately thought of him as an intellectual, and therefore right, just because he had the correct leather patches on the elbows of his jacket. In reality, the people didn't really care what it was that Tengis was saying. They were enraptured by the shimmering sunny yellow-orange metal. So long as Tengis ended each meeting or speech by holding aloft a large lump of it, he was sure to be met by rapturous applause, fervent adoration and professions of absolute faith. It frightened him slightly that his fellow Ongolians could be turned so blindly and he made note that, if he was to retain their loyalty in the longer term, he would need to discipline their thinking and behaviour in some way.

After that first week he knew he had to pay his mother a visit. Winning her support might not be so straightforward given their recent parting and cross words. Still, he would offer her a lump of his newly mined resource – everybody seemed to love that. Surely she would be no different.

'You can take that bloody lump of metal and shove it somewhere jolly horrid!' shouted Mrs Khaan. She threw the object at her son. 'Don't you come round here trying to recommend things to me, young man. I know the rules and you're breaking just about every one of them.'

'But, Mum,' said Tengis, 'I am trying to make things better. I am trying to get rid of the Khadists and reinstate the memory of Chinggis. I thought that was what you always wanted?'

'Don't you try and pin this one on me,' said Mrs Khaan. 'I love my Chinggis, I do, but I also know that it's them Khadists that runs things here. All this Chinggis worship will not end well, mark my words!'

'Mother,' said Tengis, 'you have just about every item of Chinggis memorabilia that's available; I thought you would be happy that I am spreading the word, encouraging everyone to share in the glory of Chinggis?'

'He's *my* Chinggis,' said Mrs Khaan. 'You and your lot keep your grubby little hands off him, will you, he's mine! I love him more than anyone else. I have loved him longer than anyone else. You lot clear off and go and find your own Chinggis. This one's mine.' And with that she slammed the front door in her son's face.

The meeting with his mother had not gone quite as well as Tengis had hoped it would. It did make Tengis feel less guilty for having been a little bit horrible to his mother, though. Despite having changed from being a weirdo school kid into a political activist cum would-be emperor Tengis had still felt a little bit bad for having walked out on his mother. She was the only one he had.

He walked away from his childhood home towards the centre of town. He needed to pay a visit to the only other person he had ever really truly cared for. Unfortunately, he had also been unduly nasty to that person in the past fortnight, too. He hoped that his meeting with Odval would work out more amicably than that with his mother.

As he wandered through the streets towards the home of Odval's parents, Tengis noticed some peculiar things. Before Tengis had left for the Steppe, in fact for as long as Tengis could remember, the people of Baatarulaan had been proudly lazy and profoundly antisocial. Few if any of the city's population would move if they could possibly avoid doing so; even fewer would actively participate in conversation with someone they didn't know. Now he noticed that there were people walking with purpose through the streets. There were people talking in groups, people chatting on street corners, people speaking in shops and people conversing in cafés. Furthermore, they didn't appear to be discussing where to score the best Khem or whom they should rob to pay for the next beetle drive. They seemed to be talking about the Ten Recommendations, the desire for change; a wish to see an end to the strict Khadist regime that had repressed them for so long. Tengis smiled. His movement was gaining momentum more quickly than he could have hoped for and more quickly than he could ever have warranted.

He could not believe just how malleable people seemed to be. It was a valuable lesson.

Odval lived with her parents and brother in the smartest district of Baatarulaan. Theirs was a home other citizens of Ongolium could only ever aspire to. It had four walls and a roof that didn't leak. Each member of the family had their own room and the family shared two bathrooms. The house also had a front door that locked and a fireplace. There were not many in Baatarulaan who could boast of such things. Only the very wealthiest and most powerful families had homes such as this and Odval's was among the finest. Their home had luxuries that weren't found anywhere else in Ongolium. It had a toilet that flushed, taps with clean running water, and, luxury of luxuries, central heating; only top Khadist bureaucrats had central heating. Tengis and his mother had shared a two-room apartment all his life. They shared a small bedroom. A larger room served for cooking, eating and living. Their bathroom privacy comprised a makeshift curtain held up by washing pegs. The bathroom! There was no bath to speak of. Like most people in Baatarulaan, Tengis and his mother washed in the river. The river was frozen solid six months of the year.

Although Tengis had visited Odval's home many times, he was nervous. He and Odval had been sincere soulmates since childhood but the revelation concerning his destiny had all but blown that friendship apart. He was here to see if he could rescue their friendship in any way. He also needed someone to talk to. He needed somebody to share things with. His first week in Baatarulaan as Tengis the Politician had been more than a little eventful. He needed Odval back in his life. He just wasn't sure whether she would want him. He knocked loudly on the door and stood back, his hands clasped behind his back fidgeting madly.

Tengis could hear the door being unlocked from within. It

opened. A tall dark-haired man with an enormously wide and bushy moustache answered the door. It was Odval's father. Odval's father liked Tengis. If he could ever have allowed himself to entertain the notion of his daughter being married, it would have been to Tengis. He respected Tengis's intellect and self-belief. Odval's father was also a man of politics. With Tengis's newly acquired political capital he was more than welcomed into his home.

'Good afternoon, Mr Enkh,' said Tengis.

'And a good afternoon to you, young Master Khaan,' said Mr Enkh. 'We have been a busy chap, haven't we? I am most impressed by your words on reform. Although a devout Khadist, I recognise when change is required and you seem to be a man who has the ideas, belief, direction and energy to enable such a change. And what is that marvellous yellowy-browny-orange shining material everybody keeps talking about? Not that I'm interested in it. Your words are clearly far more important. Do you have any of it with you? Can I see it? Where did you get it? Is there more? Can I have some?'

'What are you doing here?' said Odval briskly. Despite the harshness of her tone, Tengis was glad to see her and equally pleased to avoid Mr Enkh's oddly insistent line of questioning. He had always thought of Mr Enkh as a principled man; this metal he had mined seemed to have a strange effect on even the soundest of minds.

'I came to see you,' said Tengis. 'I wanted to know if you could forgive my leaving you the way I did.'

'Is that meant to be an apology?' asked Odval.

Her father knew it was safer to retreat to the safety of his library than come between his irate daughter and her prey.

'If it is then you can . . .'

'I am not here to fight,' said Tengis. 'I am also not here to apologise for anything I said about my beliefs but I am sorry about the way I spoke to you. You deserve more than that, especially from me.'

Tengis moved towards Odval and tried to take her hand. Although only a short time had passed since they had last met, Tengis felt as though he had grown and matured far beyond his years. Upon seeing Odval, he knew that he no longer merely wanted her friendship. She was more, far more. He looked beyond her curt glare. He could only see the beauty in her eyes, her smooth face, her glistening dark hair, her perfectly formed figure. A sudden sense of longing filled him; he needed to hold her close to him but was too afraid to move closer – afraid that, if he held her, he would never be able to let go. His breathing became deeper, his self-control vanished.

'Why are you staring at me like that?' asked Odval. 'And why is your mouth hanging open? Do you have any idea how stupid you look? And what's all this silliness about Chinggis? It's one thing to dream about an emperor; it's another to use his name as a means of communicating your ideologies, and quite another altogether to believe that you are an emperor. I assume you still think that you *are* an emperor?'

'I do,' said Tengis enthusiastically. He was daydreaming and utterly oblivious to what Odval was saying.

'If you persist with this line of thought,' said Odval, 'then I absolutely insist that, if we are to be friends, only friends mind you, that you pay a visit to Doctor Todd the Mind Minister. I've done some thinking about what you said. I have never had reason to doubt you in all the time we have known each other, but your outburst at school was frightening. If I agree to be friends with you, will you promise to make an appointment with Doctor Todd?'

Tengis said nothing but closed his eyes, puckered his lips and moved closer to Odval. He was still very deeply enjoying his daydream. Not quite knowing what to do, Odval stuck her forefinger between his lips and wiggled it around a bit. It felt odd but it also had the desired effect of waking Tengis back into the present.

'Absolutely barking!' said Odval. She leaned in and kissed him on the cheek. They both blushed.

'Friends?' asked Tengis.

'Friends,' confirmed Odval.

She cuddled Tengis. Tengis laid his head on her shoulder. She was warm and he thought she smelled good. Everything had worked out just as he had wanted.

13

'I can make a decision,' mumbled Lily.

Only her horse Lucky could hear her. They had been riding across the Steppe towards Baatarulaan for two days and hadn't seen a single person. If you were all alone, the Steppe could make you feel even more so. However, it had given Lily ample time to think about what her spirit guide had been telling her.

'Silly horse, why can't you talk?'

Lily still had so many unresolved questions. She hoped that going to the city would help answer them. It was the first time Lily would have been to Baatarulaan and, although she thought of herself as braver than any of the herders she lived with, the idea of being in a place crammed with so many people intimidated her. Still, her father had been going there since he had been young. Unfortunately, her father had been imprisoned on his last scavenging outing. Lily hoped that, as well as addressing her questions, she might be able to find her father and help him return to the herders. He was after all their rightful leader; she had only ever agreed to take the role on a temporary basis.

Lily and Lucky continued plodding across the vast open arid plain. Snow began to fall. In Ongolium, snowfall was light. There was lots of it but, because of the dryness, snowflakes were tiny. They rarely had an opportunity to lie on the ground before they evaporated back into the atmosphere. Today the environment was allowing a sparkling carpet to be formed. It crunched quietly under Lucky's hooves. His dark shoes glided gracefully across the glittering ground.

Riding around a rocky outcrop. Lily could see that the horizon had changed. Lucky let out a loud snort of disapproval. All her life Lily had only ever seen the Steppe on the horizon. She was now presented with what looked like man-made mountains; each was uniformly perpendicular. Instead of wide opening valleys and space there was barely a gap between the mountains. It seemed as though cliffs fell away sharply from each mountain before rising up into the next. The vision occupied the central part of the Steppe lying in front of her. Either side it stopped suddenly. Its centre was its peak, the mountains there rising higher than the rest. Above the artificial mountain range there hung a thick, dull-looking cloud. It was unlike any cloud she had seen before. It was far lower than she would normally expect to see clouds, and seemingly made of a different texture, although from this distance it was hard to tell. What puzzled her most was why the cloud seemed to be attached to the man-made mountains at various points where what looked like rocky towers rose into the sky. But Lily was not afraid. Her first sight of Baatarulaan had filled her, rather, with a sense of wonder and adventure. She spurred on Lucky, who very reluctantly moved a little faster, but not much.

As Lily neared the entrance to Baatarulaan she was able to better absorb what she was seeing. There were no mountains. She could see wooden and metallic structures that looked as though they were filled with people. In her experience people lived in small gers. Here she found herself confronted by buildings up to six storeys high. The drab grey stone structures were packed full of people. Every window had a dank light on the inside showcasing at least one, but more often two or more, citizens sitting blankly in their homes. The tracks between buildings were equally busy. People walked here and there purposefully, their hands shoved deep into their pockets; few, if any, took notice of other people around them. They walked fast and bumped into one another grumpily. On corners, small groups of people stood warming their hands against the cold over barrels filled with flame. The more Lily examined the city the less she was able to find any soul.

Anxiously Lucky strode deeper into Baatarulaan. It was not noisy but there was an eternal din that rang through Lily and her steed's minds. They were used to the contemplative silence of the Steppe. In Baatarulaan, the hubbub of chatter, movement and general day-to-day doings of the city's one million inhabitants were enough to generate a din that forbade peacefulness. Lucky snorted deeply and then sneezed violently. Lily patted his neck fondly. She was feeling the same way.

The city had a stench that was both unfamiliar and repugnant. It was the smell of a million lives spent living too closely together in unsanitary conditions. Lily's ger camp had occasionally stunk of horse or camel dung, but Baatarulaan took things to a completely different level. Lily could tell that the sides of the well-worn tracks were to be avoided at all cost. For many decades the townsfolk had used the gutters as a dumping ground for their more odious household refuse. In turn, the city leaders had long felt it was better not to do anything about the reeking remnants. In their opinion, they were so toxic that given time they would rot themselves away. It was their attempt at embracing environmentalism and they made much of it in the media.

Lily dismounted and, patting Lucky's head, tied some dried herbs to his reins. He showed an immediate improvement. Walking slowly, she led him on, her eyes wide in wonder.

'Excuse me,' said Lily. She tried to grab the attention of a passer-by. The first man ignored her. 'Excuse me,' she said again. The second man cast her a look of contempt before walking away. 'Please, excuse me,' said Lily to a lady carrying shopping bags filled with newspaper and empty canisters. The lady grunted and pushed past her. 'These people are so rude!' exclaimed Lily to her horse.

As Lily examined them, she noted that the menfolk of Baatarulaan were far more stocky and rounded than those she had grown up with on the Steppe. They had gruff faces that Lily feared shielded an even more gruff temperament within. Most of them dressed in the same long traditional del robes made of felt worn in the countryside, although the urban versions were more ornately decorated. On their feet the men wore thick leather boots that were designed for warmth not looks. In contrast, the women of Baatarulaan were beautiful. Several inches taller than the women who lived in the herder communities, the city ladies proudly wore what Lily presumed to be the latest fashions. They were far slimmer and carried a less pronounced bosom than their countryside cousins and their facial bone structures seemed designed entirely to give aesthetic pleasure.

'Hey you,' said a voice. 'Hey you, young woman. You new here?' A grubby-looking man walked out of nearby shadows towards them. Both horse and rider backed away. 'You new here? Where you from? You're not from round here, are you?'

'Hello, sir,' said Lily, 'we have just arrived. We . . . we . . . we are from a different part.' Lily didn't want to disclose that she was a herder. Her father had warned her that Baatarulaan's residents were highly suspect of anyone from outside the city limits and the city's rulers would immediately imprison anyone of that variety. Lily had presumed this was why her father had not returned to their camp.

'Which part?' said the man. 'District 4? District 11? Possibly District 13?'

'District 8,' said Lily. Eight was her favourite number.

'Oh,' said the man, 'that'll be why you have the horse. How are the crops this year? We gonna get any food? What about this, can I buy your horse; it sure looks tasty?'

The concept of eating horsemeat – let alone Lucky – filled Lily with horror.

'My name is Lily,' said Lily. 'I am in this area on business.' Lily didn't really know what business was but knew that people who wanted to sound important tended to say they were on business regardless of what it was they were doing. 'Important business,' added Lily for effect.

'Wow!' said the man. He whistled theatrically. 'Why didn't you say?' He made an exaggerated bow in her direction and doffed his filthy cap. 'My name is Drudger. It be a pleasure to be meeting you. I am at your disposal.'

Lily prayed she would be able to dispose of him soon. On the other hand she needed help finding lodgings and some place to stable Lucky. She figured there was little harm in asking Drudger for assistance; he seemed an all right kind of person and had been the only one to stop and talk to her.

'No problem,' said Drudger. 'I know a lovely little guesthouse, perfect for a lady of your standing. They've got a stable, too, from memory, though it probably ain't seen no horse in our lifetime. You don't get many horses round here, not live ones at any rate. Anyways, follow me.' Drudger shot off, walking fast along some of the darker, narrower tracks that weaved their way between the oppressive buildings.

Lily followed hastily with Lucky in tow. She only just managed to keep up with Drudger as he wove left and right around corners that made Lily dizzy. An hour previously Lily had never been on a street. She was now finding herself chasing a stranger, turning tight corners in semi-darkness along busy streets in the middle of a noisy, smelly city while trying desperately to give off the impression that she knew what she was about. In a matter of minutes she was completely lost. Her only option was to keep Drudger in her sights and follow him wherever it was he was leading her. This was not an altogether appealing option but at that particular moment it was the only one she had.

Eventually Drudger stopped. 'I'm sorry about the rush, miss,' said Drudger. 'You never know who is following you in this place. Anyway, we're here.' He opened a rickety gate that led into a small muddy yard.

They had a reached a dead end. On the three sides ahead of them were tall buildings reaching up towards the sky. Behind them Lily noticed that they had come through a hole in another equally imposing building that led back into the labyrinthine passageways she had been chasing Drudger along. No natural light found its way here, but at least there was quiet and the stench of outside seemed to be kept at bay. There was very little that was striking about the place but it had a sense of order and peace that Lily had yet seen elsewhere in her short time in Baatarulaan. A door on the ground floor of one of the buildings creaked open and a large man peeked around it nervously.

'Who's there?' he said.

'It's me,' said Drudger, 'and I've brought a friend. She needs somewhere to lay low. She arrived today on horseback. Says she's on "business".'

Lily could tell by the way Drudger spoke that he really hadn't believed her story for a second. Now that they had stopped rushing through the underbelly of Baatarulaan, she also realised that there was no way she could retrace her steps. Lily moved closer to Lucky who reciprocated. They wondered what sort of trouble they had got themselves into.

The larger man came into the yard and headed towards them. He had a troubled face but Lily didn't think he looked dangerous; certainly not nearly as devious in appearance as Drudger, now that she had a moment to look at him. The men clasped one another as old friends, spoke briefly and then turned towards their quarry.

'I am Danyal,' said the large man. He offered Lily his hand. She wasn't quite sure what to do with it. Placing hers next to his, he took it and shook it firmly. Lily thought that this was very off and tried to understand what it represented and where it had come from, particularly the shaking bit. Herders raised their hands to one another until they were close enough friends to embrace. There was never any shaking of body parts.

'Hello, I'm Lily,' she said.

'I believe you are not from around here?' said Danyal. 'It is not my place to judge people or show prejudice, so I won't ask you where it is you are from. However, I need to know one thing. Are you a Khadist?'

Lily had absolutely no idea what that meant. She had heard of Khad from the tales Chuluun and the other nomad elders had told her. She knew there was a legend relating to Khad that involved Outsiders but was a little hazy on any further details on the subject. Danyal watched her confused reaction. 'I shall take that as a no, shall I?'

'I should say,' added Drudger. 'Poor thing doesn't seem to even know what Khadism is!'

'Not poor at all,' said Danyal, 'I'd call her lucky.' At this Lily's horse raised his head.

'That's his name,' said Lily. She stroked her steed fondly.

'It seems as though he is too then,' said Danyal, 'having such an honest young lady as you looking after him.' Lily blushed, she had never been called a lady and, having heard what a lady was, seriously doubted whether she really was one. Lily hated dresses, formal etiquette and even cake. 'Here, let me.' Danyal nestled his head close to Lucky's.

111

'In some places they call him the man who whispers into the ears of horses,' said Drudger quietly.

'Why would people call him that?' asked Lily.

'He has a special way with animals,' replied Drudger.

They watched as Danyal led Lucky away through a door adjacent to the one he had exited. It led to a stable that had been built inside one of the buildings. Lucky seemed happy to be led to his new shelter and was delighted when Danyal offered him a large bucket of leftover food scraps and, more excitingly, a king-sized equine bed of hay. Danyal closed the door as he came back outside and then, to Lily's surprise, pressed a latch that unlocked the top portion of the door. This he swung open, before tying it to the wall. Lucky appeared in the opening, his mouth masticating food that Lily was certain she didn't want to see. He seemed to be content and as a result Lily relaxed. She knew that her horse was a very sound judge of character.

'You can stay with us,' said Danyal. 'It's not much but it's away from the chaos of Baatarulaan. It's warm, we have some food and we have complete privacy. Nobody bothers us here. Please, won't you come inside?'

Danyal ushered his guests, beckoning them to follow him. Lily cast a glance at Lucky who was still munching happily then followed her host indoors. Baatarulaan had not been what she had expected. The people had been rude and seemed to be gruff and unhappy and they lived in buildings that appeared to be more suited to animals. Lily was happy she was a herder. Happy that her home was on the Steppe in the fresh open air. She could see no attraction in living here, yet it remained a place of wonder to be explored further. She also needed to unravel the words on the box and try and find her father. After three days riding across the Steppe, Lily's only thoughts drifted towards getting some sleep and more immediately to the aroma that was flooding downstairs from Danyal's kitchen.

14

With Odval by his side, Tengis's confidence knew no bounds. Baatarulaan had always been his home but never a home he was particularly proud about. For almost a decade he and Odval had discussed how they would change the world for the better; change the world for the good of other people. In the space of a few weeks Tengis had begun to do just that. Guided by his intellect and logic; counselled by the voice in his head, and buoyed by his special friend Odval, Tengis felt he was winning considerable support for his Ten Recommendations as well as his aesthetically pleasing colour schemes. However, in reality he knew that it was really the shining sunny metal that people had fallen in love with. He had to ensure there was a plentiful supply so that he could leave tokens of his faith with the appropriate townsmen who could curry favour in his direction. He didn't view this as corruption; he was merely helping to spread the faith. People seemingly worshipped the metal and, if he could strategically place quantities of it more widely, then the people's faith had more to focus upon. Odval approved of his scheme. She hadn't quite understood the subtleties or implications of his actions. She firmly believed that Tengis was doing good and doing it in a good way.

'You know,' said Odval, 'politics and religion are not so very different. Both encourage people to have faith.'

'Absolutely!' said Tengis. 'Perhaps people don't really know what it is they have faith in but they seem keen on having faith all the same. Also, both politics and religion encourage faith with the same promise of some future reward, which again people are largely uncertain of but equally enthusiastic to worship.'

'Don't be so sarcastic,' said Odval. She sometimes wondered whether Tengis was serious when he said things like that. Tengis was a good man but he did have his secrets.

Despite forging a strong relationship with one another, Tengis had decided to keep all details relating to the source of the shimmering material from Odval. He told himself that this was to keep her safe but knew that he simply didn't trust her enough. He didn't trust *anyone* enough. He had also seen the effect the substance had had on erstwhile sound minds. Mr Enkh had been someone whom Tengis had always looked up to and yet even he had fallen for the allure of Tengis's metal. Tengis worried what effect it might have on Mr Enkh's daughter and really didn't want to tempt fate by finding out. He kept the exact location of the intimidating metallic substance close to his chest (in a small leather pouch with a cat on it that his mother had given him for his eleventh birthday). It was easy to keep a secret from her. Odval was a busy woman. Being part of an important family came with certain social commitments, even in a city as far removed from civility as Baatarulaan.

Tengis had succeeded in winning an important ally and friend. With Odval on side he felt he would be able to do anything. So far everything had gone well.

'Have some fun,' said a voice suddenly from inside Tengis's head. 'You've earned it. You have done everything so well. The people are with you. Go and have some fun.'

'What do you mean?' asked Tengis. 'I don't have time for fun. Anyway, fun is what I am trying to stop. Fun is a Khadist trait. I am Chinggis, I am certainly no Khadist.'

'There must be some people that have annoyed you,' said the

voice. 'There must be those that made your life difficult before you unearthed the shimmering promise and mined the Ten Recommendations?'

Tengis thought for a moment. There certainly had been a group of people who had never treated him with the respect he had always known he was due. There were those that had always kept him, and Odval, on the outside. A group of people that were more Khadist in their sheepishness than any other Tengis had encountered. He headed for his school, a spiteful smile spreading across his face. He rubbed his hands together to warm them against the cold, pulled up the collar on his coat and trudged purposefully through the snow.

'Hi,' said a former schoolmate.

Tengis shouldered his way past him into the playground. There were a dozen or so young men and women milling around. They were all the same age as Tengis but his new sense of function set him above the others.

'Whatcha!' said another former schoolmate. 'How you doing, weir– Tengis?' He looked embarrassed at his near mistake.

'I am very well,' said Tengis, 'exceedingly well now that you ask. What about all of you; what have you been up to over the past few weeks?' He spotted that a few of the former school mates were wearing blue, white and black badges that declared 'What counts is what works' and 'Our objectives are radical'. Others had long cheaply knitted woollen scarves that read: 'Our means are modern'. The remainder had scrawled graffiti on to their school bags citing: 'Change is good'. All of them had a silken pendant of sorts in the same colour as his mystical metal. Tengis knew that these same people were the ones that for years had tried to run him out of school. Now that he had gone it seemed as though they were suddenly enormous fans of his. He smirked satisfactorily. His former classmates shuffled about uneasily. Age counted for little. Tengis was their superior. Of that there was no mistake.

'We've . . .' said one of the girls. 'We've missed you.'

'I bet you have,' replied Tengis. He remembered the same girl having thrown his school books into the river a few months previously. 'I bet you have.'

'We love what you are doing,' said the same girl. 'You are an inspiration to all of us. You always have been. Your words are amazing; and as for that wonderful metal . . . Where did you discover it? It's truly awesome!'

'What do you make of my *words*?' asked Tengis. The voice in his head whispered silently to focus on the words and not the metal.

'Err,' said the girl.

'Umm,' said another boy.

'They're brilliant,' said a different girl. 'The Ten Reconciliations are just what we need. The metal stuff too, though; that really is quite breathtaking. Do you have any with you?'

'I'm glad you like the TEN RECOMMENDATIONS,' said Tengis. 'Now, which of them would be your favourite?'

'Err,' said the girl.

'Umm,' said another boy.

'I have a favourite one,' said a smaller boy who was standing behind the others. Tengis remembered it was this runny-nosed rich young man who had been responsible for making up so many amusing songs and ditties about Tengis and Odval. 'I think there is one about not killing people?' It was a question as much as a statement. He looked for Tengis's affirmation. Tengis nodded slightly. Much to the small young man's delight he continued. 'Not killing people is a good thing. Killing people would be bad, very bad. Wouldn't it?' Again he sought Tengis's response.

'What about you?' said Tengis. He pointed to the largest

116

boy – a boy who on more than one occasion had taken delight in slapping Tengis's head or shoving him very hard in the back. 'Which of these words do you believe in, big man?'

'There, there's one about children, isn't there?' said the large young man. He was quite obviously frightened of the newly empowered Tengis but wanted to state his mind. 'I believe in that one.'

'Why?' asked Tengis. He was surprised that his former school mate knew any of the Recommendations and was particularly surprised that he would select that one.

'I, I, I,' said the young man, 'I never knew my parents. I had to live with an aunt and uncle who were horrible to me. It's not my fault I'm stupid. It's not my fault I'm in trouble all the time.' The young man turned and ran into the school. A couple of his friends laughed but were quickly called to task by the others.

'What is his name?' asked Tengis.

'Tchoo,' said the others.

'Interesting,' said Tengis, 'very interesting.' He mused over what he had heard. 'What about the rest of you? Are you with me? Are you willing to stand up against the Khadist bureaucrats? Are you willing to make a stand for all that our country once stood for?' The group stood staring at Tengis with a befuddled look upon their faces.

'What?' said the shorter boy. 'What are you talking about? We just like your shimmering shiny stuff. We'll do whatever you want if you have that. I don't know about the others but I haven't a clue what you're talking about with all that Khadist bureaucracy, what-our-country-once-stood-for stuff?'

Tengis was shocked. Then the penny dropped. All education in Baatarulaan was geared around the advancement of bad behaviour and ill repute. People knew about Khadism but they didn't really know what it was. They believed whatever they were told and always had done. Now that they were being presented with something more tangible to think about it was almost too much. However, it also played to Tengis's advantage. He had seen what power he had when he wielded the sunny substance. So long as people believed in that he had their attention, he had their support, he had their faith. Tengis walked back towards the city centre feeling that this had been one school reunion he would remember for a long time.

'How easy is this?' asked a voice in Tengis's head. 'I really had no idea people these days would be so simple to bring on side. If I'd known how strong the lust for wealth and mystery had become, I would have tried this again centuries ago!'

'What do you mean?' replied Tengis. 'I am Chinggis. How could anybody else have achieved what I am achieving in so short a space of time?'

'Calm down, relax,' said the voice. 'You *are* a marvel in your own way. You are far more scholarly than I ever could have been and your reputation as a bookworm appears to be making your claims sound ever more plausible. We are a wonderful combination, you and I!'

Tengis reached the square that had long marked the centre of Baatarulaan. Around its edges flapped large flags in support of New Chinggism. People sat huddling from the snow around fires. All were in deep conversation, or at least as deeply in conversation as people in Baatarulaan were capable. As Tengis walked among them, only a few recognised him. It was his words and more importantly the shimmering yellow-orange that were the hallmarks of New Chinggism. Those that did know his face turned immediately away and whispered to their co-conspirators, who would in turn peek a look at the leader of their movement. Occasionally Tengis would pass a sheltering group of people and hear a cry of 'Change is good!' or 'All hail the shimmering shiny metal!'

It was a bitterly cold night. Better to be in company than alone. Odval was attending some Khadist event with her father. There was not much to burn. The Khadists had removed all tree-like vegetation centuries ago in fear of would-be assassins. People were burning whatever they could possibly lay their hands on –broken tables and chairs, paper . . . even candles. Anything that would provide some respite from the invading chill. Temperatures in Ongolium fell below freezing during October to March. It was February. The temperature rarely rose above minus twenty during the day. At night it could be as low as minus forty. Dusk was upon them. The disparate groups gathered into a larger group trying to retain body heat among one another. The shops of Baatarulaan had not been restocked in years. The average person survived from what scraps and morsels they could scavenge. Even wild dogs seemed to have a better-balanced diet than your typical Baatarulaanian.

Normally, the square would be empty but now, it seemed, people wanted to be with others. People wanted to talk about the Recommendations Tengis had brought them, even if few knew who he was or what the Recommendations actually were; few honestly cared. There was a sense of electricity charging the air. Tengis could feel it forcing its way through the biting cold on to his skin.

Bonfires were combined into a larger central flame around which several hundred people sheltered. Scarves and hats were drawn tightly over faces. Tengis was pleased there was no wind. That would have been too much. The fire began to diminish. People looked around anxiously at one another.

'Speak, you fool,' said the voice in Tengis's head. 'Quickly, take the initiative. Tell them what they want to hear.' Some people at the fringes began to walk away in search of heat.

'Everybody!' said Tengis. He stood upon the last remaining wood before it was burned and drew himself into a manly posture. 'I know that some of you are aware of who I am. There are many of you who do not but who do know of my glimmering substance.' This grabbed the people's attention. 'My name is Tengis Khaan; author of the Ten Recommendations; miner of the shimmering metal; loyal servant of the true Khaan dynasty. Son to a wronged mother; patron of a ruined city; and I will help my people, on this day or the next.'

People stopped moving away. Others gave a little cheer before falling back into silence. All looked up at Tengis, not really understanding what it was he was saying but very eager to hear what else he might utter. He was speaking with such conviction, and he was the owner of the glimmering stuff, so his meaning must be riddled with glorious wisdom. Tengis didn't know what else to say.

'Quick!' said the voice in his head. 'Quick, you have them; keep them! Now is your chance! Seize the moment!'

'I know that many of you are cold and haven't eaten properly for a while,' said Tengis. People around him murmured in accord. 'I also know that many of you have long been unhappy with the way in which Baatarulaan has been governed.' More people nodded in agreement. Nodding also helped people keep warm so Tengis wasn't sure if they really were agreeing and quickly carried on talking. 'I know that you feel that you've been let down. I know that you feel that those in power have abused their station; that they have taken and kept what should have been shared among you; that they are only interested in looking out for themselves.'

People were moving closer to him to make sure they heard what he was saying. Others came streaming out of nowhere from all across the square, drawn towards Tengis and the throng.

'Many among you have no place to call home; or at least no place with warmth and running water.' Some people began to voice their approval. 'Who among you has not grown sick of the Fun Brigade and the perpetual fun they keep poking at you?' More voices spoke in approval. 'Who is not tired of worshipping false idols for fear of persecution and having to find ways to make life bearable? Who would not be free from the tyranny that has held you tight and bound you in its addictive substances?'

Tengis's words were met with applause. He was enjoying this. The voice in his head was enjoying it even more. He started to use more body language, pointing at the crowd to highlight particular words, raising both hands upwards to promote others.

'Who among you would not be rid of Khadism for ever?' The audience exploded in a din of cheering and clapping. People had forgotten they were cold and hungry. Tengis had helped them forget.

'Who is with me?' said Tengis. He was hoisted upon the shoulders of men. 'Who will follow the Ten Recommendations?' There was some applause. 'Who will follow the shiny yellow metal?' There was uproar.

People streamed forward to touch him. This was the reception Tengis had wished for, more than anything. The voice in his head sat quietly in silent, conceited contentment. The plan was working.

Tengis allowed his followers to embrace him. He was their new leader. He needed to act as such, showing grace, humility, strength and honour. To keep the people warm he incited a raid on all the city's libraries to purge them of the inhuman, and often gratuitous, magazines that adorned their walls. For food Tengis decreed that all homes of Khadist sympathisers be emptied of nutrition for the greater good. New Chinggists would oversee fair and equitable distribution. He encouraged people to declare that night the last night of Khem. Going forward people would be free to be themselves, to have their own will. Tengis gave them the strength to do so. Instead of taking Khem, all addicts would be encouraged to drink from a special chalice made from the sunny orange substance. As they drank addicts would be promised salvation; their bodies purged of craving, their minds filled with obsession.

Fearing for their property and knowing in which direction power was shifting, the wealthier members of Baatarulaan declared their support for New Chinggism. Over the course of the week following the Square Dance, as Tengis's initial meeting had come to be known, they welcomed him into their homes. The wealthy poured syrup on to his tea and into his ears. Tengis had never felt so accepted. People, rich and poor, believed in him. People believed he was doing good. People believed that his wondrous glistening material would eradicate evil. He was enjoying having power. There was too much for him to do alone though. He needed assistants and assistance was closer than he had realised.

Given his ability to procure almost anything, Tengis made Odval's father High Minister for Economic Affairs, whose remit included wealth, nutrition and physiological needs distribution. Mr Enkh set about establishing unions for each area, who went almost immediately on strike because they felt that the other union must have been receiving better entitlements. To break them Mr Enkh had procured a number of photographic images of each union leader in an untoward predicament which served well to keep them in line. Mr Enkh was a very resourceful man. The people felt happy.

Oldortar (or Oldortar the Clown as his friends still called him) was a natural choice as Chief of Staff for Safety and Security. He had been in charge of the Fun Brigade for years. So as not to confuse people who supported New Chinggism, one of his first objectives was to rename the Fun Brigade as the Leggie on account for the fact that they walked everywhere. He also undertook a special review of the House of Fun (renamed the House of Hurt), the result of which was that any resident being entertained for Chinggist 'crimes' was released immediately so long as they served in the Leggie. Almost immediately the residents of Baatarulaan no longer feared their protectors. The people felt protected.

Tengis had in mind someone special to place in charge of promoting the Ten Recommendations. One Saturday afternoon when people were otherwise occupied he went in search of that person. Knocking on a large wooden door belonging to one of the top Khadist bureaucrats, Tengis brushed the dust from his waistcoat. The door opened.

'Err, hi,' said the voice of a young man. 'What, what are you doing here? Have I done something wrong?'

'Hello, Tchoo,' said Tengis. 'I have a proposition for you. One I think you will feel obliged to accept.'

So it was that Tchoo left his hated guardians and became Head of Self-Actualisation. Tchoo would have a free, relatively free, rein with which to market and advance the Ten Recommendations using his honesty, charm and a little bit of bullying. Tengis knew that enemies could sometimes become the most loyal of friends.

The most important role was the easiest for Tengis to fill. There was only one person in the world he would or even could trust as his closest advisor – that was Odval. She accepted graciously. On her first night in office she would become more than simply a spiritual mistress. Tengis moved into the Enkh household. Tengis even managed to persuade his estranged mother to move into a centrally heated hut in the garden (she had refused resolutely to live under the same roof as her rapscallion son and his hussy vixen).

It was a kind of family and it kind of worked. Important

visitors would come to the house to pay their respects and pledge their allegiance to the New Chinggist movement. The first council meeting of the New Chinggist Upper Guard (Tengis and his four confidants) was held in Mr Enkh's sitting room. Tengis's mother supplied hot chocolate and nibbles. The top agenda item was driven not by Tengis but by his team. They wanted him to force the Khadists along the road to democracy. They insisted that, with the support that Tengis had managed to garner over the previous month, there was no way anyone could successfully stand against him in an election. He would be voted in as President Of Ongolian People. It was a new role; a democratic role. His Council insisted it would win favour with the people far longer and less shakily if Tengis agreed to become the first elected President of Ongolian People. Just thinking about the marketing campaign filled him with dread; he could envisage the short-form name he would be given.

It was true the Khadists had completely misread the situation when Tengis and New Chinggism had first appeared. Like so many of the bad smells that lingered in Baatarulaan from time to time, they thought people would simply get used to it and eventually forget it was there. They had underestimated the way in which Tengis had been able to sway sentiment in his favour with his clever words, marketing prowess and shining shimmering substance. They knew their days were numbered. Many Khadists refused to give up but many more changed their allegiance to New Chinggism. Tengis only too readily accepted their commitment to his cause. Those Khadists that remained turned to spreading lies about Tengis. They would say he slept with his horse, even though everyone knew he didn't have one. They would say that he was an Outsider in disguise, even though everyone remembered seeing him running around as a child. They would even stoop so far as to say that his father was a devout Khadist, which happened to be true but was no longer of any consequence to Tengis who had never actually met him.

'What are you going to do about all these rumours?' asked Odval after they had shared a particularly robust and steamy mug of hot malted chocolate.

'Gossip is worse than poison,' said Tengis. 'I need to find a cure, and quickly.'

In reality, however, he had more pressing matters to deal with. He had built a team who worshipped him and who wanted him to force the Khadists to play the democratic card. The problem was that Tengis was enjoying being in charge. Power was beginning to go to his head. He still believed absolutely in New Chinggism and the Ten Recommendations but he also believed that to cement this absolute faith he needed to rule absolutely. He wanted to be an emperor. He wanted to use his shining metal as he saw fit. He had little desire to listen to what his Council was telling him and he had most definitely absolutely no desire to become their primary POOP. He wanted to be a number one.

15

Lily felt like a different person after a good night's sleep. She was a different person. When she had woken up yesterday she had only even known the Steppe; now she was staying with strangers in a hidden corner of Baatarulaan. She felt oddly liberated. After checking on Lucky, who had evidently slept as well as she had, Lily went in search of breakfast. As she ascended the stairs a scent she had not known hit her.

'Good morning,' said Lily. Both men were already waiting for her at the table. 'What on earth is that wonderful smell?'

'That'll be the coffee then,' said Drudger. 'Watch yourself, though, it's strong stuff.' He poured Lily half a mug. She tasted it. She loved it. 'So what *are* you doing in Baatarulaan? I know Danyal is too polite to ask but I ain't.'

Two strangers had taken her in, fed her, stabled her horse and given her a safe roof to sleep under; the least Lily could do was talk to them. She figured that if they had been untoward characters that her person and few belongings would have been taken before now.

'I am a herder,' said Lily. Both men looked at her, astonished. They had never seen one before. 'I'm not a freak,' remarked Lily. She felt as though she was being examined a little too closely and she didn't like feeling like a specimen of sorts.

'I'm sorry,' said Danyal. 'We've never seen a real herder before. We hear stories about them but they don't seem to come to Baatarulaan often since they were outlawed. Why the

Khadists want to keep everyone within the city limits is beyond me. I always felt there were far too many people in too small a space with no room to breathe. The only herder I've heard about in recent times was Baatar. They say he would sneak into Baatarulaan in the dead of night and pilfer goods and belongings for his people. He was popular in the taverns. They say he could drink like a camel, eat like a yak and sing like a wolf. Word is he got captured, though.'

'That would be my father,' said Lily. The men looked shocked. 'It certainly sounds like him and he was, rather is, called Baatar. Do you know where he is now?' Both men looked at her pityingly and shook their heads.

'I'm afraid he got taken to the House of Fun,' said Drudger. He took a sharp intake of breath as he said the words.

'What's that?' asked Lily. 'It doesn't sound so bad.'

'What do you know about this place?' asked Danyal. Lily confirmed their suspicions that she knew very little. They felt it was important she did know what sort of place she was visiting and set about informing her of the Khadist regime and the city Khad had created, not omitting any of the fun elements the bureaucrats felt were so important.

'But you don't laugh like that five times a day,' said Lily, 'do you?'

'Absolutely not. We keep away from most people,' said Danyal. 'We help out with things here and there.'

'You could say we live on the fringes of society,' said Drudger. He nudged Danyal knowingly. His friend ignored him.

'You must be careful,' said Danyal. 'There is nothing but evil in this place. Especially now.'

'Why?' asked Lily. 'What's going on at the moment?'

'As I said earlier,' continued Danyal, 'the Khadists have been running the show here for centuries. People have never really liked them but they were told by the Khadists they had been given so much freedom it was difficult for them to fight back. They were told that it was they who had made the rules, that it was they who had insisted that life be full of fun and laughter. The Khadists were smart when they started. If the people had fought back they would have felt that they were fighting themselves. Instead they put up with it. They put up with all the discipline, all the things that are wrong with this city. Instead, they made things worse. The people figured that, if they could live as they wanted to, then they would live for themselves – greedily, hungrily, evilly. Control people too much and they are so afraid they'll commit suicide. Give them enough rope and they will also hang themselves. Those bureaucrats knew exactly what they were doing. By giving them freedom they "permitted" the people of Baatarulaan to become addicted to living as they wanted, addicted to gambling, to prostitution, murder, rape, drinking, disrespect and, of course, Khem.'

'I can't believe it is human nature to act like that,' said Lily. 'And what's Khem?'

Danyal explained that it wasn't human nature to behave like that but, if those in charge manipulated people the right way, then they could force them to behave that way. Those in charge had found the people easier to manipulate if they were living by their own self-proclaimed freedom, and of course the people in charge had also invented Khem.

'Why doesn't someone just stand up to them and tell them that it's not fair?' asked Lily.

'People are simply too scared,' said Danyal. 'They know that there is every chance they'll end up in the House of Fun.'

'There is Tengis,' offered Drudger. Danyal shot him a look of contempt.

'He is not to be trusted,' said Danyal spitefully. 'Nothing can be built upon sand and it is nothing but sand that he buys his power with.' With that Danyal sloppily scooped brunch into their bowls and they sat eating in silence.

'I need some fresh air,' said Lily. Now that her stomach was filled she had time to think. Her fellow herders might live a simple existence when compared to those in Baatarulaan but at least they lived an honest, virtuous and respectful simple life. Lily needed time to absorb what she had heard; everything she had experienced in the preceding twenty-four hours. After petting Lucky and assuring him that they would be going home as soon as she had found some answers, and hopefully her father to boot, she set out through the alleyways. Before leaving, Drudger had messed up her clothes with some oil, fats, mud and blood, then ripped her trousers a little, given her an odd wide-brimmed hat that was slightly crooked and a thickly set wooden walking stick that could double up as a weapon if required. It made her look far more like a city dweller than the Steppe girl she was.

The streets of Baatarulaan were as busy and chaotic as they had been the previous day. Lily may have been awestruck when she had arrived but now that she knew how people behaved in this town she was afraid. However, she was not afraid enough that she would pass up an opportunity to find out what the golden box containing Chinggis's words might have really been saying. People ignored her as she walked along the busier roads. They would have done so normally but now that she had been dressed à la Drudger she was almost invisible. She scoured the city for signs of cats, tigers, bells and fish. Now that Lily knew about Khadism, she also looked for its signs in a bid to better understand the evil.

The more that Lily walked among the people the keener she understood that they weren't naturally aggressive. These people were scared. They were trying to conceal themselves in the crowd. They didn't want to be noticed. Those that did raise their heads above the parapet of people were either in the employ of some group called the Leggie or trying to force others to buy their presumably illegal wares. Lily noticed that some of the salespeople were peddling Khem, and she stayed well away from them. Although she spent the entire day looking, she saw no signs of anything she was looking for.

Arriving at a square she presumed marked the centre of the city, the atmosphere was different. It was more charged. People were talking frantically with one another; speaking close to one another so as not to be overheard. The Leggie were there in great numbers milling and mixing with the throng of city inhabitants. Before she could move away, Lily found herself getting caught up with the movement of the crowd and pulled further into the middle of the square. Oddly-dressed people with frightened faces cast her quick glances. None of the gazes lingered but there was a haunted expression behind every look. Nobody looked healthy. The glowing ruddiness she had grown up accustomed to simply did not exist in this place. City people's pallor paled in comparison.

Lily stepped out of the human current that had swept her into the square and stood next to a group of older residents huddled around a small fire. Two of them grunted to acknowledge her. The other three nodded in her direction. She did likewise. Nobody wore anything other than a deeply fixed frown.

'Did you hear what he did last night?' asked one of the group. His fellow conspirators shook their heads. 'He only went and nailed a copy of the Ten Recommendations to the door of the Khadist Chamber.' His co-connivers gasped. 'He wrote something underneath, something along the lines of: "To the Fat Cats of Baatarulaan, this is your Diet of Words; may you choke on them." Can you believe it? Tengis is really standing up to them. I thought when he came with his Recommendations he was just another lunatic that would surely end up in the House of Fun . . .'

'Don't you mean the House of Hurt?' interrupted one of the others.

'Yes, of course,' said the original speaker, 'House of Hurt. Anyway, with that shimmering stuff he seems to have won over a lot of friends. It's a bit like the story of Chinggis and the Five Fish.' His fellows remained silent. 'You know, the one where he feeds his entire army with a few enormous fish. Well, Tengis is doing the same. He's managing to win over all the influential and wealthy people of Baatarulaan, as well as us by the way, with just a few lumps of that yellow-brown-orangey substance. I don't know how he's done it but he's got everyone believing those Recommendations of his.'

'You sound like you don't believe in the Ten Recommendations?' said another man. The group turned to look for the original speaker's reaction; Lily presumed they all felt the same way.

'Of course I do,' said the original speaker. 'Anything is better than the Khadist freedom movement. I would rather have rules and regulations than none. As for the youth of today, if I had my way they would all spend time in the Leggie learning all about discipline.'

'Who is this Tengis?' asked Lily. The group turned to look at her more carefully. She pulled the brim of her hat down further over her face and repeated the question in a pretend deep voice.

'What do you mean?' asked one of them. 'How can you not know who Tengis is?' Her question had made the group suspicious.

'I know who Tengis is,' said Lily. 'I just wonder who Tengis really is; like inside. Who is the man? Where has he come from? That sort of thing.'

'Oh,' said the original speaker. 'They say he was born and raised in Baatarulaan but when he was twelve he was spirited away from the city and schooled in the outside world.'

'What, in another country?' asked one of the group.

'No,' said the original speaker, 'somewhere a whole one hundred miles from here. Can you imagine it; being a hundred miles away from Baatarulaan?' Lily bit her tongue. She knew that she could travel almost that distance in a day if she really pushed Lucky hard. Her home was a good three days' ride from here. 'They say he learned how to think for himself; how to debate; he was taught the martial arts that have been forbidden under Khadism; as well as geography, history, literature and woodwork. It was while on a field trip that a voice is said to have spoken to him and taught him about the shimmering glimmering stuff as well as the Ten Recommendations. They even say that Tengis isn't really Tengis anymore. There are rumours that he is . . .' He beckoned the others to move closer so that he could whisper. 'They say that he is Chinggis Khaan himself!' Lily was floored. She could hardly believe what she was hearing.

'Do you think Chinggis Khaan is really here in Baatarulaan?' asked Lily. She had pushed herself to the front of the group and was speaking directly with the original speaker. She couldn't accept that she would be able to find answers so easily or that she had a real opportunity to meet Chinggis. He heart exploded in a flurry of excitement. 'Please, do you believe he is here?' She grabbed the lapels of the original speaker's coat.

'No I don't,' said the original speaker. He took hold of Lily's hands and pushed her away from him. 'How could he? He has been dead for almost eight hundred years. Tengis is just a shrewd politician who is going to save us from the tyranny of Khadism. What's it to you anyway? Why are you so keen? I haven't seen you here before; are you a Khadist spy or something?' He made to grab Lily but she narrowly ducked away and was soon lost from him in the crowd which had been swelling further as Lily had been listening to the group.

Wherever she turned, there were faces turned to one side of the square. She was too short to see over the heads in front of her. Standing on tiptoes, Lily could see nothing more than hundreds if not thousands of heads staring at a space that seemed unusually darkened. People jostled her out of the way as they sought to get closer to the front. She lost half of her disguise. It didn't matter; people weren't interested in her. The only thing that mattered was what was in the darkness ahead of them. Lily was confused. She could not imagine what was going on. The crowd was beginning to get out of control. People were pressing hard against one another in a bid for a prime position. Some shouted agitatedly at others who were being overly forceful. Lily felt the pulse of the throng quickening. Violence seemed only a heartbeat away.

From deep within the darkness ahead of the swarming multitude came a noise. It was barely audible above the din of people but they soon quietened in heady anticipation. A steady drum beat quelled the restlessness of the masses. Nothing but a solid beat resonated around the square. Everybody stood stock-still facing the source of the sound. There was a crescendo as the beat sped up. Lily looked around, almost everyone was standing with their mouths gaping, eyes fixed in a glaze that was half panic, half sublimation. Startling white beams shone upwards in four huge columns of light. Enormous flags unfurled all around coloured blue, black and white. The crowd half closed their eyes but were so afraid to miss a thing that they readily risked blindness.

Lily tried to see what was on the flags but the light was too strong. The beat intensified. Boom-boom-boom roared the deep drums; and then the drumming stopped dead as the lights became less intense save a solitary focus on the centre ahead. Rising from behind the plinth rose a man. As he ascended he kept his head facing downwards. His face was set in serious contemplation. His hands were stuck to his sides. He wore a black suit and matching cap with a blue armband. The moment he reached the height he hesitated and as the drums beat out a deafening final, one-off 'boom' he lifted his head to face his people.

'I love you, Tengis!' yelled a girl near to Lily moments before the crowd erupted in a volcano of molten emotion. Tengis theatrically lifted both his arms above his head to embrace the crowd. They responded in kind. Some screamed; others began to chant his name. Then came the drums again, now accompanied by trumpet blasts. The noise built and built until the noise was again deafening. Then it stopped. Tengis stepped forward and there was silence. He was about to speak. There was a universal hush.

'I am Tengis Khaan,' said the figure. 'I represent the Chinggist movement and the Ten Recommendations. I bring you the sparkling metal and I offer you salvation!' The figure lifted a large piece of shimmering metal above his head. The swarm chanted its approval. Women fainted, men screamed and children picked their pockets. The assembly acted as though under a spell. Tengis continued decanting further vitriolic verbiage. People cried his name and shouted whatever words he orchestrated them to.

After what Lily had heard earlier she had dearly hoped to see Chinggis Khaan. The person presenting himself in front of her was not he. This was a bad man. Once upon a time her stomach had begun to move whenever she was close to Chinggis in mind, body or soul. Tonight she simply felt sick. This person might purport to be Chinggis but he wasn't. Whoever he was, she felt he had to be an imposter. She listened to his words and they were delicately laced with slivers of spitefulness. She knew that Chinggis would never speak of hatred.

'In a good word there are three winters' warmth,' continued

Tengis. 'In one malicious word there is pain for six frosty months. Let us give the Khadists an eternity of frost.' The figure said nothing of substance. People didn't seem to care. So long as the figure held aloft the glittering metal they would do whatever he wanted. Lily had to get away. She was being filled with a hatred that she knew would consume her absolutely if she didn't leave the rally that moment.

As Lily fought her way through the crowd she glanced above them to the flags that caged the square. Taking in the carefully designed imagery, Lily almost tripped over. She was not certain but she thought she could see the roaring head of a tiger sitting on the back of a horse. She began breathing shallowly. Her palms became hot despite the freezing temperature. Suddenly she burst out of the crowd. Landing on the pavement, she sat looking up at the flags. Lily now had space and time to assess the flags. She had not been mistaken. Atop the body of someone she presumed to be Tengis was the head of a fierce tiger animatedly roaring to the sky. Unless Lily was mistaken, she knew that she had unearthed something important, something that related to Chinggis's words: the real words of Chinggis, not those she had just been forced to listen to. She raced back to Danyal's yard faster than she had ever run before.

'People say they like change,' said Danyal a little later as he poured her a cup of delicious coffee, 'but they don't, not really. They just want to be told what to do and how to live their lives. They just want to belong to the group; they don't want to stick out from the crowd or be noticed. So long as whoever is telling them what to do lets them lead a life that is in some way acceptable then the people will support them. They don't like people that are different; they certainly don't like anyone who doesn't belong to Baatarulaan, so you need to be extra careful. Imagine coming home dressed like that!' Lily looked down at herself – she had lost all of her disguise and the traditional herder clothing beneath, worn to ward of the cold, was revealed for all to see. She knew that wearing a deel would make her utterly conspicuous.

'I saw a tiger on a horse,' said Lily. 'Can you tell me anything about that?'

'That man disgusts me!' answered Danyal. 'He has taken the insignia of Chinggis, the horse, as his own and had the gall to place himself atop our only true emperor. How can he even think of doing that? It is despicable. He clearly sees himself as the new emperor. He thinks he is working with or joined in some way to Chinggis and that together they will forge a new empire. An empire free from Khadism. Now that this shiny new stuff is around, everyone wants a piece of it. From what I can see it's nothing more than a piece of rock but the way that Tengis has been flashing it about it has become invaluable overnight. I don't trust that guy. As for his so-called Ten Recommendations – fluff and nonsense! That Tengis has no substance. He is nothing but a tailored marketing machine, too young, too big for his own boots, too powerful too soon with too little sense of realism. All he's done is ask questions about Khadism. One idiot can ask more questions than ten wise men can answer. How he's done what he's done I have no idea but he has won the support of everyone, especially the elite few. They're scared he will incite theft of their property. They may account for a fractional percentage of Baatarulaan inhabitants, but they hold almost all of the wealth and certainly all of the power. They truly are fat cats.'

For the second time that day Lily checked herself. She wasn't certain but she felt as though the feline factoids that she had heard must surely relate in some way to the words she had received via Elder Chuluun. She made a note to check the scroll when she was alone that night.

'What can we do about it?' implored Lily. 'What I saw tonight was dreadful, truly terrible. If Tengis manages to take over from the Khadists, why don't the people realise that all they'll be doing is swapping one corrupt regime for another? Why isn't anyone trying to do something positive?'

'Well, we are . . .' said Drudger before Danyal cut him off mid-sentence. Lily looked at them both perplexedly.

'We have known one another a mere day,' said Danyal, 'I need to know that I can trust you, even though my heart tells me that I can.'

'Of course you can!' said Lily. 'Anyway, you have more on me than I on you. You might be harbouring me but I'm the one that faces arrest simply for being a herder.' Danyal and Drudger nodded to one another secretly agreeing upon something unseen and unheard.

'There is a group that is making a stand against both Khadism and New Chinggism,' said Danyal. He sat down on a stool opposite Lily wearing a serious face and looked deep into her eyes. 'We are but a few but we have the backing of a secretive and powerful city magnate. We operate outside the boundaries of society, dwell beneath the surface of the city and have faith in matters some deem beyond the realms of reality. If you are introduced to our brethren, you can never leave them; no matter where you are, you will always be one of us. We will always be with you even when you do not see us. We are secretive to others but openly transparent among ourselves. We fight against tyranny and have been fighting against it for almost eight hundred years. My family were all members of the order, as were Drudger's. We both come from a long line of fighters. We might not look like much but we know more than anyone can possibly imagine and thankfully infinitely more than anyone ever suspects. Are you willing to learn more?'

Lily nodded eagerly. Anyone that was against Tengis and the Khadists had to be good news; nothing could be worse.

'Follow me,' said Danyal.

Lily dutifully followed Danya and Drudger downstairs, out into the yard and into the stable, where Lucky lay snoring. Quietly moving aside some hay they unearthed a trapdoor. Drudger opened the trapdoor and disappeared down inside. Danyal beckoned Lily to follow. She hesitated.

'Where are we going?' she asked. Leaving the Steppe had been difficult, growing accustomed to Baatarulaan had been demanding; being asked to go underground for the first time was almost too daunting a prospect.

'Trust me,' said Danyal. He reassuringly placed his hand on Lily's shoulder. She glanced across at Lucky who lay obliviously dreaming of the Steppe.

'Where are we going?' repeated Lily. She really did not feel comfortable about entering a secret underground tunnel with two men she had only known for a short while. Danyal smiled at her knowingly. He knew exactly where they were heading. He turned and faced her, a broad smile beaming across his face. It immediately relaxed Lily. Even before he spoke she felt comforted. She could tell that wherever they were going it was a good place filled with friends who would help them. He started to speak:

'We're going to Millie's.'

16

The passageway was far longer and far darker than Lily had expected. She thought about her faithful horse Lucky who was sleeping somewhere far above her. He was the only link she had back to her life on the Steppe. Everything else in Baatarulaan was alien, particularly its politics and religions. Subjects she was unwittingly taking a crash course in. Drudger led the way carrying a flaming torch above his head. Danyal stayed near Lily to make sure she felt safe. The flickering light set spectral shadows dancing across the walls. It was damp and cold but at least the stench of Baatarulaan was locked firmly outside. Other than their footsteps the only sound was a million water droplets falling nonchalantly from the tunnel roof and splashing in an ordered, almost orchestral manner on to the muddy puddled passage below.

'Not much further!' shouted Drudger.

He was right. There was a short ladder leading up the side of a wall where he stood. Climbing it, he knocked hard on a wooden hatch in the passageway ceiling. Lily had no idea who Millie was but she knew she was heading to meet her. She trusted Danyal and, despite his shady personality and dodgy dress sense, even Drudger seemed to be earnest. Presently they heard a knocking from above. Listening carefully to the pattern of sound Drudger responded with a series of knocks – some hard, others soft. The trapdoor was lifted and the murky passageway flooded with light from above.

'Right ho?' asked an invisible voice from above the trapdoor.

'Left ho ho,' replied Danyal. A hand was thrust from the light and Danyal took it. Lily felt uneasy. 'We are with friends,' said Danyal as he was pulled out of sight into the luminosity. Lily saw his hand reaching down towards her from beyond the trapdoor. 'Please, you have to trust me.' Danyal pulled Lily into the light. Drudger followed closely behind and shut the darkness behind them.

Lily peered around at her new surroundings as her eyes readjusted to the light. She was in a splendidly furnished home. The room into which they arrived appeared to be a hallway, though she wasn't certain – she had never been in a real hallway before. It did have a staircase, though. In front of her a particularly fanciful one swept widely upwards before splitting left and right towards the top to a mezzanine that overlooked the hall. An impressive front door that looked heavily fortified stood guard behind her. Around the walls were large tapestries that hung behind enormous urns containing plants, walking sticks and umbrellas. A heavily designed chandelier hung overhead. Lily guessed that it had to contain over a hundred candles.

The arm that had helped pull them into the room belonged to a stocky broad man who wore a bushy beard and broad grin. The man wore a garishly coloured shirt, baggy shorts and sandals, even though it was freezing outside. He laughed a good deal and when he spoke had an accent Lily had never heard before.

'All right but?' asked the man in his strange brogue.

'But what?' replied Lily. The man laughed and ruffled her hair before shuffling off to stand beside the tallest boy Lily had ever seen. He didn't have a beard but his hair was shaggy and unkempt. Both men shared a joke that seemed to be about Lily and laughed privately. Four others entered the room and clapped their arms around the tall boy and man with the odd

140

accent. The tall boy proceeded to poke them in the stomach, using his height and superior strength to his advantage. All of the men and boys were young, strong and each had either a beard or a shaggy head of hair. The tall boy continued to annoy his compatriots. Lily felt that the tall boy was very childish. The man with the interesting twang scratched himself in a peculiar fashion. Although they looked quite unruly, there was something about these fellows that Lily found both fascinating and comforting. She sensed that they would look out for her if looking out for was ever required.

'Lily,' said Danyal, 'please can I introduce you to the Hairy Hordes.'

'Hello,' said Lily. She thought their name was amusing and tried not to laugh as she looked at the furry rabble in front of her. 'How do you do?'

'At your service, ma'am,' replied the Hairy Hordes as one. 'It be a pleasure to be making your acquaintance, so it be.'

'And I yours,' said Lily. She had never heard six gruff people speaking in unison before. It sounded almost musical.

The tall boy punched the man with the weird burr and they all immediately began play fighting. The rolled around on the floor punching, kicking and pulling at one another. In any other setting, Lily would have been frightened but their fighting was accompanied by raucous laughter. Lily looked to Danyal and Drudger, who both shrugged their shoulders and smiled.

'Boys!' echoed a woman's voice from upstairs. 'Settle down and behave!' The Hairy Hordes instantly stood quietly to attention. The voice was not cold but was strict; it wasn't a harsh voice but it conveyed strength. Lily craned her neck looking for its owner.

Presently a lady appeared and began slowly and gracefully to descend the staircase. She wore a long green dress that trailed two steps behind her. Upon her head was a tall felt hat that folded upwards in layers and was studded with emeralds. One delicate hand covered in a satin glove that swept up a thinly toned arm carefully touched the banister; the other cradled a small bundle of grey fur that much to Lily's surprise began to move. A slender cat with deep-green eyes yawned nonchalantly. The Hairy Hordes stood erect, trying their best to control themselves and not punch the man next to them. Drudger also stood to attention, respectfully holding his chin higher than he had lifted it since Lily had met him. Danyal stepped forward enthusiastically.

'My lady,' said Danyal, 'how are we this fine day?'

'All is as good as it can be,' replied the lady. 'Is this the girl?' The lady gestured towards Lily.

'My lady,' said Danyal, 'may I present Lily. She is one of us. She has come from outside. She has bravely ridden across the exteriors to Baatarulaan. She knows the dangers but believes, as we do, in justice.'

'How do you do?' asked the Lady. Lily began to curtsey although didn't know why. 'No, no, none of that please.'

The lady took a gentle hold of Lily's elbow and brought her closer to her. Lily noticed that the lady was considerably more mature than she had first thought. She had exciting dark eyes set in a face that seemed to hold a millennium of wisdom. The cat purred gently in her other arm. The lady let the cat down and it curled itself around Lily's ankles. 'Don't mind Jasmine; she's really quite gentle. My name is Millie. So you're a shaman?'

'I prefer shawoman, if it's all the same,' said Lily. 'You have a lovely home. It is much grander than anything I have ever seen before.'

One of the Hairy Hordes began to snigger. Millie shot him a glare and his smirking was immediately stifled.

'Thank you, I like it,' said Millie, 'it's not what I'm used to but it's home. I see Jasmine likes you. She has exquisite taste, so I am sure we shall become the very best of friends.'

'I hope so,' replied Lily. She really did. Millie was an intimidating character and Lily was sure she wanted her on her side; the thought of Millie as an enemy filled her with dread.

'Come,' said Millie, 'let us walk. Danyal, please, come too.' She offered Lily her left arm and Danyal her right. The three slowly ambled off into the house. Behind them the Hairy Hordes pounced on top of Drudger who eagerly began bashing them around the head. 'Boys will be boys,' Millie commented indulgently. 'Let me show you around.'

Millie gave Lily a tour of her home. She explained the many stories that lay behind the multitude of portraits, paintings and tapestries that adorned the walls. Millie's family was an ancient and illustrious one. It dated back to the time of Chinggis's reign. Her foremother had been Chinggis's agriculture and industry advisor. Over the centuries Millie's family had nurtured their skills. They still provided the majority of food and fuel for Baatarulaan but had long ago pledged their allegiance to the Chinggists. Canvases depicted enormous fields of corn beneath transparent roofing; mills and production units were embroidered into huge wall hangings. There were many corridors each filled completely with works of art that showed in detail the extent of Millie's heritage and current commercial dealings. Lily was awestruck. She quickly realised just how important, influential and rich Millie was.

Businesspeople first and foremost, Millie's family had grown sick of the Khadist regime imposing higher and higher taxes on their produce and claiming ever more ridiculous reasons for stealing property for its own people and purposes. As time passed, Millie's activities had become increasingly secret from the Khadists. The regime was keeping the best of what Millie had been producing for itself, while the people of Baatarulaan were given only the most meagre rations. The Khadists preferred to keep their people doped up and unhealthy as possible, in the belief that this would induce enough lethargy so as to avoid causing resentment or rebellion.

As they strolled through the mansion, Millie told Lily how much she wanted the people, her fellow townsfolk, to live well. She had developed a means of privately engineering enough surplus supplies to provide for the neediest people of Baatarulaan. Some distance outside of the city, and far from the prying eyes of the Khadists, she had established two enormous complexes. Each building was three storeys tall with three hundred chickens on the top floor, a hundred goats and sheep on the middle floor, and a hundred cattle on the ground floor. The waste from the animals was collected using an intricate sluice system and carried to an adjacent collection tower. Inside the tower the waste was carefully managed. The energy it produced was powerful enough to provide the energy needed to keep the animals warm but also to provide power for several acres of covered fields where crops, vegetables and even fruits were grown. This more than satisfied the needs of the animals and was increasingly becoming the staple source of food for the residents of Baatarulaan. What was more, Millie gave the food away for free. Her production plants cost almost nothing and she needed no money.

As she listened, Lily was overwhelmed with admiration. Danyal, too –although he had heard about Millie's doings many times before – never failed to be impressed.

'So what can we do?' asked Lily. 'I know the Khadists are bad but I fear that Tengis could be even worse. There is something about him that makes me terribly scared.'

'Don't worry,' said Danyal, 'we have a plan.'

'My young dear,' said Millie, 'I understand. The Khadists have to go and Tengis is the means of achieving this change.'

'But,' said Lily anxiously, 'he is a bad man. He cannot be trusted; I heard what he said at the Square Dance.'

'We had our people there, too,' said Millie. 'What he stands for is irrelevant; what matters is that he gets the Khadists out.'

'Our sources have reliably informed us that Tengis intends to bring about change through means of a democratic, open and fair election,' said Danyal. 'Our spies tell us that Tengis's advisors are pushing for him to blow apart the old regime. They want to see it replaced with what they feel the people want; a freely elected leader who will promote the teachings of the Ten Recommendations.'

'You're mad!' said Lily. 'Tengis is evil. He will never let the people have a say in what happens to them. He is as bad as the people who imprisoned my father. You don't seem to appreciate the danger he presents.'

'I don't underestimate the love you have for your father or your drive and desire to find him. Please don't underestimate us,' said Millie. 'Of the good people we have an understanding; fools like Tengis we appreciate and keep a large stick upstairs especially for them.'

'What do you mean?' asked Lily.

'We have the Hairy Hordes,' said Millie.

'But,' said Lily, 'they are only six men, they might be tough and like fisticuffs, but the Khadists and Tengis both have far more and better organised support.'

'You'd be surprised at just what the Hairy Hordes are capable of,' said Danyal. 'They practise the ancient art of guerrilla warfare. That's why they get called Hairy. No one outside of this house knows their identity and no one ever can. The Hairy Hordes believe in fairness for all, food for everyone and fighting for fun, or rather fighting against the kind of fun that Khadists have been promoting. They are a formidable force.'

'You are underestimating Tengis,' said Lily. 'I saw the way the people took to him. They are so eager for a change from Khadism that they will take up the mantle of anyone who can assure them of a different future regardless of what that future might be. They are blindly following him.'

'He has some powerful allies,' said Millie, 'but we have stronger allies – truth, honesty and justice. No further harm will befall Baatarulaan so long as we remain true to those friends. We will win out. I have a good deal of experience dealing in strategy and tactics. Business, politics and battle are not so very different. We may not have a numerical advantage but we can make that work to our advantage. Trust me, please?'

Lily found that there seemed to be a lot of people asking her to trust them but she also realised that she had little choice. She gave way, and the threesome continued their tour of Millie's home and returned to the hallway where the Hairy Hordes had prepared lunch.

Boys being boys, the lunch they had prepared consisted of cheeseburgers and milkshakes.

'Where are the greens?' asked Millie. 'What have I said about healthy eating?'

'There's lettuce and gherkins in the burger,' said the Hairy Hordes as one. 'That counts, doesn't it?' Millie shook her head.

Lily bit gleefully into the burger – it was delicious. She found herself extremely hungry after her tour. It had been enlightening but, although it had filled her with hope, she was also afraid that they were taking Tengis too lightly. She couldn't explain it, but Lily was certain that Tengis was a bad man; she also knew that worrying about Tengis was going to be the death of her.

'How's the food?' asked the Hairy Hordes.

Lily mumbled her approval between mouthfuls. The tall boy-rabbit punched the leg of the man with the odd accent.

17

After finishing her second cheeseburger Lily needed some fresh air. Saying thank you to Millie and her men, she assured them that she would work with them to bring about justice so long as they helped her find her father. They agreed that they would meet later that day at Danyal's yard to discuss their plans further. Leaving by a secret exit that led Lily through a maze of passages to a main road, she looked back and found that Millie's exuberant home was completely hidden by the squalor that surrounded it. Turning away, Lily set off out into the city streets. She found herself less intimidated than she had been previously. Whether it was that she now has the support of friends, and the Hairy Hordes, or just that she was getting used to the place, she couldn't decide. Baatarulaan had at first felt like a frightening city but the more time Lily spent there the more she realised that it was the city that was frightened. She had the luxury of not having been born and raised in fear of the Khadist regime. Unlike the Ongolians who lived there, Lily firmly believed that people should and could have a good life. She wanted to understand more about them. She couldn't understand why they had become so bad; why they were so very different from the people she lived with and why they behaved so differently from the way she believed people should behave.

Passing nearby the scene of the Square Dance Lily noticed that there was pro-Tengis graffiti daubed on to nearby walls. A crazed man high on Khem chanted the Ten Recommendations from his addled mattress refuge. Lily pulled up her collar and hurried onwards. Leaving the square, she entered a district she assumed was for the wealthier city dwellers. Well-kept apartment blocks stood behind gated fences guarded by heavily built new recruits of the Leggie. They watched Lily suspiciously as she hurried past. While she wanted to take in her surroundings, she did not want to be conspicuous. Tugging her hat further down over her face, she hastily walked past the leering guards.

Ahead of her Lily saw a large group of people milling around outside another guarded gated estate. The winter was biting hard as snowfall began to fill the air. Still more people joined the mob. The people carried placards bearing pro-Tengis slogans and chanted wildly: 'Tengis, Tengis, he's our man. If he can't do it, no one can!' Lily lurked near a smaller gate on the adjacent wall. The heat of the rabble radiated into the harsh cold. Lily pushed herself against the wall as she sought shelter from the wind. Her eyes were fixed on the crowd. She wanted to see if she was able to understand their behaviour; they were acting just like the herds of wild horses she had been brought up to train. As she watched, Lily noticed something coming towards the smaller gate next to which she was huddled – three men flanking another over whose head a jacket was placed. Lily was alone in observing them; no one in the throng noticed the movement. As they neared the gate to unlock it, the coat was removed. Lily immediately recognised the man it had been shielding.

'You!' hissed Lily. All self-control evaporated and she lunged towards Tengis. The men who had been flanking him held her fast. 'How can you dare pretend to be Chinggis Khaan? What do you know about him? You are nothing. Chinggis was noble and wise; you are filled with hatred and spite.' The venom in her voice was clear. Her eyes visibly glowed with poison.

'Who exactly do you think you are?' asked Tengis. 'You look quite pathetic.' He had never seen Lily before but immediately loathed her. The pit of his stomach lurched as acid boiled within and rose up in his throat. He choked back his anger. Tengis needed to appear in control at all times. His supporters expected it. Still, this mysterious woman invited an unknown beast to rear its head. He wasn't sure why but something within his dark soul told him that he absolutely hated her. He wanted her dead but knew he couldn't lose face by simply choking her there and then.

'I am Lily,' said Lily, 'and I am not some petty little person you can bully and boss around. I have no idea who you are but I absolutely know that you are definitely not Chinggis. No one will believe you; people will see through you.'

Some of the stragglers on the fringe of the throng outside the main gate started to drift towards the girl who was being held by the guards dressed in black. Lily fought hard to hold her nerve.

'I don't think so,' said Tengis. 'Anyway, what on earth could you possibly know? Nothing, that's what!' Tengis nodded to his henchmen to drag the girl away. He would deal with her some-place else, some place more private. As he did so the remainder of the mob started to circle Tengis's private party. They started to chant his name. The guards were unable to move.

'Tengis! Tengis! Tengis!' chanted the crowd.

'Listen,' said Tengis. He beckoned for Lily to move closer. 'Listen, do you really think that people don't believe in me? Watch this.' Tengis turned to face his crowd. 'Who do you love?'

'TENGIS!' screamed the crowd.

'What do you want?' asked Tengis.

'THE POWER OF TEN!' roared the crowd. They were enjoying this impromptu rally enormously and most of them couldn't wait to get home and boast about it to their friends.

'Who do we hate?' invited Tengis.

'KHADISTS!' yelled the crowd. Hearing that word a few began to shout 'boo' and screech wolf-whistles. One more intrepid member moved forward with a Khadist flag and set fire to it. The throng bellowed their approval and braver men jumped on top of the flaming flag. Tengis turned towards Lily and sneered. He lifted his hands towards them, intimating their raucous support.

'What do you worship?' declared Tengis. From his pocket he snatched a lump of his wondrous shimmering shiny substance and held it aloft for all to see. It shone brightly glistening in the evening air.

'THE ORANGEY YELLOW SUNNY STUFF!' boomed the crowd. Some among the crowd squealed in delight and held their tight fists to their mouth. The people were becoming frantic with excitement. Tengis's henchmen looked on worried that he was about to start a riot.

'Who's the man?' hurled Tengis.

'CHINGGIS!' shouted the crowd.

'I can't hear you,' said Tengis. 'Who's the man?'

'CHINGGIS! CHINGGIS! CHINGGIS!' cried the crowd. Although they only numbered one hundred their yells could be heard far afield throughout Baatarulaan. Tengis crossed his arms and smugly soaked up the plaudits. He turned to Lily. She did not look impressed. Her face still spat toxic anger in his direction. His stomach heaved again as the furious acids roared within his body. Although Tengis retained a calm serenity on his face, he was raging inside.

'You are an imposter!' shouted Lily. 'The real Chinggis would never seek attention like this. He was an honest and just man. You are a manipulative bully!' The crowd began to grow quieter. The populace of Baatarulaan was renowned for its fickle nature.

'How dare you doubt my integrity!' bellowed Tengis. His

reflux was getting the better of him. Being the possible president in waiting was taking its toll on him.

'Integrity?!' screamed Lily. 'Integrity?! How can you stand there and talk about integrity? Have you even read your so-called Ten Recommendations? Please, enlighten us by telling us what particular aspect of those pathetic words shows an ounce of integrity. You have simply taken the words you think people want to hear and shaped them into false promises that are so fluffy they can be interpreted as you see fit. You have no substance, no integrity and no place even thinking about telling us how to act!'

'You have no idea of my power!' said Tengis. He tried to gather himself together more calmly. 'I have the power of Chinggis Khaan within me. He and I speak freely; his spirit is in my soul.'

'Is that right?' said Lily. Although she was still fuming, she was able to stabilise her emotions a little. 'And what do you know of spirits?'

'I speak with the spirits,' said Tengis. 'Chinggis and I converse regularly.'

'Are you a shaman?' asked Lily. She knew the answer and Tengis's silence was the affirmation she had been seeking. 'You're not, are you? So, how do you propose it is that you speak to the spirit of Chinggis? Everybody knows that it is only shamans that can speak to the spirits. I should know. I am a real shaman, or rather shawoman. I do speak with the spirits and, you know, it's funny, they never mention you. Are you sure you speak to the spirits? Are you sure you're not perhaps just a little bit mad and hearing voices in your head?'

The memory of Odval's initial doubts flooded Tengis's mind. He recalled the humiliation he experienced as a result of his loved one's words. He fought to keep his anger hidden. Bile poured up his throat into his mouth as his chest clenched around his ribcage. In his cramped heart Tengis knew that Lily's words adhered to the same logic he had lived his whole life by but he also knew he was Chinggis Khaan. He was sure that he simply had to be.

'A shaman is nothing more than a witch,' announced Tengis. The crowd gasped in horror. Shamanism had long been the sacred religion of ancient Ongolium and, although rarely, if ever, practised in Baatarulaan, was still held in high esteem. Tengis's words were nothing short of sacrilege. If he knew anything, though, Tengis knew how to turn a crowd his way. 'You are a witch and that is why you are trying to undermine me. You know full well that the Ten Recommendations are the true words of the people but still you decry them. Why?'

'You lie!' shouted Lily. 'A shaman is a holy person and you know that full well. Don't you dare try and twist things.'

'My dear,' said Tengis, 'what can I say? Men and women sleep on the same pillow but they have different dreams. I am clearly a man; you are not yet even a woman. Your word counts for nothing. In case you haven't noticed, we don't believe in religion any more. The Khadists saw to that hundreds of years ago. The only thing we people of Baatarulaan worship is the right to be ourselves; the right to freedom and the right to live life according to the Ten Recommendations. We call it New Chinggism; it's a way of life not a religion. Religion is all mumbo-jumbo. Religion is the silly stuff of people that believe in magic and we know what people who believe in magic are, don't we?' Tengis turned to the crowd looking for their answer.

'WITCHES!' yelled the crowd. And before long most of the crowd were pointing at her and some were even asking for her to be burned. Lily was learning quickly just how inconsistent people in Baatarulaan really were.

'Hush, please, hush,' said Tengis. He raised his arms to calm the mob. 'Let's see what the little witch, I mean little girl, has to say. We are not barbarians here.' With each moment Tengis's reflux began to move back down inside his throat as well-spun snake oil made its way out.

In contrast, Lily's blood was boiling. She tried to break free of the guards but they held her firmly.

'Speak up, the people want to hear what magical spells you have to cast.'

The crowd eagerly awaited her words.

'If you are so just,' said Lily. She hurriedly tried to find a different tack and recalled the words of Millie. 'If you are no despotic dictator in waiting; if you are a true democratic leader of people; if you truly believe that the people believe in you; if your New Chinggism is so robust; if your Ten Recommendations really have won hearts and minds, why don't you *prove* it?'

'What would you have me do, witch?' said Tengis.

'If you have faith that people have faith in you,' said Lily, 'if you honestly believe in a future fair for all, why have you avoided talk of an election? I know that people around you have discussed it, why don't you even mention it? Surely it is the one and only way of finding a leader for Ongolium who truly represents the people?'

Tengis felt the bile in his stomach rising once more as he struggled to hold the smile on his face. He knew a smile was important.

'Are you trying to cast some spooky spell over us?' said Tengis. He theatrically pretended to be scared. People in the crowd laughed in support. 'Are you trying to summon up some long-forgotten evil demon? Is that how you get in contact with your so-called spirit friends, by telling lies? No? I think I know what it is you are doing. You are indeed casting a spell. You are spreading words of mass deception. I can't quite pinpoint which words they are but I know they are in there somewhere. When

I find them I will prove beyond all doubt that you are a witch. And what do we do when we find a witch?' Tengis turned histrionically towards the crowd, holding one hand to his ear.

'BURN HER!' shrieked the crowd, 'BURN HER! BURN HER! BURN THE WITCH! BURN THE WITCH!'

Lily was terrified. She tried once more to shake free of her fearsome custodians but to no avail. The crowd chanted louder and more fanatically as Tengis began to work it into a frenzy. Lily desperately sought a way out. Her future suddenly looked particularly bleak . . . and hot. She frantically looked for support among the crowd. Delusional eyes glared back at her deeply drunk on Tengis's fanaticism.

Towards the back of the seething throng Lily suddenly spotted movement. Six heavily set figures were slowly but firmly making their way towards her through the crowd. They wore large hats and shook their fists in the air in time with the chanting. The crowd was undeniably in favour of turning Lily into carbon. The hefty men were apparently strong supporters of burning witches. Lily watched them advance, petrified that they might be the last people she ever saw. The six men approached.

As she watched six arms pumping the air rhythmically, one of the men's cloaks fell back. The arm beneath it was far hairier than Lily had expected it to be. The men reached the front of the rabble and advanced upon Lily. Tengis, who had been busily playing the people, suddenly noticed the intruders making their way towards his captive. Lily was close to fainting with fear. The intruders suddenly threw off their hats and cloaks. Standing abreast of one another, they beat their chests and roared into the darkening sky. As they did so, one of them, a particularly stocky broad man, cast a look towards Lily and winked. She noted with joy and relief that his roar had a particularly unique sing-song lilt. The tall boy made his way over to her and shoved her captors out of the way pushing them all a little harder than was actually necessary. Picking her up effortlessly, he placed her on to his wide, warm shoulders. His fellow guerrillas continued to roar at the crowd, who scattered despite their number. Tengis stood watching on dumbstruck. Within a minute there was no sight (or sound) of the guerrilla, or of Lily.

Rushing along at dizzying speed atop the tall boy's shoulders, Lily tried in vain to figure out where they were headed but they were moving too fast. Presently they slowed and finally stopped. The group stood in the middle of Danyal's yard. Breathing hard, the men and boys began to slap one another on the back and laugh raucously. Even Lily began to giggle as her nervous system rebooted. Danyal and Millie came rushing out of the house to greet her. Drudger walked out of the stable holding Lucky's reins.

'My girl,' said Millie, 'I don't know whether you are brave, stupid – or both!'

'Imagine taking on Tengis when he is with his henchmen and in front of a mob of his frenzied supporters,' said Danyal. 'Lass, you really must have a death wish for yourself and for Tengis. Trying to attack him single-handedly, brilliant!'

'It wasn't like that,' pleaded Lily. 'I was just out walking when . . .'

'When you decided to have a go at Tengis,' said Drudger.

'Nudge-nudge, wink-wink,' said the Hairy Hordes in unison as they nudged one another heavy-handedly and blinked wildly at one another. It wasn't long before they were a jumbled mass of dusty, playful fighting.

'Honestly,' implored Lily. 'I didn't want to cause any trouble. But when I saw Tengis something came over me. I wasn't in control of myself. I couldn't help trying to attack him. It was weird. It felt as though he had somehow unstopped all of my hatred and was pulling it towards him. I could see in his eyes that he felt the same way. There was an awful and frightening connection of some sort. I really don't remember.'

'It doesn't matter what you do and don't remember,' said Millie. 'You are now very much on Tengis's agenda. The question is: are you happy being on his agenda? Would you be willing to take this battle further? From what I have heard he has already unleashed the entire Leggie to find both you and the Hairy Hordes. He has issued a shoot-to-kill mandate to all archers throughout Baatarulaan. Like it or not, you have started the fight. He will probably be forging a coalition with the Khadists, promising that, so long as they give him overall control, he will not banish or execute any of them. We are but a few, but now we have a talisman, or should I say taliswoman?'

'What?' said Lily. 'Battle? I only wanted to find my father. I really don't know what to do but Tengis can't be allowed to continue. He is evil – I will willingly do anything it takes to stop him.'

'You are not alone,' said Danyal. 'People wanted change. They will soon begin to realise that Tengis was never really offering change. There is nothing new in his New Chinggism and there is certainly nothing to do with Chinggis, not that we could see. He does have powerful friends but in time I think we will find that so do we. Unless we act soon, there is a grave danger that Tengis will take full control of Ongolium. If we let that happen, the world in which we will find ourselves is likely to be a lot more severe than it is now. As for your father, if Tengis realises who he is, I fear he will never be found. He is a clever man and a devious orator, but he has blackness in his soul.'

'Tengis has no soul!' said Lily. 'He is consumed by his greed for power and position. He appears to be so sure that he really is Chinggis Khaan. Listening to him talk was terrifying.'

'That as may be,' said Millie, 'but whereas the meat-biting tooth is in the mouth, the man-biting tooth is in the soul. You have a stronger soul and spirit than Tengis will ever be able to understand. As for now, it's not safe for you to stay here. You must leave Baatarulaan. The Leggie will be turning over every stone as they search for you. Here, Lucky is ready for you. He will know his way out of here and back across the Steppe. Wear this disguise, it may be dark but everyone will be looking for you. Good luck and rest assured, we will meet soon, I promise.' Millie leaned over and kissed Lily on the forehead. Lucky nuzzled up next to her happy to be with his mistress again.

'I have packed your belongings,' said Danyal. 'There is enough food for both of you for a week. I have also left a note explaining how to contact us in emergency. There is a map – we will meet at the point marked X ten days from now. Be safe: you are an important young woman now.' Danyal ruffled her hair and hastily walked back inside.

'He's not very good at goodbyes,' said Drudger. 'Anyways, it's more of an *au revoir*, innit?' Drudger followed Danyal indoors, wiping a tear from his misshapen face.

'Wait. What about you and the Hairy Hordes?' asked Lily, as she climbed up on to Lucky's back. 'They're not safe either. They are in as much danger as I am. They can't stay here either.'

The Hairy Hordes stood and looked at Lily. No one had really ever cared for their wellbeing before. They tried to show how touched they were by the empathy of this young woman but instead replied using the only means they knew how – they snorted loudly, guffawed and gave the fellow nearest them a jolly good kick up the behind. Wiping his shorts comically, the man with the interesting accent wandered over casually and gave Lucky a heavy slap on his rump. The horse reared up and galloped off into the darkness. Lily turned and shouted to the Hairy Hordes: 'Keep safe and may your moustaches grow like brushwood!'

18

For the first time in over a week Lily found herself alone with Lucky. A good deal had taken place since that had last happened. She was thankful of having an opportunity to take stock and think about everything that had taken place. Sitting up in her saddle, Lily wiped the sleep from her eyes. She had no idea what time it was or how long she had been riding. As she looked around her, Baatarulaan was nowhere to be seen. Even if she wasn't certain where she was, Lily knew that she was safely back on the Steppe. She bent over forwards and gave Lucky as big a hug as was possible from her saddle. People had always said he was a very fortunate horse.

Lily stretched widely and yawned heavenwards. Although they had been travelling for some time, Lily knew that Lucky would simply stop when he needed a rest; she didn't have to worry about his fatigue. Reaching behind her, Lily opened the pannier saddlebags that contained her provisions and meagre belongings. She pulled out the letter that Danyal had left with her and untied the string that bound its scroll:

Dearest Lily,
You really have been a wonder. Imagine taking on Tengis on your own – such courage! I no longer have any doubts that with you leading our charge we shall defeat Tengis and with him the Khadist regime that has shackled the true people of Ongolium since the age of Chinggis Khaan. Keep your

faith – you are the one; it is your destiny.

In your saddlebags you will find enough provisions to see you till next we meet. I have also given you a small horn. If you find yourself in danger, blow it. Although you may think you are alone, there are friends in hidden places. The influence of Millie reaches further than you can imagine.

Be at the spot marked X by midnight of the next full moon. In the meantime, while your horse is strong, travel to see places.

With deepest support, faith and gratitude,
    Danyal.

Lily finished reading the letter, rolled it back up and replaced it in the saddlebag. Although she had experienced more excitement in the past month than in the rest of her life put together, she was exhausted both mentally and physically. The last thing she wanted was anything that would cause her adrenalin levels to rise anything over 'just awake'. She looked around at the flat rocky Steppe. She counted how many birds she could see – eleven in total. In short, Lily was bored. After the excitement of Baatarulaan and the future challenges that lay ahead she didn't know what to do with herself until the next full moon appeared. It was too far for her to head back to her herder group. She also didn't want to go back until she had actually achieved something. To date she had been given a box she didn't understand yet; gone in search of her father but not found him; met some people she wasn't one hundred per cent sure she trusted; and inadvertently started a battle with somebody she utterly abhorred but wasn't sure why. Lily was rather confused. Lucky kept plodding further on into the Steppe. Neither of them was sure where they were heading but both of them wanted to get there.

Lily needed something to occupy her time. Two things came

to mind. She had a puzzle that she still remained some way away from solving – the strange ornate box and its nonsensical riddle.

She had seen a tiger. It was apparently meant to signify Tengis and the future, although other than being a strong marketing tool Lily saw little connection between the two and there had been no sign of any tigers wearing a bell. It all felt a little bit like it lacked real substance. The cats Lily had quickly identified as the rich, opulent and lazy Khadists living in Baatarulaan, but there were no fish. During the time Lily had spent in Baatarulaan she had seen people eating many weird and wonderful things but never once fish. There was also hardly any fresh water to speak of. The river near the city was dreadfully polluted and not even Lucky would think about drinking from it. This brought Lily to the Heaven and Earth conundrum. It had to have something to do with her shawomanism, but again she was unsure what. Altogether she surmised that, while she had learned many things from her first experience of Baatarulaan, she had moved no further in understanding the riddle of the box.

Deflated, she jumped down from Lucky and walked beside him. The horse stopped almost immediately. Lily saw that he was looking to rest. He wandered down to the banks of the river that flowed nearby and drank deeply. Lily was utterly exhausted. Dusk was fast approaching, which meant the chill cold of the Ongolian night would soon be upon her. Where they stood was as good a place as any to set up camp. After starting a suitable fire Lily set up camp. The tent covering Danyal had provided was oddly shaped yet enabled both Lily and Lucky to snuggle up against one another. It was a blustery frozen night but the pair remained warm. Lily dreamed about Baatarulaan and the strange way city people lived. It differed so greatly from the herder life she had grown accustomed to. She could not understand why people lived in such confined spaces so close to one another. It didn't feel natural.

Lucky dreamed about carrots and a warm bed of hay, snoring noisily as he did so.

19

Lily awoke sometime in the middle of the night. She had no idea what time it was but it was almost pitch-dark. The moon was only midway through waxing and its bulging illumination was not yet at its full power. Lily knew from her lunar charts that it had something to do with gibbons or monkeys of some sort. Lucky still lay snoring next to her. He was the largest and warmest hot-water bottle she had ever enjoyed. She made a mental note to build a ger that she could share with her steed; it was odd but it made sense, even with the fruity aromas. Stretching her arms wide and yawning she ventured outside the tent into the chill night air.

Lily knew almost every constellation in the Ongolian sky. As she wrapped a blanket around her shoulders, she sought out the Big Dipper and Carousel – they were her favourites. Settling down on to the ground, she stoked up the fire to create some additional warmth. She felt empty. Lily had so many questions yet no answers. She feared she really was turning into the idiot with so many questions that Danyal had referred to. How was *she* to know everything, though? She considered herself to be relatively young. She had never heard of any twenty-two-year-olds who really knew how the world worked despite their constant refrains claiming the opposite. Why should she have been any different? She had spent her life moving between the Steppe and the spirit world; living among her simple herder family; and sharing friendship with no other soul than a particularly grumpy yet loyal horse. Why did people have such great expectations of her? She had been made leader of her herder group simply because she was her father's daughter. The elders had confounded her by trusting and presenting her with the ornate box containing Chinggis's words. Danyal and Drudger had trusted her and taken her to meet Mille and the Hairy Hordes, who instantly knew she was the one to help them return Baatarulaan to the civic glory it had once known. Even her nemesis, Tengis, had somehow known she was his arch foe. Why else would he have acted so dastardly towards her? Why else would he have unleashed the Leggie on her and sworn to kill her if at least some small part of him hadn't realised the threat she posed to his odious plans? Even Lucky willingly carried and cared for his mistress; his equine instincts apparently sensed that she was a valuable cargo.

Lily seemed to be the only one who had not come to terms with the fact that she was destined for something more than being the daughter of a herder group leader and shawoman. She simply could not accept that she was in the middle of things. Her life had always been spent skulking around the periphery. Why should that have changed? More importantly, she was just small fry; she couldn't comprehend how she now suddenly found herself immersed in a conflict that looked set to define her entire nation. How she was at the forefront of Tengis's evil intentions was beyond her.

Lily sat and stared into the fire, huddling against the chill wind. There had to be a reason. There had to be an answer. But she felt powerless. She began to sob gently. It was the first time she had shed a tear since her father had been taken prisoner. The gentleness of her tears gave way to a heavy outpour.

Presently Lily stopped weeping. She dried her eyes with a corner of the blanket and focused on the flames in front of her. Throughout her life she knew there was only one place where

163

she could find refuge when life became too complicated. However, her last visit to the spirit world had proved less than fruitful. She may have left there feeling confused, but all the same it was time to go back. Weeks had passed since her last visit. Her world had exploded. Her life was in danger. If she was to fulfil the destiny everybody seemed to have in mind for her, she needed to find strength from somewhere. The spirit world had always been that place. It was to the spirit world she needed to return.

She placed more fuel on the fire, hoping that it would keep her warm during her inner journey. As she settled into a comfortable position, she looked behind her. Lucky had woken up and was peering at her from the tent. He nodded knowingly and winked. Lily knew that horses weren't supposed to wink, so she put it down to the bad light. Lucky seeming approval, however, had given her confidence that he would protect her while she was away. He was the only friend she could rely upon. Lily crossed her legs and lifted her face to the sky. Closing her eyes, she cleared her mind of all thoughts. Inhaling through her nose, she began to steady her breathing. Exhaling through her mouth, she found long, measured breaths. She could feel an invisible ethereal shroud surround her, enveloping her in a mysterious warmth. Clapping her hands, Lily began to beat out a regular rhythm. Opening her voice, she began to chant: 'Oohhmmmmmmmmmmmmmm . . .'

Opening her eyes Lily lifted her hands to shield them from the white glare that flooded them. It was several moments before her sight adjusted itself. Her hearing had not caught up yet and all that sounded was her steady heartbeat and deep breathing. The ground was covered in crisp icy snow, although it was not at all cold; Lily seemed to be wearing little more than light clothing. As she stood up, blood coursed through her body. Lily had never quite got used to the physical rush that came with entering the spirit world. It always gave her a sensation of great elation. She lifted her arms and turned her hands in the air. Everything seemed different here – lighter and somehow fluffy.

Once all of Lily's senses had been restored, she looked around her. As usual, she was standing near the large gate that always began her visits here. She walked along the riverside road to the half-finished bridge. Her friendly puppies bounded across to see her. She was always pleased to see them and they licked her hands and nibbled at her feet playfully.

While Lily was stroking the dogs she heard familiar footsteps walking quietly through the snow behind her. As they got near to her, she turned to face her spirit friend.

'How are you?' asked her friend.

'I have so much to tell you!' exclaimed Lily. 'I have been to the city. It is both horrible and exciting. I have met some strange yet compelling people and I seem to have somehow started a battle!'

'I know,' replied her friend, 'I have been watching you with great interest. You certainly have been busy, but are you any closer to solving your riddle or finding your father?'

'I have even more questions now than I had when we last spoke,' said Lily. 'I know you told me to stop looking for answers and to start believing in my instincts, but I'm afraid that when I've done that it has resulted in me following two swarthy, grubby-looking men into a dark tunnel, and also in my attacking a relative stranger on a gut feel that he was a really horrid person. Surely that cannot be right?'

'Did any real harm come from following your heart?' asked her friend.

'No,' answered Lily, 'not really, but I did almost get burned at the stake. Does that count?'

'I think you are underestimating your intuition,' said her

friend softly. 'Within the space of weeks you have gained a fuller understanding of your nation. You now comprehend more clearly the various factions that exist within Ongolium. You can empathise with those you feel are being treated unfairly. You have been accepted for yourself by a powerful group of strangers. They believe in you as much as I do. Most importantly, you have looked into the face of evil and survived.'

'Only just!' said Lily. 'If it wasn't for the Hairy Hordes, I would quite literally be toast.'

'But would they have saved you, had you not already won their hearts to your own?' said her friend. 'Would Tengis have been as afraid of you if you were just the simple herder woman you are still trying to convince yourself you are? Would you be here speaking to me in the spirit world if your destiny was merely to milk goats and shave sheep? You may not have unravelled your riddle but you have answered questions about yourself that you had not even begun to ask.'

'But I have found hatred!' said Lily. 'I had never hated anything or anyone before I heard about Tengis. What is that all about?'

'That is simple,' said her friend. 'There are two straight-forward explanations. First and foremost, you are a woman for whom justice is all important. You heard Tengis talk, you listened to his Ten Recommendations, you absorbed New Chinggism and immediately you saw straight through it. For you this was not about helping the people and overthrowing Khadism. This was all about Tengis using his sunny substance to attain power and control over the people. He is no different to the Khadists he purports to detest. As soon as he caught a glimpse of the trappings of power, his mind was sullied.

'Be careful, he is intelligent though. He knows that if he uses the right words and portrays the correct image the people will support him, at least at first. Tengis knows that the shimmering stuff is only half the battle; to win the people to his cause entirely he realises that he needs to offer them something new, something that promises to improve their quality of life, albeit falsely. He declares that he is at one with the spirit of Chinggis. You and I know that this is not true, but the people of Baatarulaan don't know that. All they see is someone brave enough, and rich enough, to seize control of the Fun Brigade and do so peacefully. All they hear are the words of someone that promises to eradicate a regime that has held them fast for centuries.

'Although the memory of Chinggis has been outlawed, it yet retains its age-old pull in people's hearts. When the people hear Tengis declare he has the blessing of Chinggis, together with the apparent energy his mined material seems to exude, all they see is hope. You can't blame people for having hope. It has been eight hundred years since hope last walked the streets of Baatarulaan. It has been many generations since the people last had anything to which they could pin their forbidden dreams. You can't blame the people for so readily believing in Tengis. But you *can* blame Tengis for corrupting them. You *can* blame Tengis for abusing the name of Chinggis. You *can* blame Tengis for forgetting that the people deserve justice!'

'What can I do, though?' asked Lily. 'Tengis has everybody's support and if Danyal was right, even though he has set up a coalition with the Khadists, the people are still behind him. They cannot see his duplicitous nature. They forget how almost overnight those whom Tengis had declared the enemy have become his allies. What can I do against his cunningly crafted words and that glistening substance? They have secured him the backing of the most important people in Baatarulaan. When I tried to stand against him, look what happened? I have unwittingly become an enemy of both the state and the most frightening man I have ever met. How can he claim to be in league with Chinggis? When I remember what he said, I just want to kill him. I have never wanted to harm anything or anybody before. I don't mind admitting that I am more than a little terrified. I am afraid that Tengis and the Leggie want to hunt me down and I am frightened of the violent emotions Tengis has awoken in me.'

'What if I told you that there was a way to undermine Tengis absolutely?' said her friend. 'What if I told you that you could destroy his credibility and win over the support of the people?'

'How on earth could that be possible?' asked Lily. 'When I challenged him before, he claimed that I was a witch; that I was using spells to deceive and mislead. He might have given his disciples hope; what hope do I have to give them?'

'There is always hope so long as you believe in yourself,' said her friend. 'We know that Tengis has nothing to do with Chinggis, don't we?'

'I do,' said Lily. 'You say you do too, so I guess you do, though I can't read your mind.'

'Let me tell you that I know Chinggis better than anyone,' said her friend. Lily looked bemused. 'You have long wondered who it is that I am, have you not?' Lily nodded in affirmation. 'What I am about to tell you I have kept secret for eight hundred years. What I am about to tell you I took to my grave.'

Lily stood silently, peering into the eyes of her friend, trying to see if she was able to guess what she was about to say. Her friend began to weep softly.

'Why are you sad?' asked Lily. 'You are beautiful. You are wise. You live in the most charming lands I have ever seen. And you are immortal. Please don't be upset. You have so much.' Lily moved closer to her friend to comfort her but was waved away.

'Please,' said her friend, 'please, let me tell you what I have to say. It has been so long since I spoke of it that I sometimes

168

wonder if I only ever dreamed it. I know that Tengis has no connection with Chinggis. I know that Chinggis would never speak to someone with such a foul mind. I know that Chinggis would never counsel anyone to fool the people so cruelly as Tengis is doing. I have a closer understanding of Chinggis than even his mother.'

Lily remained stock-still. Her friend stood up tall and composed herself.

'Please,' said Lily, 'tell me.'

'Chinggis and I were lovers,' said her friend. 'Chinggis and I were the closest friends can be. Chinggis and I were united on Earth and promised never to part. But Khad made sure we would never be united in death. I have waited for his return for eight hundred years. Chinggis was never committed to the ground. His death was never mourned correctly. His spirit remains stranded in some distant limbo unable to reach its final destination. Such is the way for those without proper burial. He cannot come to me and now that I am bound to the spirit world I can no longer search for his soul.'

Lily was shocked. In all the years she had known her spirit friend she had never imagined that she was such an important friend. She had presumed she was the spirit of some other shawoman, not anyone as important as the famous and falsely dishonoured Tsara.

'What happened to you?' asked Lily.

'Once Khad had spread his vile words about my fictitious misconduct,' said Tsara, 'the people were too afraid to ignore them. Within months everything that Chinggis had striven so hard to create had been turned inside out by his jealous and evil cousin. Even my closest friends and confidantes turned against me. So terrified were they of Khad's wrath they shunned me. All of them shut me out of their lives entirely. They even took my children from me. My lovely Sukh and Bolorerdene. I was deemed unfit as a mother. I, the woman who had given birth to Chinggis's rightful heirs, was made to watch as Khad took them from me and imprisoned them in a tower. Khad saw to it that my name became synonymous with dirt. Whenever my name was mentioned, people used to spit on the floor. It was more than I could bear – in the end my only hope of escape was to the spirit world to which I duly fled.' Tsara fell to the ground and broke down. Her tears melted away the ice where they fell. Lily was struggling to accept what she was hearing. On top of everything that had been happening in the real world, the spirit world, too, was now being thrown into disarray. She bent down and comforted her friend.

'I wish I could do something to help you,' said Lily. 'You have been such a good friend. You have always been there when I needed help. I would love to be able to repay your kindness in some small way.'

'How I miss my children,' sobbed Tsara. 'How could anyone deprive a mother of her children? My poor Sukh and Bolorerdene. I have no idea what happened to them. Every day I pray that one of my more kindly friends managed to get them released and that they lived long and happy lives.'

'Have you never found them in the spirit world?' asked Lily. She knew it was a sensitive question but wanted to find out what she could if she was going to try and help her friend who had done so much to help her as she had grown up. If the children had not been found in the spirit world, then they had met a fate as callous and cruel as that which had overtaken their father. Tsara remained wordless, crying into Lily's shoulder. The ladies consoled one another helplessly. They remained thus for several hours.

'This spirit world has many wonders,' said Tsara, 'but it has many drawbacks too. If only I could visit the real world and search for my loved ones.'

'What about me?' asked Lily. 'Surely I can help. I don't know where to start but with your guiding hand I could help you surely?'

'I know very little,' said Tsara. 'All I remember was Khad bragging about having sealed Chinggis in an icy tomb and my children in a tower. I have no idea where either might be located but if you could possibly help me I would be eternally grateful . . . and I do have an eternity in which to be grateful! Come, let us sit down and plan. There is much that needs doing.' Tsara led Lily by the hand and they sat beneath the tree where once they had talked briefly to Mark Anthony. Lily found some paper and a pen and they began to make notes on what needed to be done.

'I have so many things to do but have failed at discovering any of them so far,' said Lily. 'I have no tiger with a bell. There seems to be no sign of cats eating fish. Heaven and Earth still feel like very different places to me. My father is still being held somewhere but I don't know where that is. We have to look in every glacier for Chinggis; there are hundreds in Ongolium. And we must find your two children, though again I cannot for the life of me think of anywhere to start looking.'

'Have faith,' said Tsara. 'If eight hundred years has taught me anything it is that while a person might fail seven times yet they will rise up again eight times. I said before that you are special. Use your prescience; it will serve you just as I do. Think of it as a guide in the real world. Do not look to master it. Let it feel freely and when it directs you, follow.'

'I will try,' said Lily. 'What about Tengis? How will I avoid him? If I meet him again, what should I do?'

'His power lies exclusively in his highly spun words and shimmering substance,' said Tsara. 'Words can easily be out-manoeuvred by actions. When the time comes you will know what to do. As for his shiny material, I will leave it up to you to decide how best to deal with this. For now I bid you fair weather and fill your heart with my love and gratitude.'

'Please,' implored Lily, 'don't go!'

It was too late. Lily began to feel the pull back into the real world she had grown accustomed to. The invisible shroud slowly began to dissolve and she found herself sitting next to a fire. Lucky stood behind her with a startled look on his face. She braced herself in anticipation of the icy wind but it didn't blast her. They were not where she expected them to be. She looked about for her tent; it wasn't there. Standing up in the darkness, she banged her head. Rubbing it better with her hand, she listened for signs of wildlife or weather. Her ears filled with the sound of silence. As her eyes adjusted to the gloom, her mouth opened in awe. This was most definitely not the Steppe.

20

'Have you caught her yet?' asked Tengis. 'I want her found and I want her killed. There is no place in my city for heretical witches.' The guards lining the walls looked on bemused; they hadn't realised that Baatarulaan had become Tengis's city, at least not yet.

'No sign of her, sir,' replied Oldortar. 'It confirms my suspicions that there must be some underground movement that aided her escape. My men are too thorough to have missed her otherwise.'

'Evidently not thorough enough,' said Tengis.

Oldortar shrank away from him into the shadows; his guards stifled their laughs.

'All of you, get out! I want that witch found. Nobody rests until she is dead, you understand?'

Odval looked almost ashamed. She loved Tengis but ever since he had returned to Baatarulaan with the shimmering substance his thoughts had begun to become ever more corrupt. With each day that passed his savage hunger for absolute power wiped out the sound, logical mind she had fallen in love with. She feared that he no longer wanted to restore the faith of Chinggis. She feared his motives were completely personal and he had been utterly seduced by the glistening material. In the past week he had taken a new and terrifying direction. Since the moment Tengis had met the woman who was Lily he had been overflowing with bloodlust.

The man she adored who had once never been able to lift a finger in anger was craving death, violence and mayhem. She had no idea why one woman should have incited such passion in his heart and she was embarrassed to admit that she, too, longed for her demise – that this other woman could stir such emotion was beginning to claw at her heart as jealousy started to overcome her.

In the previous two days Tengis had ordered three executions. The first victim was someone who had tried to steal his glimmering metal, the second a foolish boy who had tried to start a True Chinggis movement at one of Tengis's own rallies. The last person he had hanged that week was the result of simply being in the wrong place at the wrong time. A young girl who worked in his kitchen had hurriedly been carrying Tengis and Odval's porridge to their bedroom when she had rounded a corner and bumped into Tengis as he was on his way to the bathroom, spilling the contents of Odval's bowl down his pyjama bottoms as she did so. It had scalded Tengis where he least wanted to be scalded and he had immediately ordered that the girl repay him with her life. Odval had willingly concurred; she loved her porridge on cold mornings and was most put out to have missed breakfast.

Life in the Tengis household was fast becoming less than relaxed. With Tengis rampantly seeking the blood of Lily, Odval fighting her jealous demons, the guards floundering as they sought to find Tengis's quarry, and the staff simply cowed and scared, the home was quickly shrouded in tension. The stronger Tengis's desire to capture Lily grew, the more time he spent alone seeking counsel from the voice in his head.

'You must humiliate and destroy her!' said the voice. 'She is the one person that can prevent you from fulfilling your destiny.' Tengis shared one thing with Lily: both of them were regularly reminded by their personal counsellors that they separately had amazing futures ahead of them if only they fulfilled their destiny. 'If you fail to kill that woman she will tear apart everything you believe in and sully your name for ever.'

'But how can one person possibly ruin our plans?' asked Tengis. 'I am committed to killing her but it's not because I fear she could prevent me reaching my potential. There is just something about her that makes me livid. It's as though we know each other without having ever met. She can see into my soul. What would you do? More to the point, what would Chinggis do?'

'Well, it's not about what Chinggis would do,' said the voice, 'it is about what *you* should do. The power you have at your disposal offers boundless opportunity. You can turn Ongolium into whatever you please once you prove yourself worthy to the people. I have always believed that the best way to prove one's worth to one's people is to ensure that they fear you more than death itself.'

'How can that be?' asked Tengis. 'I have always simply wanted to make their lives better; it is the New Chinggism way. My Ten Recommendations are all designed to help people live a happier life. When I wrote that people should not take things that are not theirs, I meant for them to put an end to the robberies and theft that have dogged Baatarulaan for centuries. When I recommended that people stopped saying bad things about one another, all I wanted was to create one big society that was based upon mutual respect. My suggestion to have only one belief was to unite faith in the same way that Chinggis united cultures when he was emperor. As for asking people to stop killing one another, that is because it's a job for higher authorities not the common person in the street. There has to be a jolly good reason to put an end to somebody's life. I am all about the people; I have always been all about the people; I will always be all about the people. Why would I want or even need them to fear me?'

'Was it not you who killed a girl over porridge?' said the voice. 'People will always look to their leaders to set the benchmark for acceptable and proper behaviour.'

'That was a spur-of-the-moment sort of thing,' replied Tengis. 'I really probably should have just given her a stern talking to, but my bits hurt so much that I got carried away. I promise I will try harder going forward.'

'Very well,' said the voice a little wearily. 'But have you not taken possession of everything that had once belonged to the Khadists? You have even made their head office your home.'

'That's different!' explained Tengis, 'I have formed a coalition between New Chinggism and the Khadists. It is only fair that we sought to find accommodations between us. I have relinquished threatening behaviour towards them and they have given up each and every trapping of office. I have also given up all claims over their personal possessions. I think you'll find that I have been more than generous on that account. They may have given up or amended accordingly every policy they stood for but I have kept them in power . . . Well, we share power, sort of, and they still have their lives.'

'If you are to lead by example,' said the voice, 'surely you should stop saying bad things about that girl in public, and about everyone else in private?'

'What I say in my own home is my own private business,' said Tengis. He was becoming more than a little irritated. 'I can say whatever I want in my own home and, if there are people in my home that hear what I say, then that's fine because it's my private home, and if my home just so happens to be the main office where we govern the country from . . . well that's life. It is *my* home and I can say what I like. As for that girl. That girl is beneath contempt.'

'If she is beneath contempt,' said the voice, 'doesn't that mean she is not worth feeling contempt for?'

'Don't play with my words!' said Tengis. 'She is beneath contempt in so much as she ignites sentiment that is even more base than contempt. I hate her. She is a danger not only to me but to the whole of Ongolium. If I am to do right by the people, she must be wiped from the face of this world. It is the best thing for the people. If this requires me to spread the word of her status in order to capture her, then I am only doing the bidding of the people; it is nothing personal. I would never dream of saying anything bad about anyone else unless it was for the greater good.'

'You seem to believe in many things,' said the voice. 'How are you going to convince people that believing in just one thing is the right and proper way to have true faith?'

'What do you mean?' asked Tengis. 'I only believe in doing what is best for Ongolium.'

'You say that,' replied the voice, 'but in so doing you believe in New Chinggism; you believe in harnessing the historic strength of Khadism; you believe in the strength proffered by the gleaming material, and, most of all, you firmly believe in your own ability.'

'Aha!' said Tengis. 'This is where you are wrong. All of those things are the same; they *all* relate to believing in doing what is best for Ongolium.'

'If that is the case,' said the voice, 'then surely any man in the street can declare he believes in the austerity of Khadism, the bravery of Chinggism, the opportunism of New Chinggism and in the hearty nature of the pies his mother cooks for him? Such a man could just as easily state that by believing in those four things he merely believes in what he considers are the best traits of our Ongolian heritage (especially the pies)?'

'That is not the same at all,' said Tengis. 'A man in the street does not have the right to believe in more than one thing. He should not have the time or inclination to do so. It is not his station in life to think about the bigger picture, in what is best about his country. That is the role of those in charge. That is my purpose. I believe in all things to do with this country and I believe in helping the common people understand that having faith in one single direction will make their lives far more effective and efficient. They should have faith in what it is that I say.'

'At any cost?' asked the voice.

'Yes, at any cost,' replied Tengis. 'I know what is best for the people, and when they come to accept and believe that, then they will have nothing short of the best.'

'Are you perhaps being slightly egotistical?' asked the voice rather waspishly. 'Don't you consider that what you think, say and do to be greatly superior to the actions of any other? Might it be possible that you see yourself as above all others, even those you care for? Do you think of yourself as more intelligent, more talented, clearer of thought, wiser? . . . Brave enough to make decisions others would fail to do?'

'Of course I do!' said Tengis impatiently. 'You know that full well; I have always believed that. I only mix with other people so that they can undertake the tasks I have no interest in doing. Other people are merely resources at my command as I seek to do the best for the population of Ongolium and our great country.'

'What about Odval, Mr Enkh and your other counsellors?' asked the voice.

'They are pawns,' said Tengis. 'I may care for Odval; she is somewhat special to me. As for the others, fish only see the bait not the hook – people fail to see the danger, only the profit. All of them are disposable. Ruling this country would be far simpler if I had people working for me who had no flimsy emotional attachment to Ongolium. Sentiment does nothing except cloud effectiveness. I have no time for it. I am certain Chinggis must have felt the same way.'

'Do you think so?' asked the voice. 'Chinggis was after all the most tolerant leader this country has ever known. He was democratic to a fault. He did nothing unless he had attained consensus amongst his advisors. He would not act unless Khasar, Bold and Khad agreed that it was the correct course to take. Are you prepared to share your power with those around you?' Tengis remained silent for a moment as he thought about this.

'No,' came Tengis's response.

'Are you willing to fully embrace and endorse the democracy that marked the rule of Chinggis?' asked the voice.

'No,' replied Tengis.

'Will you listen to what your advisors tell you and change your mind if they deem it necessary?' inquired the voice.

'Absolutely not,' said Tengis.

'If you are not willing to do these things,' said the voice, 'then how can you claim to be acting under the banner of Chinggis? How can you tell the world that you are against those that ruined Chinggis and his egalitarianism? How can you claim to be for the people if you are not prepared to listen to them?'

'Because I know better than they do,' said Tengis. He was becoming heated and now stared angrily out of his window across his city. 'They are corrupt. They are wrong. I am here to make things better. Only I know how to serve and protect Ongolium.'

'That truly does not sound like you believe in Chinggis,' said the voice. 'It sounds as though you have never really believed in Chinggis.'

'But,' said Tengis, 'everything I have ever done has been in consultation with you. Every move or decision I have ever made. Finding the shimmering metal, establishing New

Chinggism, winning the trust of the people, distilling fear into my enemies. Everything has been at your behest. You have been the one that has guided me since I was an infant.' Tengis's brilliant mind raced, his motor neurons exploding in a feeding frenzy as they fused hungrily in one another's electricity.

'You *are* Chinggis, aren't you?'

The voice in his head remained silent for several moments.

'*I am Khad*,' said the voice. 'How do you do? It is a welcome pleasure to finally make your acquaintance. We have much to discuss.'

21

As a child, Lily had often wondered what the afterlife might look like. Most of the images she had been able to conjure up of Heaven looked pretty much like the place where she now found herself standing. She pinched herself. It hurt. She wasn't dead. Lucky moved closer and she could smell cabbages on his breath. She was definitely alive. Everything else told her otherwise, though.

It was midwinter and Lily had known enough of them to realise that she should be shivering and diving for shelter. The temperature was not warm but it was far from cold, certainly above zero degrees. She didn't even have a jacket on. Lucky seemingly appreciated her thought and shook his rump approvingly. On the Steppe, the herders had taught Lily how to identify her location by sound – from the way the wind whistled over certain rocks, the cawing of various birds of prey, the bleating of local goats and the hoof fall of herder horses Lily had become able to pinpoint almost exactly her location within a radius of some hundred miles from the site of the winter camp. As Lily craned her neck to listen for noise, Lucky followed her example. Despite much twitching of ears, teeth clenching and exasperated concentration, neither of them could hear a thing.

Looking around in wonder she marvelled at the structure inside whose belly she now stood. The past fortnight had been the first time Lily had ever set foot inside a structure larger than a ger. Some of the buildings she had been inside were almost the same size as twenty or even thirty gers. Millie's home had to have been the same size as one hundred. As she took in the scale of the glowing room at whose centre she stood, she estimated that the space could house every single ger in the whole of Ongolium and still have space for lots more. It was enormous; even Lucky seemed to be impressed. The roof disappeared into darkness beyond the reach of the firelight emanating from the centre of the structure. The gargantuan walls that led up to the roof were roughly hewn. They looked damp and a little magical. As Lily ventured closer to them, she watched as translucent figures danced across their luminosity. There was an alien feeling to the room; it was so unlike anything she had seen before. Lily tried to understand why everything looked so strange yet eerily familiar. Stopping dead in her tracks, she suddenly recalled that she had seen this before. The walls were made from the same shimmering material peddled by Tengis. Lily gasped.

Running her hands across the walls, Lily was astonished by the softness and warmth the unusual yellow metallic substance offered. The way in which the walls captured the light cast by the fire was mesmerising. It illuminated each and every nook and cranny. The massive walls were completely uneven and irregular. There was no uniformity to the tender, polished rock face. While the substance was new to Lily, and related to Tengis, she was not afraid. The cavern felt like it should belong to the spirit world. Lily remembered that it was through the spirit world that she had arrived here. She had never known the spirit world to have exerted influence on her place in the real world. Lily wondered whether there was some connection between this cave and Tsara. She determined that there had to be but she had no idea as to what it could possibly be. Rather than think, she decided to act. Rather than mull over her predicament, she would explore further. Lily had long ago discovered that doing something was a far more productive pastime than doing nothing. Her father had once told her that, so long as she endeavoured, the Fates would favour her. So far he had never been proved wrong.

Lily and Lucky began investigating the grotto. Moving apart in separate directions around the gargantuan and nearly circular space, they each kept near to the wall and closely examined each corner carefully. Lily was awestruck by the metallic matter. With each step and flicker of flame it seemed to change shape. It didn't seem to be real. Lucky was less interested. The substance had no scent and there didn't appear to be any carrots around. He quickly became rather bored and irritable. As Lily ran her hands across the walls, she became so engrossed in the malleable material she was touching that she failed to look where she was walking and almost fell to the floor. She stumbled over a jumble of items piled on the ground in a darker recess and caught herself just in time before she joined them.

Her attention was diverted from the captivating substance. Picking through the slightly dusty articles, she tried to make sense of them. Everything appeared to have been hurriedly bundled into a large metal wheelbarrow. When Lily had staggered over the wheelbarrow, everything had scattered before her and she now sat in their midst. There were several heavier things that looked like tools but were completely different from the ones used by the herders. One looked like a weighty hammer with a stout handle. Another looked like a letter 'T' but with sharpened points. There were also smaller items that Lily was sure she had seen in Danyal's stable next to a woodwork bench, although these items seemed stronger and more robust. Lily surmised that they must all be implements for extracting the sunny substance that Tengis had so eagerly exploited to manipulate the people of Baatarulaan.

Besides the tools there were lots of books and loose leaves of paper. Lily piled them up and began to look through them. She glanced up and noticed that Lucky had completed a full circle of the grotto and had now settled nearby. Lily also observed that there was no apparent exit.

As Lily scoured through the papers and books, she made two piles. The first included those items that seemed to hold some interest. The second was for those she intended to discard, which had titles such as *Health and Safety Manual*, *Human Resource Policy* and *Administrative Logistics*. None of those sounded remotely interesting to Lily. She moved them to one side and returned to the pile that had seemed to be of more importance. It contained only two books.

The first book was titled *Historical Background to the Mine*. Opening the dusty cover, she wiped away the grime that covered the contents page. As she thumbed through the book, she discovered that the shiny substance had been found several thousand years ago by a gang of marauding Outsiders. The initial find had been a cave the size of a man. For centuries they had pillaged and plundered, digging deeper into the mountain-side. It appeared that around eight hundred years ago one of the key investors in the mine struck a deal safeguarding its future. At that time Chinggis had been endeavouring to claim the site for himself so that he could use the funds it generated to improve his empire. They had not been willing to bargain with him. Chinggis had demanded they give him over 50 per cent of the income the mine was generating. This was not a deal the miners could entertain and so Chinggis had become increasingly irate. He threatened the foreign miners claiming they had no right to be there and gained considerable support from his people. Anti-mine groups sprang up around the country. The Outsiders had been terrified. The site provided a vast proportion of their wealth; they needed it, not to survive, but to ensure they could continue the quality of life to which they had become accustomed.

Eventually the key investor struck a bargain whereby the Outsiders would be permitted to extract as much of the invaluable shiny substance as one hundred horses could carry and given safe passage home in exchange for handing over the deeds to the investor. It was an offer that had been impossible to refuse and the miners set about extracting as much of the glistening matter as fast as possible. On the day that they had finished loading up their horses, the investor appeared and the deeds were signed over to his name. The investor then told them that Chinggis was dead and that all bets were off. He then informed them that his name was Khad. Khad had clicked his fingers and the miners had been slain where they stood. The horses were taken back to Khad's palace in Baatarulaan where he used the minerals to fund his corruption.

Lily was horrified. Now she knew how Khad had managed to take over Mongolia so easily. Throughout time it seemed to her that people everywhere were easily influenced and made dishonest whenever and wherever there was an excessive amount of wealth. It didn't seem fair. Chinggis had wanted to improve his empire, working for his people. Khad had wanted to create his own empire and cruelly rule over his people. It wasn't right that Khad had been allowed to succeed. As Lily read on, there appeared to be no entries dated later than a few months after Khad had seized control of the mine. From what Lily could ascertain it seemed that Khad not told anyone about the whereabouts or source of his fraudulent wealth. When he had died suddenly, it was before he could share this knowledge. Since then, although the Khadists had remained in power, their coffers had slowly dwindled as the remainder of Khad's stolen swag was wasted upon banal bureaucracy and supercilious seediness. The mine had now stood empty for eight hundred years.

Closing the book roughly, Lily threw it away from her. The more she learned about her country's history and the unfairness of its government, the more resolved she became to taking action against it. She turned to the second book that had appeared pertinent to her. Given the length of time the mine had had no owner, the book oddly looked more recent. Between its pages were crammed small pieces of yellow sticky paper containing illegible scribbled notes that stuck out from the edge of the book. When Lily opened the book, various tatty pieces of paper fell out, each covered in faint squares some of which had numbers written in them. There was also what looked to be mathematical workings but Lily had no knowledge of these things. Mathematics had never held any real importance to the life of a herder beyond the ability to count livestock accurately, barter forcefully on price and subtract carelessly when giving change. These workings were more complicated than anything she had ever seen before. Lily wasn't particularly interested in numbers and so laid them next to the pile she had earlier discarded. The book itself looked far more intriguing and she eagerly turned the neatly scribed pages. As she read on, her mind raced faster and faster as her blood began to boil.

The book used language that had a more modern feel to Lily. She read through pages and pages that detailed the strategic plan for the mine – an outline for a massive expansion. Whoever had written this book intended to increase the size of the mine tenfold. There were sketches of how far into the mountain the mine would go. To achieve their goal, whoever was behind it planned to employ hundreds of people who could act as cheap labour. The plan was to be kept secret so the labour would be found outside Ongolium. Lily recalled the Legend of Khad; she knew that if any Outsider set foot in Ongolium ever again then Chinggis's terror would cut through them like a scythe. The Outsiders were to be kept out of sight and housed within the mine. The plans detailed the myriad of ger complexes, canteens and even a hairdresser's that would be set up within the grotto as its belly grew ever more bloated.

Lily wondered who on earth could be planning such a greed-fuelled enterprise. There was only one person she knew who had an unnervingly single-minded self-agenda to attain power at any cost, a cost that could be met through mining vast quantities of the shimmering matter. There was only one person despicable enough to flaunt ancient legend and risk the wrath of Chinggis. Then again, the person she had in mind seemed to believe that he had the favour of Chinggis, that it was Chinggis that advised him. He was also the only person in Ongolium who appeared to have ever found any of the iridescent metal. The expansion plans were hugely ambitious; his ego even more so. It was no wonder that Tengis had so keenly sought the support of the wealthiest members of Baatarulaan society. How else was he to fund his intended corrupt election?

Towards the end of the book Lily found some plans for winning over the people that Tengis had written. They contained a number of slogans he had presumably used during his road show around the upper classes: 'Greed is good – for those who can afford it'; 'If you are sick, think about your life; if you are better, think about your gold'. She now looked at the graph papers she had earlier thought irrelevant. Now she saw that they listed the good and great of Ongolium. Next to each name was an estimate of how much money they would lend Tengis. The total was a sum far more vast than anything Lily had ever heard of before. In another column Tengis had detailed the various strands of work he deemed needed to be undertaken together with related costs. The sum he planned to raise from the gullible fat cats of Baatarulaan far outweighed the amount necessary to complete the proposed works. Lily wondered what on earth Tengis could be planning with the surplus.

Flicking through other pages she saw a number heavily circled. It matched the same amount as the initial surplus Tengis would have left over. Lily glanced up the page to see what it related to. There were names listed she didn't recognise. They didn't even seem to be in the Ongolian language. Next to each was a monetary value but also another number that tended to be in thousands. As Lily read the entries detailing what this related to, she began to feel sick. Perhaps Tengis was more corrupted than she had imagined? Perhaps Tengis was planning to buy in mercenaries from outside Ongolium? Perhaps he was planning something far greater and more wicked than simply gaining the support of the people to bring him to power? If he was able to gain even half the number of hired soldiers he had outlined on the page she was reading, it would swamp the entire population of Ongolium. The Khadists and Fun Brigade may have been malicious but the martial law which Lily feared Tengis and the Leggie had planned would be infinitely more terrible.

She hurled the book against the cavern wall. Holding her knees to her chest, she rocked crazily back and forth. Her heart pumped awkwardly in her chest as blood soared through her body. She felt dizzy. She felt afraid. Most of all, Lily felt angry. She had to let the people know about Tengis. She had to raise the alarm before it was too late. She had so many things to do besides. As she thought of the best way to find her way back to Baatarulaan, she recalled where she was. While the fire had been dying down, the darkness had risen from the floor and descended down the walls from the roof. She had hoped that some semblance of natural light would become visible but nothing presented itself. She may have wanted to run to Danyal and Millie but for the time being she was trapped. Lily needed to find another way to get out.

When she had stumbled over the wheelbarrow she had only

covered half the cavern wall she had intended to. Lucky had completed his task and returned to her, and she knew her horse well enough that, had he smelled fresh air, he would have let her know. There was a distance of some forty metres that remained unexplored. Rushing to the fire before it died completely, she gathered up what unburned wood she could and fashioned as many torches as she was able. The last thing Lily wanted was to be left trapped, alone (besides Lucky) and in the dark.

Feeling her way back along the unchartered wall it suddenly began to turn away from the centre of the mine. Moving slowly Lily held the torch in front of her to light the way. Lucky followed so closely behind, Lily could hear his teeth chattering. Although he was comfortingly loyal, he had never been a particularly brave mount. His nose occasionally touched Lily's back, causing her to jump.

'Stop it, will you!' shouted Lily. 'Stop being such a silly beast!' She gently slapped his nose and he backed away an inch or two. The wall continued to bend away from the mine. Lily and Lucky walked on. Before long the fire that had lit proceedings this far went out. Lily was unsure whether it had finally gone out or if they had moved around a corner out of sight of its glow. She had expected to start turning back the way they had come, but the wall continued to bend in the opposite direction. The hand that Lily had been holding against the wall began to turn cold. She looked at it. The wall was no longer completely covered in the shimmering substance. Flecks of it riddled and pocked the grey rocks that had started to dominate the wall. Lily could tell straight away that it was normal rock; there was enough of it lying about on the Steppe. It was good to find something she recognised. Her respite was short-lived, as the path she was following began to descend deeper inside the mountain. She took a cloak from the saddlebags on Lucky's back and tied it tightly around her shoulders; it was becoming colder with every step they took. They moved onwards down inside the mountain.

Lily's head began to ache. Blood had been rushing through it unchecked for the hours since she had arrived in the cave. The sensation that started to fill her head was different. It was noisier than the gush and throb of blood. She noticed that Lucky's ears had pricked up. Standing to attention they rotated fractionally as they sought out whatever it was that had caught their attention. Lily closed her eyes and concentrated. There was sound. Following the absolute silence that had pervaded the mine Lily had not immediately recognised the noise that was filling her head. She hastened her pace but with each stride the air around them became increasingly colder. It didn't matter to Lily she was hearing a sound that she recognised. It was a sound that meant movement; it was a sound that she knew would lead them out of the mountain. Somewhere below them an underground river was rapidly raging through the rocks.

Lily was running now and noticed that the path was becoming slippery in places. Ice was starting to form on the rocks, too. Icicles began to appear cascading sluggishly from the roof. Droplets of water that escaped froze before they hit the ground. The echo of glass chandeliers swaying in the breeze tinkled up through the passageway. Lily and Lucky began to breathe with difficulty. Their breath billowed out from their mouths. Moving quickly soon became too hazardous. Lily was wearing leather shoes and the precipitation that had collected on her soles as she had made her way down began to freeze. She was walking ice on ice. Similarly, the sweat that had dripped through Lucky's hooves began to hinder their progress as it froze.

Inching their way along the passageway, Lily was relieved to see some natural light up ahead. Buoyed by her potential escape, Lily hurried on as fast as was safe. Soon enough Lily no longer needed her flaming torch. What light that had penetrated this icy interior was multiplied a million times by the glassy temple they now found themselves standing in. The room was as large as the cave had been. They stood on a bridge made of ice that spanned a raging river that flowed beneath. Lily noted that the light came from the river and knew that it must escape the mountain at some none too distant point. Escape was now only a matter of time. As Lily and Lucky edged across the frozen precipice, they entered a crystal chamber. It was even more beautiful than the cave had been. Icy sculptures tumbled down the walls from a roof that would have suited the most marvellous of fairy-tale castle ballrooms. The rushing river below lapped up the walls, frequently dragging large coffins of ice into its depths. In the centre of the crystal temple the ice from the room met the bridge they were crossing. As they drew nearer, Lily's heart didn't know whether to sink or explode.

Partly hidden within a section of ice over three metres thick Lily could see the figure of a man. As she examined the glacier further, she began to notice his features. He was tall and muscular and had long thick dark hair. He was dressed how she had always assumed a traditional warrior would have been clad. Two razor-sharp scimitars crisscrossed his back, various throwing weapons were attached to his belt, and two long knives hung by his side. Baggy dark trousers were gathered at his waist and held fast by a large clasp. A large tunic covered his broad torso and hung in places as far down as his thighs. Embroidered into the tunic were various spheres each emblazoned with a proud-looking horse bearing an ornate saddle. The man's almond-shaped eyes were closed in frozen slumber. Peacefulness clad his noble face. The only sign that all was not well with the man, other than the fact he was deeply embedded within a strangely shaped glacier, was a thin line of red where his throat had been slit. Lily slumped to the ground and held her head in her hands. Lucky cosied up close to her; he understood her distress. When Lily had found herself in the cave filled with the sunny substance she had not expected that it would lead her to . . . Chinggis Khaan.

Lily needed to speak to Tsara. It was the least she could do for her spirit friend. She began trying to steady her mind and focus upon releasing her body from its physical boundaries. She started the breathing exercises that normally eventually led her to the spirit world but nothing was happening. She tried in vain to block out the sound of the river below. No matter how tightly she closed her eyes, they remained blinded by the illuminations dancing around her in the crystal temple. Lily had never failed to enter the spirit world when she had wanted to. Now, more than ever, she needed to be there. Lily had to let Tsara know that she had found Chinggis but leaving the real world was proving impossible. Lily began to weep, her tears freezing to her cheeks as they rolled away from her eyes.

As Lily sat crying in shock, she felt the earth move. Lucky whinnied. Staring across the ice bridge she and Lucky were sitting on, Lily saw that their combined weight was too much for it. The result was inevitable: it was only a matter of seconds before the bridge collapsed and they tumbled downwards into the ferocious bitter waters below. Everything happened in slow motion as is so often the case when something terrible occurs. The ice continued to crack loudly displacing sections of the bridge. Moments later Lily and Lucky found themselves falling. Enormous pieces of ice fell between and around them. Lily could hear the roar of the river coming closer. Taking deep breaths, she and Lucky awaited their fate . . .

As she hit the water Lily looked heavenwards. The last thing Lily saw was the outline of Chinggis Khaan standing proudly in his deathly tomb. A moment later she sank beneath the river and was rapidly swept away.

22

Odval doubted whether her beloved Tengis would ever recover from the shock of hearing that all he had ever believed was indeed wrong. Until that point, Tengis had believed he carried the spirit of Chinggis Khaan in his soul. To discover that he was haunted, not by Ongolium's greatest emperor, but by the phantom of the man he had always viewed as his nation's greatest traitor was a lot to come to terms with. Tengis had shut himself away for days, refusing food, sleep or company. He had even turned his mother away. The only person Tengis would allow to be near him was Odval. He trusted her above all others. He knew that he could expose himself to her and she would not mock him. As she stroked his hair soothingly, Tengis ranted and raved. The news had done nothing to suppress his rage. If anything, he was angrier than ever.

'Why have my men not found her yet?' he demanded. 'She is one small girl; my force has hundreds of men. Do I have to do everything myself? Why can I trust nobody other than myself? You are all fools. I am the only one who can lead this country. I am its rightful emperor. I am the chosen one.'

Odval grew worried but knew better than to question her lover. As his rage had grown, so had the list of those who had lost their lives for trivial reasons. She remained silent, doing her very best to provide solace. After five days, just as Odval was about to give up on Tengis, he fell into a deep and heavy slumber. She ordered his favourite foods to be prepared for the moment he awoke.

'I can smell sausages,' said Tengis. He sat up in his bed and yawned.

He had slept for almost forty hours all the while lovingly guarded by his faithful Odval. As he started to eat heartily, he called upon Oldortar, Mr Enkh and Tchoo. Together with the omnipresent Odval, they gathered in his chamber as he wiped the last of the sausage grease from his chin. Ushering them to draw chairs around the bed where he lay he pushed away his tray and began to speak.

'My dear friends, I have not been myself. Not for a very long time. I had thought my purpose here was to listen to and serve the people. I figured that, if I set up a good team of smart people, we could implement change that would make a difference. We had thought that the Khadist regime was corrupt and wicked. We were only part right: the Khadist regime that has governed us for these past centuries was merely broken. The principles of Khadism, if you break them into their base constituent parts, are not dissimilar to those of New Chinggism. What they do both most certainly have in common and what I had failed to appreciate – and I put my hands up as the one person that should have noticed – is that they are a far more *intellectual* embodiment of what Chinggis Khaan had originally set out to achieve.

'Where he failed to fulfil his personal potential, I have an opportunity to succeed. Where he showed his frailty by always seeking consensus, I can show strength by acting single-mindedly. Where he survived less than a decade as emperor, I can last for all eternity. I have the ability to become emperor of Ongolium for all time. This will become known as the Age of Tengis and no more shall we think of ourselves as followers of Chinggis. Now that I have had time to think, we need to reconsider who it is we follow. From this moment on you will follow me and I will follow Khad.'

His advisors looked at him in awe. It was the type of awe people showed when they had just intimately witnessed something especially malevolent.

'That's all very interesting,' asked Tchoo, 'but what about democracy? I thought we had agreed you would become the first President Of Ongolium People? I thought we four would become your government?'

'My dear friend,' said Tengis – Odval noticed that the tone of Tengis's voice sounded a little too familiar for her comfort – 'you will always be important to me; it's just that I will be infinitely *more* important to you! From this moment on it is all about me. Do you agree?' Tengis looked inside the eyes of each council member.

'So we will still have a say in how the country is run?' asked Mr Enkh.

Odval wished her father had said nothing. She feared that Tengis could turn at any moment. Instead, he rose out of bed and stood naked before them. He clapped a hand on Odval's father's shoulder.

'No, not really,' said Tengis. 'As I said: it is all about me. You will retain your positions so long as you are happy to do my bidding and never question my reason.' The Council looked uneasy but knew they had little option but to concur. 'Oh, and about the shimmering substance . . .' Each member instantly perked up. Wealth always carried more weight than words as far as they were concerned. 'I have lots of it. Lots and lots. So long as you please me you will each become richer than your wildest imagination.' The Council relaxed; some of them even began to smile. 'That's the spirit,' Tenghis concluded.

'What would you have us do?' asked Oldortar. Tengis smiled a broad tight-lipped smile that creased up into his cheeks.

'My good man,' replied Tengis, 'what a loyal military general you are. I want you to summon the Leggie and ready them to march out of Baatarulaan within two days. I want you to swell the size of your force. Find one extra man, woman or child for each existing member. Release every prisoner you feel would loyally serve us and not slit our throat at the first opportunity or endanger our children in any way. Equip them all with the contents of our armoury and, once that is depleted, with anything sharp, bludgeoning or nasty they can get their hands on. Ensure that the archery legion is given particular attention; I want their numbers to swell four-fold. Do I make myself clear?'

'Yes, sir,' said Oldortar. He stood to attention, saluted in the way he imagined somebody would salute if he had ever seen anyone salute, clicked his heels and marched towards the door. 'Sir?'

'Yes, General Oldortar,' said Tengis. Oldortar swelled with pride, it was far nicer to be addressed as General than it had been to be called Clown.

'Sir,' said Oldortar, 'I have been thinking. So as to make sure we recognise everyone that's with us, should we perhaps wear a uniform?'

'Splendid idea!' replied Tengis. 'I like you all to have ideas so long as the good ones are mine. General, dress as you see appropriate. Mr Enkh here will provide you with the necessary funds and please take a little extra for yourself; after all, you're worth it.' Oldortar left the room feeling the happiest he had ever known. He was going to enjoy working for Tengis.

'Mr Tengis, sir,' said Tchoo, 'with the new direction we are taking with our political agenda, what would you like me to do? I am happy to spread the Gospel according to Tengis? I think your Ten Recommendations still stand strong as a handbook for the average person to live their lives by day by day.'

'Tchoo,' said Tengis, 'you have proven yourself a highly skilled political tactician. I would like you to ensure my name and word are revered throughout Ongolium. I would also like you to devise a strategy for the Leggie. With so many new recruits we need to think up new ways to prevent our authority ever being questioned. We need them to be too scared to question our actions. Perhaps once we have proven this in military circles we could consider rolling it out across the general population.'

'Like the House of Fun?' asked Tchoo.

'No, absolutely not!' answered Tengis. 'That was merely a childish interpretation of Khad's beliefs. By dressing up dreadful things with fluffy verbiage you remove part of the terror. In so doing you render the fear less effective. Be overt if you are going to strike fear into people's hearts. That's why I renamed the House of Fun as the House of Hurt. It is far more in line with the way Khad would really have wanted it.' A spark of warmth glowed deep within Tengis's head, as if Khad himself were affirming his approval.

'Anyway, I task you with developing the means with which to force the people to accept that what I, and we, are doing is for their good and for the good of their, and our, country. I don't want people freely addicted to nasty substances; I want people to pay heavily for the privilege. We need to bolster our revenues somehow and taxing Khem and the like seems like a perfectly reasonable place to start. Make a note to increase the pushing of drugs with respect to younger people and get them hooked sooner. I want to help the people want to help themselves. To do this they have to put all of their faith in me. See to it that this happens.' Tchoo departed leaving Odval and her father with Tengis.

'Tengis, my young friend,' said Mr Enkh, 'I always believed you would one day be a great man. Look at you now; you make me very proud. If you ever wanted to be married, you need not ask my permission!'

'Thank you,' said Tengis. 'If I ever wanted to be married, I would do so with my own permission and no one else's. Please never let me hear you being so presumptuous again. If I am honest, I am not sure that I actually need you, Mr Enkh. I have enough wealth, after all. What else is it that you can offer me?' Odval looked terrified but not nearly so much as her father. Tengis lay down on the bed again and picked at his leftover breakfast.

'I know things,' said Mr Enkh desperately 'I . . . I . . . I have friends, people in important places. People of influence. I can help you secure your rightful position as our emperor. There may be wheels I can pay and people I can oil for you . . . Please?'

'I should very much like to see that,' said Tengis absently. 'In the meantime, please go away; I am bored.'

Mr Enkh gathered himself and, bowing, walked backwards out of the room.

Once her father had departed, Odval walked over to Tengis and slapped his face.

'Don't you dare speak to my father like that ever again,' said Odval, 'you hear me? I don't care who you think you are this time. He is my father.' She made to strike him again but this time Tengis caught her wrist and twisted her hand back.

'I do so love it when you are angry!' said Tengis.

'Then it looks like we shall get along well then,' seethed Odval through clenched teeth. Tengis released her. 'You haven't told me or anyone why you are raising such a force? You always said that Lily was but one young girl. I want her killed as much as you do, but this?'

'Don't be foolish!' replied Tengis. 'This Lily has friends. My spies inform me that she has a growing number of strong allies in Baatarulaan and goodness knows how many others outside the city.'

'Outside Baatarulaan?' inquired Odval. 'There is nothing outside the city; is there?'

'You'd be surprised,' said Tengis. He smirked secretly to himself. 'There are as many people outside the city limits as there are within, perhaps even more. They are mostly ill-educated herder communities, true, but news of Lily has spread fast. Her allies in Baatarulaan have sent couriers to all corners of Ongolium to implore the herders to come together and make a stand against the evil that has kept them living like peasants and taxed them to the hilt.'

'Who would that be?' asked Odval earnestly.

Tengis raised his eyebrows. 'Oh . . .! Never mind that! I have to prevent any risk to my plan.'

'Couldn't you just send an assassin to execute her?' asked Odval.

'It's not quite as simple as that,' replied Tengis. 'It is difficult to take a wolf cub without drawing in the whole pack. Anyway, I thought a show of strength such as this might be just the thing to lift people's spirits. Since everyone became a criminal or Khem addict, things have become so interminably boring in this city; nobody has any fight left in them. We'll soon change all of that.'

Tengis's Council knew better than to disappoint him. The following day Tchoo made a lengthy slide presentation to the Counsel. His colourfully presented slides showed various ways in which Tengis could swiftly move to assert his radical new vision. Tchoo was incredibly grateful he had paid close attention in school during his business studies class. He suggested that Tengis retain much of the marketing and brand positioning that had lifted him this far but proposed some minor changes that would help him move from being perceived as a man of inclusivity towards being seen as a being of dread. His final slide received a standing ovation, even from Tengis. The new party slogan would now read: 'Believe in ideas– Tengis's ideas. What counts is what works; and whatever Tengis says will work. The objectives are radical; the means are cruel and unusual. Change is no longer necessary.' Tengis was content that his Council, who no longer actually provided any counsel, was obeying his commands. Mr Enkh ran around his master like a cocker spaniel, desperately trying to please him. Odval watched on ashamed that both her lover and her father could act in this way.

Within two days Oldortar had built and armed troops sufficiently terrible to sate Tengis's needs. As they lined up in the city centre square, Tengis inspected them. He marvelled at how utterly innocent some of them looked. He knew that a few days' marching and a few hours of bloody conflict would soon change all of that.

'Nice uniforms, General Oldortar,' said Tengis. The General blushed. He had long wanted his men to dress head to toe in black. They wore black suits with matching shiny black patent boots, black caps with shiny black brims and each soldier wore a red cotton armband carrying the insignia of a man with a tiger's head riding a noble horse. Tengis noted that that the insignia had evolved slightly too – the man now looked more noble than the horse and was whipping it with what looked like a snake. He grinned, much to the pleasure of his general.

'Splendid, splendid!' Tengis cried enthusiastically.

'Where are we going?' asked General Oldortar.

'Courtesy of Mr Enkh,' said Tengis – Mr Enkh genuflected – 'I am reliably informed that the traitor we seek and her rebellious pack have camped on the Steppe. If a donkey can recognise the tracks of a horse, then a horse can surely recognise the clumsy footprints of a donkey. From what I hear, they are hastily endeavouring to school themselves in the art of warfare. Tell me, Oldortar, what do my men know of the art of warfare?'

'Um,' said Oldortar, 'they know a nice picture of a poppy field when they see one, if that's what you mean?'

'Not exactly,' replied Tengis, 'but it hardly matters. There is no way the rebels will be any match for my men; we outnumber them embarrassingly. I will take point, just make sure your men, and women, keep up.'

With that Tengis kissed Odval, mounted his almost proud-looking horse and took his position at the head of his 5,000-strong column of soldiers. At General Oldortar's command, they began to march forwards. Immediately Oldortar regretted not teaching his wards their left from their right but at least they were moving in the right direction.

The march was uneventful. Tengis found no beauty on the Steppe. It lacked the cultural virtues he had long loved in Baatarulaan. There was no sound of torment as somebody somewhere lost their dearest mortal possessions. So far as Tengis was concerned, the Steppe was nothing more than an arid barren barrier that protected his city from Outsiders. He had hated it the first time he visited it and he hated it even more now. Those under his command may have felt otherwise but were far too afraid of him to show it. Whatever their leader said was good enough for them. In any case, most of the soldiers were too busy trying to work out how they could move the same leg at the same time as the person in front of them to be concerned about their surroundings. On their way across the deserted land there had been much stumbling and falling over.

Very occasionally the troops would come across a small herder community. The soldiers had never seen anybody other than Baatarulaan residents and had been told that all others were the evil untrustworthy Outsiders that Khad had once alluded to. They laughed at the gers that differed so much from their own shabby apartments. The herders had darker skin and immediately ignited the hatred that fear only too often instils.

Tengis knew better. Any herder community that they came across had obviously not sworn allegiance to Lily and the rebels, or else it would have joined that shabby rabble and moved on with them. Ever the tyrannical diplomat, Tengis sought out the leader of such groups.

'You can join us,' said Tengis to the leaders, 'or you can become permanently joined to the earth. Your choice.'

'Why should we join you?' asked the leaders. 'You have made our lives even more difficult than they ever needed to be.'

'Let me put it this way,' said Tengis, 'he who drinks dies; he who does not drink dies as well. I honestly don't care either way; it depends whether you want to live a little while longer or not.'

Mostly the herders chose to become soldiers. Each time Tengis departed such a community, regardless of whether he had slain its occupants or recruited them, he insisted on a large bell being pealed to ward off any bad spirits. He was aware that almost all herders believed strongly in the spirit world. Tengis couldn't be bothered even thinking about picking a fight with people he couldn't see, so, as his only concession to the heathens he encountered, he adopted a little local culture to protect his progress.

By the close of the third day Tengis's troops had marched over one hundred miles. Not a great distance for a herder, but a frightening chasm of space for the city dwellers. From his calculations, estimates and secret reconnaissance details Tengis knew he was less than half a day's march from where Lily was reported to be camped. He was also within shouting distance of the source of his secret wealth. It was a good place to establish his barracks. Sounding the bell loud above the Steppe, his general bid his troops to set up camp. Oldortar would love to have seen a regimented uniformity to the camp with a carefully designed matrix pattern running through it. Instead, he had to make do with the sort of camp he had seen built in miniature by smelly, petrol-drinking ex-corporate financiers who lived beneath the bridges of Baatarulaan. He shook his head in dismay as several not even nearly vertical flagpoles were erected in the centre of the barracks. As the flag of Tengis was raised on each, the wind whipped up and tangled them into a knotted mass halfway up. At that moment Oldortar decided that it was time to retire to his tent. He hoped that Tengis would not notice the mess and thanked the spirits that dusk was quickly falling upon them.

In the middle of the night Tengis silently sneaked out of his tent. Peering into the surrounding gloom, he made sure no one was watching him, muffled his horse's feet with rags, and rode out of camp towards the mountains. Arriving at a gorge he had known once before, he followed the natural passage through the night air. Presently he arrived at a clearing that he recognised led to his private, grotto-based bank. The entrance was as he had left it. Several large boulders blocked the doorway so as to prevent any unwanted visitors, so there was no chance that anyone had passed into his cave this way.

Tengis tied a rope around one of the boulders, its other end to his horse, and lashed the poor beast until it had heaved both of the boulders aside. Tengis stepped into the gloom and, lighting up a torch, was instantly filled with the same excitement that had captivated him the first time he had discovered the cave. The shiny metal substance shone and glimmered all around him, making the torchlight appear to lick the walls with lusty abandon.

Kneeling at the centre of the cave, Tengis closed his eyes and raised his hands towards the roof.

'Khad!' murmured Tengis. 'Khad, if you can hear me, mark my words. I am calling you from the place that defined your soul. I am calling you from the place that will define mine. I offer you my soul in the same way as you have given me yours.

We are united. We are one. As I face my enemies this coming day, help me vanquish them. Assist me as I eradicate any doubt of our might. We will once again rule this kingdom. We will once again be invincible.'

The voice in his head remained silent. It had not spoken to Tengis for some time but he knew that it was planning something. Tengis could also sense from the feeling of confidence that pervaded his body that the voice inside him agreed with his every thought, word and deed. He was as powerful as he believed himself to be. The voice in his head had always told him so.

Once Tengis had completed his ritual, he searched the cave for his planning documents and health and safety manual. Heading towards the wheelbarrow-cum-filing cabinet that he had taken great pride in organising, he saw that its contents had been spilled across the ground. Seething, he crawled among them and brought them together in one pile. Somebody had been there! Somebody had been going through his personal things!

Tengis wracked his brain but could not understand how anybody could have come through the entrance, and he knew there was no other way in. Nevertheless somebody had been here. He thumbed through the documents; they had almost all been read, apart from the less interesting ones. Somebody knew about his connection with Khad – but who? He couldn't understand how anybody could have gained access to his vault. If they had, then they surely had to be still there; he had scoured the vault and knew of no other way in or out. He was sure there were no other passageways or exits. It was impossible he knew but somehow somebody now most definitely was aware of his intentions. Somebody knew that he was planning to take absolute control of Ongolium; that he would willingly use Outsiders to apply force if required.

As he panicked, a realisation came to him. He knew beyond all doubt, ridiculous as it was, that the person who had been here was Lily. She had to die and soon.

23

When Lily opened her eyes she thanked the spirit world that it was daytime. Sunshine shone on her face, warming her ice-cold skin. Had it been night-time she would surely have perished. As she lay half in and half out of the river she wondered why it was that among all the Ongolians it was she who was being chosen for so many adventures. She speculated that perhaps everybody had so many adventures as she was experiencing but simply chose not to talk about them. She worried fleetingly that she was being ungrateful, dour and mournful by bemoaning all that happened – but only fleetingly. No one could claim to have uncovered the source of Khad's evil, discovered the truth about Tsara and found the current resting place of Chinggis Khaan all in the space of one day.

She laughed weakly. It was too much to believe. She began to doubt it was true. Lucky waded over and licked her face. His tongue was warm but his breath still smelled of cabbages. That always brought her back to reality. It also reminded her that he had shared her exploits so far and didn't look like leaving her side anytime soon. She hugged his wide neck lovingly. She might be a simple herder girl but she knew that, without the debts or ill-gotten trappings of Baatarulaan, she was richer than anyone there; and that living without the sociological handicaps that thwarted Baatarulaan's citizens she was infinitely more fortunate than they. She dragged herself out of the water, pulled herself together, lit a fire, pulled a metal canister from her saddlebag and made herself a nice cup of tea. Nothing made things better than a nice cup of tea. Lucky even forgot all about carrots when he had a bowl of tea with two lumps of sugar. It always worked.

Nightfall was approaching, as it inevitably did, and Lily began to fear for shelter. She had not expected to have been taken elsewhere in the real world after visiting the spirit world. It was a most unusual occurrence and had only ever happened once before when she inadvertently reappeared in the ger next to her own just as her parents were enjoying a particularly intimate moment. Lily had never really recovered from that. Gathering what strength she had, Lily walked to the top of the highest rise near the riverbank.

She had known the Steppe all her life but it was still forbidding to her, a vast and barren place. Peering into the distances of every direction, she dearly hoped that she would find something she recognised. It didn't take long. Three hundred metres downriver she identified a bend in the river that seemed familiar. Ushering Lucky to accompany her, they walked towards it. To her bemusement they found themselves standing at the campsite where they had been before she had last visited her spirit friend who turned out to be Tsara. Arriving at the camp, Lily ensured everything was at it should be, which it was. As she gave her thanks to the spirit world, she noticed that the moon had moved on and was becoming fuller. It wouldn't be long before she had to meet with Danyal and Millie. That inexorably would mean facing Tengis. Given that, the last she had heard, Tengis was awfully keen for Lily to die, seeing him again was not going to be straightforward.

Without spending too much time or energy trying to figure out how it was that they could have possibly rediscovered their camp, Lily bid Lucky goodnight and they both clambered into the especially odd-shaped tent and snuggled up against one another. As she lay falling asleep, Lily knew that spirits did things for a reason. That everything they did was part of some bigger plan; Tsara must have known Lily would end up back here. Lily knew that Tsara would not have endangered her when she had returned her to the cave – at least she hoped not. What she couldn't understand was how Tsara had managed to move Lucky as well, but then again Lily was only a visitor to the spirit world; perhaps once she was a fully paid-up member these kinds of things would become clearer, although she hoped that day was still a long way off.

Lily awoke the next morning with her face firmly pushed against Lucky's nose. The horse dribbled a lot more from his nostrils than she had previously noticed. Where it had oozed into her hair it was gelled back flat against her head at an interesting and mildly amusing angle. It was a tribute to Lily's spirit that she refused to be perturbed by such an event. Her horse was part of her and she part of it – such was the way of the herder. A good night's sleep had been what she had required. She couldn't remember the last time she had been able to enjoy one. It was certainly not since before her father had been captured and that had been weeks ago.

While it remained extremely cold, the sun shone strongly and she was able to absorb at least a little warmth from its rays. Lily left Lucky sleeping; he was particularly bad in the mornings and even more so if a good dream about carrot fields was disturbed. Having rekindled the fire, she prepared a meagre breakfast of stale bread and mutton. Almost every meal eaten by herders in nomadic camps consisted of mutton, mutton, mutton or mutton, though sometimes as a treat they ate mutton, but only on very special occasions. That morning Lily boiled some mutton scraps along with some dumplings consisting of mutton tail (which was almost entirely fat). Mutton helped herders build up a tolerance against the freezing temperatures they had to endure on the Steppe. It also removed one of the more problematic predicaments that have plagued mankind since its birth, namely – what to have for dinner.

Sitting next to the fire, Lily looked at the 'to do' list she had drawn up with Tsara. It seemed to be getting longer every time that she thought about it. She was sure that wasn't supposed to be the case. Although she had no major new items to add to it, she had discovered many factors that added colour to the old ones. She now knew far more about Tengis and his true intentions. She knew what happened to Chinggis and how Khad had seized power. She knew that she was being helped by at least one other person from a different world, which always made her feel more than a little special. She also knew that she was as yet nowhere nearer to fulfilling her destiny and, although she didn't really know what that was going to entail, she did know that she needed to keep on going. Fear would get her nowhere.

Since she had left Baatarulaan a good deal had happened. Before she started to forget it all, she jotted it down alongside the existing action points. It was still several days before she would be able to speak to Danyal and she had no idea how long it would be before she was able to speak to her herder community. She also hadn't been able to revisit the spirit world and speak to Tsara since she had found Chinggis in the crystal temple. Lily was bursting to speak to somebody but from the middle of the bleak Steppe she knew this was highly improbable. Talking to a horse was all very well but Lily had quickly discovered that it tended to be a largely one-way conversation.

As Lily sat wondering how she would be able to communicate with her allies Lucky joined her by the fire. He neighed knowingly. Lily had never been able to figure out how but her horse seemed to know what it was she was thinking most of the time, especially on the odd occasions when she was mad at him. She stroked him fondly before returning to her thoughts about making contact with those in Baatarulaan, the herder community and spirit world.

Lucky drifted away. Reaching a slight rise behind the camp, he whinnied noisily to grab Lily's attention.

'What is it, Lucky?' asked Lily. She was feeling a little irritated and in no mood to play games. Lucky whinnied again and swished his mane manfully. Just as Lily was a about to scold him she noticed that several other horses were slowly making their way up from the other side of the rise to join Lucky. As Lily watched on, the four horses acknowledged one another by rubbing noses affectionately. Lily was not entirely certain what it was she was seeing, but her instinct began to form an impression. At any other time and under any other circumstances, Lily would have dismissed her thinking out of hand, but given what she had already encountered nothing seemed too far-fetched.

As she watched on, the horses formed an equine parade and side by side walked towards her. Each new horse was unsaddled but had a saddlebag. None of the new horses had any distinguishing features other than their natural beauty and a label sewn on to each saddlebag. As Lily walked from left to right inspecting each of the three new horses, she logged that the labels read: 'Mr Danyal, Baatarulaan', 'Elder Chuluun, Steppe', 'Tsara, Spirit World'. She gasped. Lucky looked down at her, a smug grin spreading across his muzzle.

Immediately Lily knew what she was to do. She grabbed paper from Lucky's saddlebag and began to write three identical letters to her allies. She was confounded as to how but knew that once again somebody in the spirit world must be providing some assistance. There had been too many strange occurrences for them to have simply been born of chance. Lily set to writing three copies of the following letter:

My dearest friends,
Since we last spoke there have been a number of important
developments. Some of you know a few of the details. I will
endeavour to recount all and everything as it stands at this
moment. Though it might feel strange and unusual, please let
me assure you that everything I say is true and that, unless we
act swiftly, then our future, as well as that of the entire nation,
is in grave danger.

As a shawoman I have spent a great deal of time in the spirit
world. My guide there, whom I would trust with my afterlife, is
Tsara, lover of Chinggis and wronged Empress of Mongolia.
Together we have been trying to unravel the riddle that was
contained within the box that was given to me by the elders of
my herder community. While the meaning of some of the words
is evident, others remain hidden.

In order to unravel them further, and in order to find my
father, I set out for Baatarulaan. The city is as I had always
imagined it to be, perhaps worse. However, in that place of
despair I have made great friends who believe in me and I in
them. Danyal and Millie, together with Drudger and the Hairy
Hordes, have helped me see the dangers facing our country.
We are no longer simply fighting against a Khadist regime. A
terrible but talented man called Tengis is making a bid to seize
control of the city under the guise that he is Chinggis Khaan's
presence in the real world; he calls his movement New
Chinggism. He has devised a doctrine which promises every-
thing yet would deliver nothing. He has also uncovered a
source of unrivalled wealth in a material more corrupt than
anything we could imagine. He has combined his false words
with his 'sunny substance' to great effect. The people of
Baatarulaan are easily swayed and he is well on the way to
winning support from the majority.

However, I have also discovered that this substance is the

same vile material with which Khad used to overthrow
Chinggis's empire eight hundred years ago. Tengis has unearthed a seemingly limitless supply. How Tengis discovered
the mine remains a mystery but he plans to raise enough
investment from the fools in Baatarulaan to enable him to mine
more mineral wealth than has ever been known. He intends to
keep his endeavours a secret known only by himself and his key
stakeholders. More terrible yet, he intends to employ Outsiders
to undertake the work. We are all aware of the Legend of Khad.
Some say it is little more than a myth, but if it is not, the fury
of Chinggis may be wrought on us all. Which brings me to the
latest development in my adventures.

After I had discovered Tengis's plans in his mine I looked for
a means of escape. As I did so I descended deep into the glacial
pits of the mountains. There, entombed in ice, I discovered the
body of Chinggis Khaan himself. He has been close to us all for
all this time. (Tsara, he looks more handsome than I could ever
have imagined him to be; I am sure you will be reunited soon.)

And so to work, my friends. The last news I had about Tengis
implied that he was combining the Leggie with all other
manner of militia and as well as any willing volunteers from
among his ardent supporters. He has also ensured the loyalty
of the Khadists. It is truly frightening the power he wields
so long as he controls that shiny substance. Although it is
perceived he will fight an election, albeit corruptly, and assume
power, I know that he plans to buy even stronger protection
from outside Ongolium which he will use to rule absolutely. If
this happens, the future of our country is dark. But we are not
without hope.

At present he is relying entirely on the power of his oratory
skills, the ignorance of fickle, greedy minds and his shiny
substance. Other than the most wealthy and greedy, people
have not wholly committed themselves to his cause. He remains

vulnerable until he garners support from outside Ongolium and commences his mammoth mining project.

I firmly believe that if we gather as one we will be able to make a stand against him. We may not have the numerical superiority but we have honesty, truth and justice on our side. I judge that those bedfellows will help us gather support from among the people of Baatarulaan. Once we make them aware of his true nature and intent, they will come to our side. If it is battle that Tengis is seeking to prove his dominance, then I am happy to lead us against him. Justice will prevail. The Khadists, and New Chinggists, will finally be driven from our land and the memory of our true emperor will be reborn.

I know of the perils involved for all of you but implore you to believe in me. If we fail to seize the moment, our nation will be lost in darkness for future millennia. Now is the time. Bring together all the forces we can muster. To Danyal and Millie I ask that you seek to swell the Hairy Hordes into an even more formidable fighting force. To Elder Chuluun I beg that you speak swiftly with the other herder communities and marshal every able body. My dearest Tsara, I ask that you do whatever you can from the spirit world. I seem unable to find a doorway to your world at present but feel that we will be joined again imminently.

To you all I say good luck, good will and good speed. Let us meet at the point marked 'X' three days hence on the night of the next full moon.

Lily.

Carefully packing the letters into each of the saddlebags Lily inspected the horses before they set off. A short black stallion was intended for Baatarulaan. Lily felt it was aptly coloured; black seemed a popular colour among the city's residents. She kissed the stallion on the nose and it set off. To her herder community Lily was sending a dappled mare. The horse had a fearsome face with a temperament to match; even the normally over-amorous Lucky had kept several paces away from her. The horse gave Lily a knowing nod before disappearing towards the horizon.

The horse proposed for the spirit world was a white stallion of whom Lucky seemed rather jealous. Lily brought the two horses together. Given her love of Tsara, it felt important to Lily that both beasts accepted one another. The white horse seemed particularly fond of Lucky and struggled to avert his gaze from Lucky's rear. This really didn't make Lucky feel any more confident, no matter how handsome and fashionable the white horse was. Lily tightened the patent black-leather saddlebag and was astonished at just how well its colour and design coordinated with the overly manicured mane of the stallion. The horse accepted her compliments gratefully and, swishing his mane in Lucky's direction, gave Lily's horse a wicked wink before galloping away.

'What a show-off!' said Lily.

Lucky nestled his head under her arm. He really did like his mistress. The pair settled back into their camp. There were four days before the full moon arrived. They would need as much rest as they could afford before then – although neither of them were quite sure why.

24

The full moon rose high above Ongolium. Across the Steppe the silhouette of Lily riding Lucky slowly came into view. She was heading back home towards her winter campsite. She and Lucky were now a full day's ride from the river that had helped them both escape the strange interior glacier. Rounding the last of the enormous boulders that acted as sporadic landmarks for her winter camp, Lily turned her head expectantly, excited about seeing her home again. It had been a long time since she had first set out for Baatarulaan and much had happened. Searching out the horizon for the cluster of gers, Lily was dumbstruck. Normally there were no more than a dozen gers; more than enough tented homes for the seventy or so members of her herder community. As she looked towards the camp, she stopped counting at one hundred gers.

Some of the younger herder children rode out to greet her.

'Lily!' they cried.

Although she had spent most of her life as a stranger among her people, Lily was still loved. Since she had become leader of her community she was revered. The children jumped from their horses to embrace Lily and Lucky. The herders taught to ride from an early age and such acrobatics which may have seemed incredible to city dwellers were second nature to those who lived on the Steppe.

With one swift movement Lily jumped from Lucky and stood

cuddling the children. Lily reminded herself how good it felt to be home. Her home had changed, though; there were hundreds if not thousands of strangers here.

'What's going on?' asked Lily.

'They started arriving two days ago,' replied the children.

'Who are they?' asked Lily. She looked around at the strange faces. They looked familiar yet distant.

'They say that they are your friends,' said the children.

Lily ventured towards the mass of people milling around and near her ger. She noticed with relief that her door was still closed; she had meant to do the dishes before setting off but hadn't quite got around to it. A huddle of men sat on the ground nearby.

'Excuse me,' said Lily. 'would somebody mind telling me what on earth is going on?'

'Lily!' cried Elder Chuluun, who now ran towards her with a surprising agility. 'My girl! How happy I am to see you! Please join us.'

'Elder Chuluun, please,' said Lily, 'what is this?' She waved her hand around the camp.

'They are here for you!' continued Elder Chuluun. 'They received word and they came. Does it not please you? We have been watching your activities in Baatarulaan closely. Matters are far worse than we had imagined. It appears that Tengis is in league with Khad. We must stop him and quickly. If he gains the ascendency, it will be too late. Please sit here. May I introduce you to the other community elders?'

Elder Chuluun made the appropriate introductions to leaders from neighbouring herder communities. His final introduction was to two faces Lily knew well and was relieved to see. She ran towards them.

'Millie! Danyal!' exclaimed Lily. 'You're here!'

'Well, "X" marks the spot,' said Danyal, pointing to Lily's ger.

Its roof had a cross motif in red stitching spreading across the thick felt cover.

'It's a full moon, is it not?' asked Millie. 'That was the arrangement, unless I am mistaken?' She hugged Lily close to her chest. 'You have many friends. But come, sit with us. We have a long night ahead of us. There is much to prepare before we face Tengis. We are having . . . what did you call it again, Elder Chuluun?'

'A *quriltai*,' replied the old man.

'It's an assembly of tribes,' continued Millie. 'It's what the herder communities supposedly do while they are preparing for battle. Come, sit, listen in. Elder Chuluun is quite the quiet little strategic mastermind.'

Lily joined the assembly. After the initial joy of meeting one another, silence soon descended as they began to discuss tactics.

'We are outnumbered,' said Elder Chuluun, 'but we are nomads; they are city dwellers. I mean no disrespect by that.' He offered his hand in peace to Millie and Danyal. 'Your Hairy Hordes are hardly typical city dwellers; they are far more like us nomadic herders. We are used to endurance and fortitude. We are hardy soldiers willing and incredibly bloody-minded – in both ways. We number almost eight hundred. I suspect Tengis will bring almost double that number, although we won't know until we see them. As expert horsemen, I propose that at least sixty per cent of our number act as light infantry carrying bows and arrows, two for every man, as well as our usual sabres for closer-range combat. The remaining forty per cent will act as lancers and attack the heart of Tengis's troops. Does anyone have any questions?'

There was a general murmuring in agreement, although Lily could sense that they were uncomfortable about their numerical disadvantage.

Elder Chuluun was aware of this, too. 'Do not worry. We will remain mobile. There is no way Tengis's men can come close to our riders. Our mobility will enable us to readily outmanoeuvre them and take control of the battle. We need to pit what strengths we have against our enemy's weaknesses. Our riders will draw their troops out into the Steppe where our lancers will plough into them.'

'What about the Hairy Hordes?' asked Danyal. 'Where do you want us?'

'I want you with the lancers,' replied Elder Chuluun. 'You will act separately, as you are always wont to do. I don't want to advise such a robust fighting outfit, but once our riders infantry have drawn the enemy into the Steppe, perhaps the Hairy Hordes could lead the charge into their midst?'

'It would be an honour,' replied Millie. 'We will not disappoint you.'

'Although there are likely to be more of them,' said Danyal, 'it does sound as though we have the upper hand.'

'Don't undo your bootlaces until you have seen the river,' answered Elder Chuluun. Danyal scratched his head, though he presumed he had just heard something profound.

'If we are finished, can I take some rest?' asked Lily. 'I am exhausted.'

'You have four hours,' said Elder Chuluun. 'We march out of camp at six. If my estimates are correct then the enemy will be camped an hour's march from here near the mountains.'

Lily excused herself as the members of the gathering bid one another goodnight. After Lily had seen to Lucky, she entered the family ger and lay back on the furs that lined the rear of the tent. Within moments she had quickly fallen into a deep sleep. That night she dreamed about Tsara. Her spirit friend assured her that all would soon be well. She also confirmed that it had been she who had helped corral Lily's supporters together; she who had sent the horses and she who would look after her tomorrow during the battle. Although it was to be Lily's first encounter with warfare, the prospect exhilarated her and her dreams were filled with thoughts of her imminent victory.

At some point during the night Lily awoke with a start. The camp was silent except for the occasional sound of snoring and breaking of wind, though whether human or animal it was hard to tell. As Lily tried to block the noises from her mind she began to hear something else. Something more distant. It was a sound she thought she recognised but wasn't sure where from. The sound was deep and heavy. It did not sound human. The noise pulsed regularly across the plain rhythmically beating time. In between the cadence was something else, something unknown. A throaty *blong* accompanied the tempo every three or so beats. It was an altogether more frightening noise. The fearsome sound poured across the Steppe into the encampment. Lily pulled the furs close around her and wished that Lucky was keeping her company. Eventually Lily fell back into slumber.

Lily managed only a couple of hours' sleep. She was awake and washed long before Elder Chuluun had requested roll-call. She opened a trunk that her father used to store his clothing. Lily had lived next to the trunk all of her life but never actually opened it before. Casting aside camel-hair cloaks and blankets she dug deeper. Eventually her fingers grasped what she was looking for. She pulled out a lacquered boiled leather tunic from the trunk. It would help protect her torso from arrows, knives and swords. From deeper in the chest came a helmet, the top of which was metal but whose lower portion was leather with straps for attaching it to the tunic. With both hands she pulled out metal leggings that formed from tiny overlapping iron plates that looked a little like fish scales. These two had straps for attaching them to the tunic and also footwear. Lily felt around for anything else and to her surprise she touched something soft. Drawing whatever it was out from the wooden container she found herself holding a one-piece silken undergarment. She was utterly lost for words. She had not expected this. She stared at it aghast.

'I am sure you are wondering what that is for,' asked Elder Chuluun. For a big man he was strangely nimble. He had quietly opened the door to Lily's ger and watched as she prepared for her first battle. 'It is meant to be worn beneath your armour and boots. If you are shot at distance by an arrow, it is unlikely to penetrate the silk. Even if it penetrates your skin the silk will likely hold. Given Tengis may use poison, this will help protect you, and should you be unlucky enough to be shot, the silk will help the healers extract the arrow safely from your skin. It's quite clever really.'

Lily was relieved. She preferred this logical explanation to the others that had been milling around her head.

Elder Chuluun helped his leader dress for battle. Attaching her leggings to her boots, he looked deep into her eyes and wished her good luck.

Having forced herself to eat some fried mutton in pastry, Lily sought out Lucky. One of the camp dogs that had been following her began to whimper; Lily threw it a piece of her mutton *khuushuur*, which was gobbled down gratefully. The dog seemed to nod to her before rushing off in search of more scraps. Lily looked up to see Lucky looking on embarrassed that his fellow animals could act so pitifully.

'Dogs will be dogs,' said Lily. She poured some warmed oats into Lucky's feed and he began chomping contentedly. As he did, Lily began to prepare her horse. Elder Chuluun had gifted her his own personal horse armour. It was made of the same lacquered leather that covered her chest. She tested the leather and felt comfortable that it was light and supple enough to ensure maximum mobility. Once Lucky had finished his break-fast, she jumped into her saddle. Pulling a warm fur cloak across her shoulders she rode out of camp just as others were starting to wake. The moon began to be usurped by daytime rays of light.

'Choo, choo!' shouted Lily, kicking Luck's flank.

Lucky was not used to being told what to do and shot off at an incredible pace given his short legs. Lily knew that Steppe horses, which were shorter than their European cousins, vehemently refused to break stride even when they galloped. When moving at speed she thought they looked as though they were speed-walking at double time. Lily had no fear that they were flying fast, though. If herders were hardy souls, then their horses were far tougher and more resilient than even the armour they wore. Life on the Steppe was difficult enough for the herders who had gers to shelter them from the minus-forty-degrees wintry storms; horses simply had to grin and bear it. Lucky sped on in the direction of the mysterious sounds Lily had heard during the night and which had continued ever since.

Reaching the top of a rise in the Steppe, Lily stopped. She looked across the plain towards the mountains from where she could still hear the noises of last night. Sure enough, just as Elder Chuluun had predicted Tengis and his troops were camped in the shadow of the crags. There were many tents. Not gers but simple silk-sheet tents. It wasn't the tent material that caught Lily's breath; it was the incredible number of them. Elder Chuluun had said they would be outnumbered but rather than two to one Lily estimated that there were more than ten times as many tents as there were among her people. She scoured the makeshift enemy barracks, taking in everything she could see. There were very few horses, which surprised her, but there were wide wooden walls holding thousands of enormous pikes. The thorny sharp points sat hovering over the white silk tents beneath. Their teeth frightened Lily. The noise continued, though if anything it was even louder. Combing the camp, Lily looked for its source. The steady thudding was coming from enormous drums that were each being beaten by two sturdy soldiers. *Blong.* The origin of the horrible new noise eluded her momentarily.

Peering from tent to tent, Lily sought out the horrid din. *Blong.* Men hurriedly rose, readying themselves for the day that lay ahead of them. *Blong.* It was a scene not dissimilar to the one she had just left; albeit with a lot more people involved. *Blong.* Focusing on the centre of the camp Lily noticed one tent that was far larger than the others. *Blong.* Flying from its roof was a huge flag depicting a lion-headed man riding a noble horse. *Blong.* As she stared at it venom coursed through her eyes. *Blong.* Adjacent to the tent was a large wooden plinth painted red. *Blong.* Resting on top was an enormous axle. *Blong.* Below the axle sung a mammoth bell. *Blong.* It seemed to be made from the metallic substance Lily had seen Tengis hold aloft in Baatarulaan. *Blong.* Soldiers clamoured around it enraptured by both the noise it was making and the shimmering substance from which it was made. *Blong.* The bell's huge clapper swung below ceaselessly, keeping time with the drums surrounding it. *Blong.* Lily could see no point in the noise other than to wreak terror among those who heard it. *Blong.* It seemed to be working.

Lily raced back to her camp as fast as Lucky was able.

'Elder Chuluun!' cried Lily, 'Danyal, Millie, everybody, come quick.' She jumped from Lucky, landing in a run of her own. The elders and tribal delegates moved in around her. 'Tengis is camped near here. Very near. We need to get ready, now!'

'Was there anything else?' asked Elder Chuluun. 'Before we send our encampment safely into the Steppe is there anything we need to tell them? Did you see anything of note that might give us advantage over our foes? Do they have any siege weapons?' Other soldiers began to group around the smaller circle and grow outwards.

Lily was reluctant to tell them what she had seen but needed to. 'No, there are no large weapons. However, there are *lots* of them.'

'We know that,' said Danyal. 'Elder Chuluun said that last night.'

'No!' shouted Lily. 'There are thousands of them. Each of us will have to defeat ten men if we are to win today. If we are to be victorious, then we have to fight harder and with more ferocity than we think imaginable. We will win. We fight for justice. We fight for what is right. We fight to restore the greatness of our nation. We fight to defeat the evil that has claimed control for too long. We fight for Chinggis Khaan!' People everywhere began to cheer. 'Everybody; to your horses. They have come to the Steppe.'

The soldiers roared their approval. All around, the sound of metal rang out as helmets were strapped on, swords picked up, last adjustments to armour made and above them all the dreadful 'Blong.'

'Hairy Hordes,' shouted Danyal, 'file in behind me.'

Fifty enormous men with extra-long arms slumped into a semblance of order behind Danyal. Each wore a thick metal helmet and in each fist they carried an enormous curved sabre the size of a small boy.

'Archers, cavalry!' yelled Lily. 'You are with me. You know what to do.'

Over five hundred horsemen shouted their approval.

'Lancers!' shouted Elder Chuluun. 'About turn. Ready.'

Almost four hundred of the biggest men, each heavily weighed down with armour and carrying a razor-like lance and matching sabre, formed units of twenty behind the Elder.

'My friends,' roared Lily, 'you have come when asked to defend what is right. You have come to make a stand against the Khadists who have left the comfort of their city and seek to eradicate all that is left that is just in this country.' Far and wide her supporters bellowed their approval. 'We shall defend our Steppe whatever the cost may be; we shall fight on plains, rocks, mountains, rivers and in the foothills. We shall never surrender and even if – which I do not for the moment believe – this Steppe or a large part of it were to be subjugated and starving, then our brethren further afield, armed and just, will carry on the struggle until in Chinggis's good time this New World with all its power and might, sets forth to the liberation and rescue of the Old.'

A thousand soldiers raced across the Steppe towards the mountains.

'Blong.'

25

Tengis stood surveying the Steppe that lay out before him. To his right two thousand archers stood ready to rain hellishness upon the enemy. To his left four thousand foot soldiers stood itching to fight. Ahead of them four thousand pike men stood formed in twenty rows, their pikes already dipped to meet their foes. Across the plain stood his nemesis.

'Look at her,' said Tengis. 'Who does she think she is?'

'She is just a girl,' replied Oldortar. 'We shall make short shrift of them and be back here in time for sundowners!'

'Do not underestimate that girl,' said Odval, who had accompanied her lover. 'We women are more powerful than you men believe. You can stand here with your troops and mock her but she is dangerous. What is a joke for a cat will be death for a mouse.'

'Yeah right,' answered Oldortar, 'a powerful woman; just like a watery desert. An interesting prospect, possibly imaginative, but definitely non-existent!'

'Quiet!' demanded Tengis. 'We must crush these upstarts. They must know who their emperor is and they must learn how to love him, or at least fear him.'

'There are so few of them,' said Mr Enkh. 'I calculate you only need to use half of your troops. You could have the others start digging for you. Where was it that you said that substance was? Somewhere in these mountains, wasn't it?'

Odval glared at her father. Since he had first set eyes on the glimmering metal he had become increasingly deranged. She had barely spoken to him in the last ten days. Everything he said or did related to his getting hold of some of Tengis's wealth. She knew that her lover was no fool and that his patience would run out soon enough; though not as soon as it did. Without saying a word Tengis pulled his sabre from its scabbard. Without speaking to him or even looking in his direction, he cleanly relieved Mr Enkh of his head.

'Insubordination will not be tolerated,' said Tengis. He wiped the blood from his sabre on Oldortar's sleeve. 'Neither shall greed.'

He looked at Odval. She bit hard on the inside of her lip. Tasting blood in her mouth, she widened her gaze to prevent any tears from welling up. Odval knew that to show emotion at this moment could leave her feeling several kilograms lighter.

'Give us the word and we will attack,' said Tchoo. 'See the men? The Leggy is eager to please you.'

'They are eager for this more like,' said Tengis. He held a huge shard of the glimmering metal substance above his head. To a person every one of his troops ogled the metal and drooled before shouting out inanely. 'While I control it I control them. Very well, Tchoo, you may start.'

Tchoo raised his hand; an action that was repeated by more junior soldiers down the ranks towards the pike ranks, most of whom were scarcely fourteen years old and began to march badly forward.

'It is time,' cried Tchoo, 'for us to destroy them!'

'A great general once asked whether people should know when they are conquered,' said Tengis. 'The general answered "Would you? Would I?" but I simply say: "yes, they should." He pulled down the visor of his helmet and walked towards his command post overlooking the Steppe below. His Council stood nearby awaiting his orders; all except Mr Enkh who lay with a look of eternal bewilderment upon his face as it looked at the body it recognised lying nearby.

26

Tengis's pike ranks marched onwards out of time. In their midst the mammoth bell swung atop a dozen horses who looked particularly unsettled. Elder Chuluun stood watching events unfold. Tengis and his troops were defended to the rear by the mountains. It would be impossible to mount the encirclement attack he had been planning. He knew that the only real chance they had would be to maximise the effect of his cavalry. He watched the pikemen moving in a band away from the craggy shadows into the Steppe. He noted how bunched together they were. The Leggy was nowhere near as well drilled as his own army but there was so many of them he wondered what chance Lily's supporters really had.

Danyal and Elder Chuluun had little military experience but then again there had been no skirmishes or real fighting in Ongolium since the Khadists had come to power. This was one of their preferred statistics, even if they forgot to mention it was largely due to the complete disappearance for ever of anyone contravening their wishes. However, Danyal and Chuluun were both intelligent, shrewd men. They knew that a day on which a battle was being fought would be noisy. They correctly surmised that most people really wouldn't be able to hear themselves think, let alone hear themselves sticking a sharp object into another person. To counteract this they had devised an astute means of communication. All signals to their troops would be delivered by a series of banners each with pertinent words embroidered into them in gilt. Green would signify 'left', red would mean 'fight harder', checks would denote 'please cause confusion' and polka dots would indicate 'please bash the chap on your right on the head and knock him unconscious'. They also insisted that their troops not make a sound while they fought. This had less to do with communication than respect for Chinggis who had, despite many ill-founded rumours to the contrary, always fought in silence.

Elder Chuluun signalled for Lily to set out with the cavalry (orange flag inscribed 'Yavyaa'). The Steppe air was suddenly overflowing with the din of thunderous hooves as the Steppe horsemen cantered incredibly quickly towards their enemy. Lily had ridden out with half of her Mangudai cavalry warriors, the others remained out of sight. Save for the occasional cry of 'choo' to encourage an irksome horse, the riders remained silent. As they neared the pikemen, the horsemen's silence intimidated the enemy. Yards from the jagged rim of pikes a yellow banner embroidered with the words 'Zogs Ereg' was raised. The entire company of horsemen led by Lily stopped and immediately retreated.

The pikemen's collective mentality changed from intimidated to confused to excited to 'Let's get them' in a matter of seconds. Without waiting for orders the entire shambles of pikemen surged after the cavalry. They truly believed they would catch the horses since the horses were only walking, albeit rather quickly. As the thick band of pikemen poured after the ambling equines, the faster runners among them rallied ahead. They were no longer a perceivable single unit of men. Once the enemy had become suitably spread out, a black banner was raised titled 'Odoo'. In response, Lily turned with her men and charged into the dispersed pikemen. As Lily turned back towards the enemy, the remainder of the cavalry arrived from behind the rise. They approached the enemy from either side attacking the Leggy on multiple fronts. The pikemen were so exhausted from running that they were barely able to lift their heavy weapons. With a curved sabre in each hand, the cavalry-men ploughed through the disparate Leggy, dicing through them devilishly.

Ten minutes after Lily had left Elder Chuluun's side her cavalry had killed almost a quarter of the pikemen. It was proving tiring work. Leaning down to hack off somebody's head, arm or sometimes leg was exhilarating yet very strenuous. As time drew on some of the cavalry began to fall off their steeds from sheer exhaustion. Once on the ground the terrified Leggy would stomp on them till they moved no more. An increasing number of riderless horses could be seen running, or trotting fast, off into the distance. A blue banner was raised. The cavalry raced back to their own troops to take stock and regroup. Tengis was visibly fuming. Elder Chuluun watched as the headless leader of the pikemen ran away from his emperor, pursued by his head which flew through the air after him.

On the battlefield ahead of them Danyal could see that two and a half thousand pikemen were straggling in disarray, their one and only battle tactic utterly obliterated. He knew it was his time to star in the proceedings. Without waiting for a banner he thwarted protocol by sounding a particularly shrill whistle. This was met by a fantastic roar as the entire body of Hairy Hordes lolloped down the slope towards the straggling pikemen.

As Tengis looked on, the bodies of his men were hurled through the sky cannonballing into other members of the Leggy. He was bewildered as to how so few men could account for so much damage and knew that many would owe so much to them. Through the scenes of carnage Lily spotted the man with the interesting accent. As he tore the limbs off some poor unfortunate soul that had crossed his path, he gave her a wink. She smiled but turned red. She was ashamed that she knew people who were capable of such aggression with so much good humour, even if it was in the name of Chinggis and justice.

Looking back at the Hairy Hordes, her mood changed. Simultaneously two of the Hairy Hordes would link arms. A third would run towards them and jump. The other two would catch him on their hands and then catapult the third into oncoming enemy. Each shot would account for half a dozen Leggy. The third man was having the time of his life. As he bowled through oncoming Leggy he giggled more headily with each hit. Other Hairy Hordes would link arms and run at the enemy as a long line of hairiness. This had the effect of quite literally mowing the enemy asunder. Lily found herself clapping with glee as she watched these overgrown boys finally finding an opportunity to turn their play into practice.

With each passing second a significant percentage of pike-men disappeared. Each member of the 'Double-Hs', as they liked to be known, had notched up at least twenty men, marking each hit on their arm with the blood of their foes. The pikemen were almost no more. Roars began to be raised among the Hairy Hordes. They were running out of people to fight and were making it known that, unless someone came and had a go, they would go and find someone themselves. The battle was going far better than Lily or any of her supporters could possibly have envisaged.

Although it was a strikingly sunny day, Lily looked upwards as the sky suddenly darkened. And then the roaring stopped. When Lily looked back at the battlefield she was greeted with horror. Every single one of the Hairy Hordes lay on the Steppe floor. Steel arrows protruded from arms, backs and heads. There were no casualties, only fatalities. Faster than a Steppe horse could walk downhill the entire body of Hairy Hordes had been wiped out. Of their number only Danyal remained and he had long retired from the battle. As the shock wore off, he tried to run to his brothers but Drudger held him back.

Tengis looked on smugly. Lily's supporters were sure they could see him muttering to himself. Little did they know that Khad was in his head directing every move made on the field of battle. Tengis turned to his right and gave a knowing nod. The head archer bowed low in response. He knew the emperor would reward him in no small way and hoped it would include some of the shimmering stuff. Tengis flicked his hand. The head archer's eyes opened wide with delight. He was being given another chance to prove himself. The air began to fill with the heavy twang of two thousand bowstrings being pulled taut. A moment later a gigantic 'shoosh' sounded the imminent arrival of two thousand arrows. Most of the arrows fell short of Lily and her troops but they made their announcement clearly. Any steps taken further forward would be well within their range. The volley did manage to kill any remaining pikemen, however. Tengis would later refer to this as an 'acceptable risk'.

Elder Chuluun looked shocked; he was fast running out of ideas. Danyal was still a gibbering wreck and every time he looked at his fallen friends he screamed maniacally. Drudger took up position next to his friend and slapped him hard whenever he felt he was about to scream. Between slaps he worked with Elder Chuluun and Lily to devise a course of action.

'I . . . I . . . I don't know what to suggest,' said Elder Chuluun. 'I don't know what went wrong.'

'They bloody well massacred us,' said Lily, 'that's what. We haven't got time to mull this over right now. The game is afoot. Look over there, Tengis is just waiting for us. He knows he has the numerical advantage. He knows we have to take the game to him.'

'We have tried my two preferred tactics,' said Elder Chuluun, 'neither "separate opponent" or "retreat into ambush" appear to have worked very well, have they?'

'Stop being so damned self-obsessed!' shouted Millie. 'Listen, my father used to read me the old stories about Chinggis Khaan. I seem to recall a few rather amazing manoeuvres he successfully executed.'

'Please,' implored Lily, 'tell me, we have to act now. The longer we give Tengis, the more he will think he has the upper hand. Confidence is half the battle. If our troops were to discover how we are acting they would lose all faith in us.'

'Let me see,' said Millie, 'there is the "moving bush" and the "lake formation". They're good from memory.'

'Are we fighting a battle,' asked Lily, 'or are we running a dance school?'

'Bear with me,' said Millie. 'The "moving bush" involves multiple attacks on multiple fronts. It asks that commanders orchestrate repeated small skirmishes intermittently at differ-ent fringes to draw the opponent into a more strung-out for-mation.' The ladies looked across the battlefield. Tengis had reformed his troops. His foot soldiers had taken up position ready to repel any attack but equally well placed to readily march upon any advancing enemy.

'We could try it but I don't think that'll work,' said Lily.

'Well, what about the "lake formation"?' said Millie. 'That one sounds nice. From what I can remember successive waves of attacks are undertaken along the enemy front. Each line, or wave, attacks and withdraws filtering through the next wave on its attack. It sounds a bit complicated, doesn't it?'

'We are also working against an enemy with far greater numbers than we have,' said Elder Chuluun.

'So,' said Lily, 'when it comes down to it we don't actually have a plan, do we? I can't believe we have been through so much; lost so many good people, and we are sitting here unable to think of something to do. So much for my illustrious destiny.'

'Who's navel-gazing now?' asked Elder Chuluun. 'We still have most of our forces. We will try a simple approach. We will send out the lancers up front. The cavalry will cover the flanks and launch forays against them using their bows and arrows.'

The plan didn't sound particularly imaginative to Lily but she realised that they had little choice at this juncture. Sheer weight of numbers reminded Lily why a good imagination was critical. Her troops were being easily repelled by Tengis's. Although the lancers were able to take out the front line of his troops as soon as their lances had struck an enemy, they were held fast. His foot soldiers simply walked over the bodies of their fallen comrades and cut down the lancers where they stood. Tengis's soldiers may have lacked any formal training but there were so many of them they simply formed a wall of bodies that Lily's army could not overcome. Elder Chuluun began to talk about retreat.

'We cannot leave!' said Lily. 'What about all those people that have laid down their lives today? Are we simply willing to run away when the going gets too difficult? We must persist.'

'Lily,' said Millie, 'look out there. We are taking heavy losses. If we leave now, we still have a semblance of a cavalry and I'm sure some of our lancers will escape. We can live to fight another day.'

'How can you stand there and talk about escape?' cried Lily. 'You know as well as I that, if Tengis is seen to be victorious today, his following will be unassailable.'

'We have no choice,' said Elder Chuluun. He gave the order for the 'Zogs Ereg' banner to be raised sounding the retreat.

Blong.

But Lily could not give up. She mounted Lucky and rode towards the centre of the fray. As Elder Chuluun and Millie looked on they watched a young woman hacking her way through enemy lines. Danyal broke free of Drudger. He watched in horror as Lily cast aside hewn limbs and Lucky trampled across fallen corpses. With a sabre in each hand, Lily forced her way towards the bell, and towards Tengis. Between strikes she caught glimpses of him. He was sitting watching her progress and with a contented smile upon his face. She noticed a woman by his side sneering at her. Had Lily had an aerial view she would have realised she had almost one thousand men between her and Tengis and it was Tengis who owned the stock of shimmering metal.

Pre-empting a retreat, Tengis had sent out his cavalry to outflank any escaping lancers longing to return home. They were dealt with savagely. With the cavalry beginning to turn towards Elder Chuluun and the remaining survivors they had no choice but to hastily beat a retreat away from the battlefield. Lily's supporters turned back to look at the battlefield one final time. Rising above the foot soldiers they could see the furious figure of a young girl fighting from horseback. Although it broke each one of their hearts, they had to leave. Spurring their horses they evaded the approaching enemy cavalry.

Lily continued to hack away at her foes. She and Lucky were almost completely covered in the blood of the vanquished. Even if she had wanted to, she would never have made it back to Elder Chuluun and her supporters. She had no intention of doing any such thing. She had not even noticed that they had left the battlefield. *Blong.* While she breathed she would honour the name of Chinggis Khaan. *Blong.* Through bloodstained eyes she looked for Tengis. Catching sight of him she watched as he calmly stood up. *Blong.* Moving down from his imperial plinth he walked slowly towards a group of soldiers that sat idly watching the action. *Blong.* Lily struggled against the mounting tide of foot soldiers. *Blong.* Lucky's legs were beginning to feel heavy. His flank had been sliced open. He knew that he was not long for this world. *Blong.* Lily looked up again towards Tengis.

As she did, she saw him looking down the sights of a crossbow. *Blong.* An object came rushing towards her and knocked her clean off from Lucky's back. *Blong.* The foot soldiers were soon upon her; thrusting swords into her carelessly. *Blong.* Lily felt Lucky fall near to her. Reaching out a severed arm, she searched for him. *Blong.* As Lily touched Lucky her steed looked one last time into his mistress's eyes. He was crying. *Blong.* A sword was thrust deep into Lucky's neck; his eyes remained open as his life vanished before them. *Blong.* Lily closed her eyes. Nothing made sense. There was an emptiness where she hoped she would find peace. *Blong.* As the foot soldiers continued their frenzied attack she realised that she had lost. She offered herself to the spirit world and prayed that Tsara would look after her. *Blong.* All sound vanished. Darkness fell upon her. *Blong.*

Once Elder Chuluun and Lily's supporters had reached a safe distance, they stopped. Tears rolled down their faces. The old man turned back towards where they had come. 'The winner has many friends; the loser has good friends.'

27

Lily opened her eyes. There was no sign of the battle, which came as an enormous relief. There was little sign of anything unusual. Slowly she came to realise that she was standing in the spirit world, though she wasn't certain whether she was here by choice or not. She walked towards the bridge where she normally met Tsara. She hadn't seen her spirit friend for some time. She was excited at the prospect of catching up with her again. Her spirit friend had been the only person Lily had ever been able to talk freely with. Among the herders, sentiment was seen as a luxury. Friendship was based upon one's ability to be useful to and help another; not empathy. Lily had always loved her father but she would never have described their relationship as close. Lily's spirit friend had been there to lean on whenever darkness had come; she hoped that she would be somewhere nearby now.

Lily tried to figure out if she had come to the spirit world in a trance or some other way. She could not bring herself to consider what that other way might have entailed. She hoped beyond hope that she was in a trance. The puppies that she had come to care for were in the spirit world. There were various odd-looking spirits walking around, although, much to her dismay, there was no sign of Mark Anthony. Lily knew that it could only be a matter of time before her friend would turn up. She knew there was no point in fretting over it. Her friend had obviously been busy doing something else recently. In the meantime Lily decided she would make herself look presentable. She couldn't remember the last time she had taken a proper wash. She walked down the side of the bridge towards the water. Her bare feet felt soothed by the cool grasses that grew there.

As she bent down towards the river, she thought she caught a glimpse of Tsara. Sitting upright, she looked up and down the river for a sight of her friend. She decided she must have imagined it. She cupped her hand and drank deeply from the cool water. It tasted heavenly. Lily dangled her feet into the river. The gentle current washed away her worries and she was bathed with a feeling of rest. She stooped over the riverbank to wash her hair. As she leaned in close to the water she opened her eyes. Lily screamed and moved away from the river. She edged her way closer to the edge. She took a deep breath and looked over. She let out a short cry. Staring back from the riverbed was the face of her friend. She sank back away from the water's edge. Shaking her head, she tried to find a rational explanation. Lily knew that her spirit friend was just that, a spirit; she knew that spirits were already dead. What she couldn't understand was why her friend was lying at the bottom of the river. She peered over the edge once more. It was definitely Tsara. As she began to move away she noticed that Tsara's face moved with her. She closed one eye. Tsara did likewise. Lily opened her mouth as wide as she could. Tsara followed her every move. Finally Lily reached out to the water and shook its surface. It became evident that there was nothing beneath it. Lily was looking at her own reflection but her own reflection had taken on the appearance of Tsara.

Lily was confused. She may have been a shawoman, but she was no conjurer nor was she a philosopher. Whatever had caused Tsara's face to be reflected from her own had to have some straightforward explanation. Much as Lily explored every possibility there was only one that made any sense. She and Tsara must have had some link more profound than simply being friends. As the sun rose higher into the sky, Lily continued to look for an explanation. Presently she saw a man walking up the riverbank towards her. He was walking with purpose. When he was close to her, his face lit up. Tears began to well in his eyes.

'How long I have waited to see you,' said the man. He stretched out his arms and approached Lily, who backed away.

'Who are you?' she asked. 'I have never seen you before.' Lily knew this to be true but there was something about this man that seemed somewhat familiar. Again he tried to embrace her and again she side-stepped his advances. He laughed at her.

'You really don't recognize me, do you?' he joked. 'After all we've been through and you say you don't know me. Have you any idea how much that hurts? Especially after all these years?'

'No,' replied Lily. 'Who are you? I think you must have me mistaken for somebody else. My name is Lily. I am a herder and shawoman. I am here to speak to my good friend Tsara. I need her help urgently. An evil man is threatening to destroy my nation, my father is missing in prison somewhere and I have a stupid riddle that doesn't seem to mean anything.'

'Tell me about this friend of yours,' asked the man. He stood leaning against a tree, one hand in his pocket. He was not taking the situation nearly as seriously as Lily.

'Tsara?' asked Lily.

'Yes,' replied the man, 'that's the one.'

'Tsara is the closest friend I have ever had,' said Lily. 'She has been my friend for as long as I can remember. We have grown up together, although with her being a spirit she hasn't really changed very much. She is kind and wise. She believes in justice, like I do, and she has been helping me as I strive to destroy the criminal that is threatening my country.'

'Tell me,' said the man, 'is she beautiful like you?'

'Please, stop being childish,' said Lily. 'I'm sure I don't know what you're talking about. Though yes, Tsara is beautiful. She is the most beautiful woman I have ever met.'

'Does she have a husband or boyfriend, this Tsara, this friend of yours?' asked the man.

'Yes she does,' replied Lily. 'She is the partner of none other than Chinggis Khaan, the greatest emperor my country has ever known. So you had better be careful; I hear he is a very jealous type. If he were to catch you trying to woo his lover, he would probably kill you.'

'Oh, I'll make sure I stay well away from him,' said the man. 'He sounds like a right sort. What about you? Are you OK? When I saw you earlier you looked like you had seen a ghost, which given this is the spirit world wouldn't be a complete shock.'

'It's nothing,' said Lily.

'Come on,' said the man, 'spit it out.'

'Well,' said Lily. 'I am not sure how I got here. Well, normally I come here through a trance – I'm a shawoman, after all – but this time it feels different. I remember sitting on my horse, Lucky. I remember fighting for my life. I remember seeing that despicable man and then . . . nothing. What do you make of that?'

'You do know what sorts of people come here?' asked the man. 'This is a place for the dead. I know that you shame–sha-people are able to visit, but to actually be here. To taste things, smell things, feel things. To be here like that, you have to be, well, dead.'

'But I'm not dead,' said Lily. 'I can't be!'

'Have you tasted anything since you arrived?' asked the man. 'Have you felt any strong emotions?' Lily couldn't deny that she had. As the realisation crept over her she began to cry. The man moved towards her and held her in his arms; her head resting on his shoulder.

'You have been dead a long time, my darling,' said the man. 'You have been dead and alive and are now back once more.'

'What do you mean?' asked Lily, although she was beginning to understand what it was that he was about to say.

'I have known Tsara for many years, centuries,' said the man. 'She and I lived and loved together. We have been kept apart thanks to my vile cousin who prevented my soul from reaching its final destination. He and I have been fighting in limbo ever since. Tsara was trapped here in the spirit world and I apart from her in limbo. Our hearts ached for one another. The only way Tsara and I were able to be able to be reunited was if somebody in the real world was able to find my physical body. Nothing more. No need for ceremony. My soul merely needed someone, preferably somebody good, to see what had become of me. For centuries I have tried to find a way to get to Tsara. I love that woman so much. She was my life and is my eternity. *I am Chinggis Khaan.*'

'How do you do?' replied Lily. She felt a little silly at not having realised this sooner.

'Nobody came forth to help us,' continued Chinggis. 'We were alone and destined always to be so. Finally Tsara agreed that she would make the journey back to the real world. We could bear to be apart no longer. She found a mother who was dying. As her soul parted, Tsara promised to look after her daughter if the mother allowed Tsara to live the woman's life on earth. The mother willingly agreed and Tsara was reborn. Born into a humble herder family. Born somewhat different to those around her and never quite able to understand why. Do you not remember? Can you not remember who you really are? You are Tsara! We are together once more and this time for all time.'

Lily had stopped crying and Tsara now began to look up into the face of her beloved Chinggis.

'How was it possible that I talked to Lily and she talked to me for all those years?' asked Tsara.

'Recall what happened when you looked in the river a moment ago,' said Chinggis. 'All those years you have simply been talking to a reflection of yourself. Your power as a spirit gave Lily the power of a shawoman. You were basically two parts of the same person. You lived as a nomadic herder, although it was not your true home; you were borrowing her body.'

'We cannot leave the herders alone to face your cousin,' said Tsara. 'I have tried but I have had no success. Perhaps if people were to discover that your spirit still looks after them, they would have the courage to fight on?'

'You have been successful,' said Chinggis. 'Our union is a source of success. Let us fight this battle side by side. Let us return to the real world and wipe my cousin and his minion Tengis from the face of humanity.'

28

As Tengis and his troops had made their way back towards Baatarulaan, their swagger had been even greater than it had been when they left. Not only had they successfully dispersed the risible herder force but they had slain their enemy's inglorious leader. When asked if they should take her body to her people, Tengis had ordered his soldiers to leave Lily's smashed and bloodstained body where it lay, next to her equally bloodied steed. If cameras had been invented, Tengis would have taken a dozen trophy shots for his wall.

Soldiers marching homewards boasted to one another about what they would do with the wealth that Tengis had promised them.

'I'm going to buy me a dozen horses,' said one.

'I'm blowing the lot on fermented mare's milk and lusty ladies,' said another.

'At least one thing's for sure,' said their captain, 'none of us will have to eat anything other than fresh food ever again. Gone are the days when we scavenged the refuse of others trying to find a meal.'

'Cor,' said the first soldier, 'real grub and we don't have to do nothing to get it!'

'Sounds too good to be true, don't it?' said the second. 'Sounds like there is such a thing as a free lunch.'

Nearing the city Tengis demanded that his shimmering bell be rung as they marched through the streets. He wanted to create a fearsome impression.

'I think I need a new name,' said Tengis.

Odval, Oldortar and Tchoo looked at him in a puzzled manner but none of them were brave enough to ask why. 'I was thinking about calling myself the Baatar Tiger; how does that sound?'

'Wonderful!' gushed Tchoo. 'It really captures your essence.'

'I think it is a name that befits the defender of Ongolium,' said Oldortar. He was not given to an emotional response.

'There is much from that name we can use to our advantage,' said Odval. She was still to shed a tear for the untimely loss of her father but did not blame her beloved Tengis for slaying him. She believed in Tengis and what he was trying to achieve. She was also finding herself increasingly attracted towards the prospect of being empress.

'Anyway,' said Tengis, 'I have sent some soldiers ahead to start whispering my new name around Baatarulaan and let people know about my unprecedented victory. If my calculations are correct, and they usually are, by the time we enter the city the gossip circuit will have been covered a dozen times. Everybody will be in the streets to welcome home the Baatar Tiger.'

As soon Tengis arrived back, he dismissed his Council. The past few days had been tiring and he was certain he never wanted to leave the Baatarulaan again. Despite all his bluff and bravado, Tengis remained a young man. It was still a few months until his twentieth birthday and while he relished the power he wielded he sometimes longed for childish things. He called for his mother.

'My boy!' cried Mrs Khaan. 'I heard about your victory; what a clever young man you have become. I am so proud of you!'

'Thank you, Mother,' said Tengis. 'I am still your son, though; nothing has changed.'

'Oh but it has,' replied his mother. 'Now that you have defeated the herders, you have united the people. You are the first true emperor we have had since Chinggis or even Khad. You are also the richest and that's important.'

'Wealth is but a tool,' said Tengis, 'nothing more.'

'But what a beautiful, beautiful tool!' said his mother. 'You must use it to ensure the people do not want change. You must make the people fear change; fear you. Do you have any of the shimmering substance with you? How I would love to see some. How I would love to touch it; feel its golden smoothness against my skin. It would be an honour.'

Despite her affection for him, Tengis could sense that his mother had become as enthralled with the metal as Odval's father had been. However, he knew he could never harm his mother. Too many delicious breakfasts lay long in his memory. Instead, he gave her a small lump of the glimmering matter and sent her on her way. He made a mental note only to call upon her for birthdays and other special occasions; her mind was being drawn elsewhere by his riches.

With his mother gone, Tengis felt alone. He knew that this was one of the less pleasant trappings of success and he didn't really relish the prospect. Even Odval was somewhat distant since he had chopped off her father's head. Tengis thought she was being petty. Searching his mind, he instead sought out the voice in his head – Khad.

'Aren't we doing well?' asked Khad. The voice sounded particularly jovial.

'It depends how you define "well",' said Tengis. 'If you define it as having no friends, no family, a mild sense of guilt for having beheaded your potential father-in-law, and a fear of the people that are supposed to be frightened of you then, yes, I guess you can say things are going well.'

'Don't you worry,' said Khad, 'you'll soon find out that being on your own has its merits. It gives you a certain improved sense of mobility with regards to decision making. You watch. Being alone will make you even more powerful. People will fear you to an even greater degree. Baatar Tiger? Love it!'

'What now?' asked Tengis. 'Things could not be better but I know that times are not always the same; the grass is not always green.'

'I think we should ramp up our plans,' said Khad. 'If my memory serves me – though after eight hundred years it does get a little foggy – then the next step is all about fear.'

'Are you sure we should be doing this?' asked Tengis. 'After all, your legend . . .'

'My legend was built on poppycock,' said Khad. 'If we are to rule this country with a rod of iron, then we need more than just the mined material. We need to have control and power over everyone, including those close to us.'

'But,' said Tengis, 'the legend says-'

'I know what the legend says,' interrupted Khad. 'I did write it. From what I recall it was meant merely as a means of keeping people away. I didn't need other foreign minds interjecting their points of view. So long as they stayed away I could hold sway over the Ongolians. Did you receive a response to your letters?'

'Yes,' said Tengis. He was acting a little sheepishly. He was about to take a step that even he thought was possibly one too far. 'As we speak there are five thousand troops crossing the frontier. We will have an army of privateers at the city gates by the day after tomorrow. The Outsiders are coming to Baatarulaan.'

Far away, just as Tengis spoke those words, there was a large cracking noise. Somewhere deep within a cavern, far underground in an icy grotto, the glacial rock began to splinter. Shards of frozen rock fell from around the glistening chamber, crashing into the rushing torrent that flowed beneath. From within the rock a figure that had been entombed in ice for centuries slowly began to lift its arm and reach for its sword.

29

It had been exactly what Chinggis had been waiting for. As he walked hand in hand with his beloved Tsara, a rush of cold air began to embrace him, seemingly pulling from within his abdomen. He barely had time to explain what was happening before he was sucked from the spirit world. With an ear-splitting *crack* Chinggis abruptly opened his eyes widely. He was no longer walking in the spirit world, or even in limbo. For the first time in eight hundred years he was in the real world. It felt good. He felt alive. He felt an enormous feeling of rage course through his body. His muscles clenched and, as they did, the ice that had been so tightly frozen around him exploded into the grotto. He fell on to an icy outcrop and let out a blood-curdling cry of anger.

As Chinggis looked around him for someone to kill, he felt something move behind him. Turning swiftly, in one movement he spun and drew both of the sabres from the scabbards that were tied to his back.

'Stop!' cried a voice.

Chinggis did not know where the voice came from and, although he hesitated, he remained fully alert.

'Stop. Breathe. It's me. It is Tsara.'

Chinggis looked around for the voice. His brain and brawn struggled to catch up with the thoughts his newly reacquired soul were sending them. As he scanned the icy expanse, he could see no living creature – neither human nor animal. The only life that shared the cavern with him was a sleek falcon. It flew close to him. As he was about to strike the bird, it spoke. 'Chinggis, it is I, it is Tsara. Remember me. Wake up.'

Chinggis hesitated and then his tension began to subside. He sat on the ice. Confusion flooded his defrosting mind. He was finding it especially difficult to think clearly after eight hundred years in the deep freeze.

Tsara rested nearby and began to inform her lover why he was there; why she was there. She explained that as his soul had been sucked back into the real world he had urged her to find a means of following. He knew that when he awoke he would be ready for battle. That had always been the way for Chinggis. Tsara recalled several embarrassing instances when they had been staying with friends and Chinggis had gone sleepwalking with his sword. Trying to explain why a pack of well-trained and much loved guard dogs had all been decapitated had been a challenge. That was not important now, though. She had to concentrate on resetting Chinggis's mind. She needed to reunite his soul with his physical body. As she focused on his body, she remembered just how good it felt and was guilty at once upon a time having been so childish in the presence of a Roman general.

In time Chinggis returned to himself. His body had been saved from the ravages of time thanks to being incarcerated in ice by his vile cousin. His thinking returned to its previous sharpened heights. The only thing that was unsettling Chinggis was that he was in love with a falcon. No matter how hard he tried to find a reason, he kept thinking about how difficult it would be to kiss a bird of prey.

'My love,' said Tsara. Chinggis blanched slightly at hearing this from a falcon. 'We must move quickly. Your being released from your icy tomb means that Outsiders have crossed into Ongolium. Tengis and Khad must be moving ahead with their plan to strike fear into the people in order to keep the peace and maintain control. They must be stopped!'

Chinggis backed away slightly from the bird but the icy outcrop he was sitting on wasn't wide. It looked as though it had once been a bridge and he considered trying to jump across until he remembered he was trying to evade a bird – such a plan would be futile. Although he was uncomfortable talking to the bird, some small part of him did understand that somewhere inside the beast was the soul of his beloved Tsara. It was just a little unappealing.

'What is that you would have me do?' asked Chinggis. He was finding it difficult speaking to a bird. Tsara could tell and hopped on to his shoulder just to see how he would react. Of course, Chinggis was an emperor so he barely flinched. When she moved closer for a light peck on the cheek that was a different matter.

'We must gather our troops,' said Tsara. 'When the herder communities hear that you have returned they will come out in force.'

'Is that not what you tried with Lily?' asked Chinggis. 'That didn't seem to go too well.'

'We only managed to get a fraction of the communities to join us,' said Tsara. 'People are too scared of Tengis and Khad, but with you back they will stand up against them. We also lacked a clear strategic military mind. A sleepwalking troublemaker you may be but you are also the greatest military tactician ever born, or even reborn.'

'What about you?' asked Chinggis.

'I have a favour to return,' said Tsara. 'Lily willingly helped me when she had no need to. The least I can do is to pay back that favour by finding her father.'

'How do I get out of here?' asked Chinggis. 'I can't tell you how much I long to see the Steppe, to feel fresh air against my skin. This icy prison has been a hell. But how do I get out?'

'That's easy,' replied Tsara. She jumped to the ground and began scraping at a narrow fissure on the ice ledge with her talons. Before Chinggis was able to understand what was happening, and long before he was able to do anything about it, the protrusion began to give way. Large sections of ice fell all around him. Chinggis remained momentarily suspended in the air before gravity took control. He fell backwards towards the water.

'No, please no!' said Chinggis, 'I can't swiiiiimmmmm . . .'

Tsara flew around the cavern until she was quite sure that her lover had safely escaped his confinement and then followed his route along the icy torrent, which was not easy for a feathered creature. Fortunately she had pre-empted this need and coated her wings accordingly with a waxy substance to prevent freezing. By the time she reached the Steppe and had flown for a few moments she was fully recovered. Enjoying the use of especially acute vision, Tsara scoured the desert plain for her mate. She could see him hauling himself out of the water a kilometre or two away. She knew he would be fine so long as he used his head. He always had been; it was only when he had followed his heart that Khad had been able to assassinate him. Leaving him to find the nomadic herders, Tsara flew off towards Baatarulaan.

The city was no more attractive from the air than it was from the ground. A thick smog hung above the myriad of cramped and insalubrious buildings, making it impossible even for a falcon to see clearly. Soaring between gaudy apartment towers, Tsara scanned the buildings for signs of Lily's father. She knew that the group formally known as the Fun Brigade had once established something called the House of Fun, so she hunted for signs of a prison. As she circled one of the darker quarters of the city, she spied a solid tower set behind fortified walls.

There seemed to be no streets leading up to the walls while behind them an area of open scrubland formed a further barrier for anyone foolhardy enough to try to reach – or escape – the ominous-looking tower. If he was held here, it was no wonder that Lily had been unable to track her father down. Tsara, though, had an advantage; she could simply glide in and land somewhere near the tower.

Landing on the ledge of a barred window, Tsara took stock of her position. There were Khadist guards patrolling the outer wall but none seemed to be watching the courtyard around the tower. The walls were twenty metres high and had only one gateway which was manned by four sentries. The enormous portcullis gate was operated from a room nearby. Those on the wall concentrated their efforts outside the wall, so confident were they that nobody could ever get that far. Tsara knew that men were fallible, though; she just needed to figure out how to take advantage of this when the time came.

Turning her attentions back to the tower Tsara easily fitted between the bars and entered the dungeon within. There were five floors with one large open room on each. Inmates seemed to be able to move easily between floors using large stone staircases. From what Tsara could make out there were no doors in the tower. The only door was the exit on the ground floor which was made of thick wood and bolted from the outside.

Tsara flew from floor to floor. Decrepit-looking individuals caked in filth cowered in corners. Some played games with chicken bones. Others sat in circles silently. Others talked. There was no light and no warmth. The tower was a bitter place. Tsara felt her soul being corroded with every second she spent there. On the top floor Tsara found three people and immediately recognised the soul she was seeking. It had the same glow she had come to love while she had been alive within Lily. The man she was looking at was almost as much a father to her as he had been to Lily. He sat with two companions quietly contemplating their fate. Tsara flew between them and came to rest beside Lily's father.

'I have news of Lily,' said Tsara. She hadn't been at all sure how to open this discussion, what with her being a bird.

The three men turned to stare at her calmly. They had all been in the tower so long that their sense of wonder had all but disappeared. Tsara could empathise. After a mere five minutes she could understand how that could happen in the tower. 'Are you the father of Lily?'

'I am Baatar,' said the man. 'I am Lily's father. What do you know about my daughter?'

Tsara was a little surprised by his lack of emotion but had come to appreciate that nomadic herders could little spare time for emotion as they eked out an existence on the Steppe.

'I am sorry to have to tell you,' said Tsara, 'but Lily is dead.'

Tsara felt guilty at saying this. Lily had never really existed in the greater scheme of things but her father had not known that. Again Baatar remained emotionless.

'That is indeed sad news,' said Baatar, 'but why have you come to tell me? Are you a shawoman?'

'No,' said Tsara, 'I am from the spirit world. How can you manage to live here?' Tsara knew the stupidity of her question the moment it escaped her lips but her understanding of life and eternity was founded upon emotion; none of the people in the tower had any.

'What choice do we have?' answered Baatar. 'Anyway, once you have locked your door, you are the emperor in your own domain. It is how we cope.'

'My name is Tsara,' she said. 'I was the lover of Chinggis Khaan.' The two other inmates stirred at this mention.

'I see,' said Baatar, 'you were the mother to Chinggis's children, at least to the two he bestowed his name upon?'

'Indeed,' said Tsara. She was beginning to discover that birds were able to shed tears. 'Sukh and Bolorerdene were my children.' The two inmates shifted closer to her.

'Sometimes from bad news there comes good,' said Baatar.

'What do you mean?' asked Tsara.

'You have informed me of my daughter's death, tragic but part of life's pattern,' said Baatar. 'I can now reunite you with the offspring that were so cruelly taken from you by Khad. Please come closer.'

The circle moved towards Baatar. The two inmates who had remained silent so far came into Tsara's sights – they had noble faces.

'Tsara, may I present to you Sukh and and his sister Bolorerdene. They are from a long line of Khaans who have been kept prisoner in this tower. Indeed, you may find many other relatives in this hellish place. The true blood children have retained the same name throughout time awaiting the return of their mother.'

Looking into their eyes Tsara sorely wished she was in human form so that she could embrace the descendants of her offspring. She had to make do with letting them stroke her head, which was a little demeaning.

'We must get out of here,' said Tsara.

'Impossible!' said Baatar. 'Many have tried, and all have failed.'

'Do not give up so easily,' said Tsara. 'I can do things unimaginable to humans. Meet me at the exit.' Tsara flew off through a nearby barred window.

Baatar looked reluctantly at Sukh and Bolorerdene. All three shrugged their shoulders before begrudgingly trudging their way down through the squalor towards the doorway. The tower had sapped all hope from them but they figured this interruption by a bird from the spirit world was at least a distraction from their normal dreary routine. They stopped when they reached the thick wooden door. Nobody stayed on the ground floor; it was too cold and was largely the domain of rats and other vermin. As they stood in the dank darkness, they heard something clawing at the door outside. A scraping noise was followed by a heavy clunk. A chill breeze pushed the door ajar as snowflakes invaded the tower. Baatar looked at his friends with wonder. It was the first time any of them had felt hope since their arrival. For Sukh and Bolorerdene it was the first time in their lives. Baatar pulled the door open and the three rushed outside into the blizzard. Tsara circled expectantly around their heads.

The falcon flew ahead of the escapees. They slowed as they approached the portcullis gate. Baatar watched on in amazement as Tsara swooped between the guards, dislodging their helmets and causing them to give chase. She was clearing the way for them. Opening the gate a fraction, the falsely imprisoned trio slid underneath and out into the scrubland. Clinging to the shadows cast by the surrounding buildings they headed for freedom.

It was a straightforward escape that took no longer than half an hour. Once he was safely away from the tower and guards, Baatar wondered why he had never thought of it previously. But then he had never had a talking falcon to assist him before. Tsara led them towards Danyal's yard, where Millie waited to greet them.

30

Sukh, Bolorerdene and Baatar were treated by Millie as returning heroes. She fed them sumptuously and gave them the finest rooms in her home to sleep in. Returning to the kitchen she sat back down at the table.

'How are our plans progressing?' asked Tsara. 'Fill me in on what happened after the battle.' Danyal, Drudger and Millie were each more than a little sceptical about the talking falcon but it seemed so strange a thing to happen that they accepted that it had to be true.

'So,' asked Danyal, 'let me get this straight. You are a falcon but you are actually not; you're a spirit called Tsara that claims she was Chinggis's lover and also claims that she was Lily while Lily was alive, bless her soul, and have come back to the real world in the shape of a falcon to resurrect Chinggis and save Lily's father before engaging in battle intent on destroying Tengis?'

'Yup!' said Tsara. 'That's about it.'

'Oh, OK,' said Danyal, 'for a moment there I thought you were going to come out with some far-fetched story. So what do you want to know, Tsara/Lily/falcon – what should we call you?'

'Tsara would be just fine, thank you,' said the bird, a little peeved by this cool reception. 'The last I remember you safely evaded Tengis's cavalry on the battlefield. What happened after that?'

Danyal and Millie explained the aftermath of the battle. Together with the nomadic soldiers they had escaped to the safe camp Elder Chuluun had sent his people to before the battle. Once they had regrouped, they realised that over a quarter of their number had perished. Rather than losing heart, it had given those who had survived a renewed sense of outrage. There and then all present pledged to continue their struggle against Tengis and to fulfil their promises to Lily.

Danyal, Drudger and Millie had returned to the city. It had been most harrowing for them. When they had set out for the Steppe they had had the jovial company of the Hairy Hordes; the return leg was made in abject silence. Since they had been back in Baatarulaan they too had been calling for support against Tengis. Although it was dangerous to speak out openly against the Khadist regime, they had succeeded in swelling their numbers significantly, selecting a new horde from among the lowest echelons of Baatarulaan's underworld. Elder Chuluun, too, had vowed to travel widely and rally support among the outlying herder communities. He now knew the extent of Tengis's troops and that they needed to bolster their numbers dramatically if they were to stand any chance against him.

Once Danyal, Drudger and Millie had finished their account, Tsara replied in kind telling them what had happened since Lily had been killed. It served to fuel their desire to take action. She also informed them about Chinggis. They all agreed that, accompanied by Chinggis, Elder Chuluun would have no difficulty engaging other communities to join their cause. They had been expecting word from Elder Chuluun for a few days, and Danyal had begun to worry about the delay.

Everyone was exhausted and so agreed to retire for the night. Tsara was given a blanket to stand or lie on; she still couldn't decide which was more comfortable. Danyal had thoughtfully placed a cuttlefish shell, some wholegrain seeds and an eggcup filled with water near the blanket.

Waking early the next morning, Lily's father Baatar was the first to venture downstairs. He had never been in a house of more than one storey other than the prison tower and Millie's home was ever so slightly more impressive than that place. He walked from room to room wondering what on earth the pictures in wooden frames depicted; he had a business brain, not an artistic one. Back in the kitchen he awkwardly bid Tsara good morning. Baatar doubted he would ever get used to speaking to a falcon. As the pair stood in silence, a hasty rapping noise came from the outside door. Peeking through a crack in the wood Baatar saw that a young boy stood on the step hopping on the spot excitedly. He opened the door a little.

'Yes?' enquired Baatar.

'Sir, sir,' exclaimed the young boy. 'I have news for you, sir. It comes from a long way away, if you know what I mean.'

'I'm afraid I don't,' said Baatar. He took the letter and started to close the door. The young boy wedged his foot in the frame preventing it from closing. 'What?'

'Sir, sir,' said the young boy, 'the man that gave me the letter said that you would give me a coin for my troubles if I delivered it as fast as I could.'

'From what I can tell,' said Baatar, 'you're late.'

'Not my fault, sir,' said the boy. 'I had to find the man with the letter; he wasn't where he was supposed to be.'

'I fail to see the point,' said Baatar, 'the only thing I shall give you is a piece of advice – don't be late in the future!' With that Baatar shoved the boy's foot out of the way and closed the door hard against the outside world. He watched contentedly through the window as the young boy began to make his way away before opening the door and flipping a small shaman trinket in the child's direction. Elated, the boy ran off.

As the echo of the closing door rang out of the kitchen, Danyal and Millie entered the room.

'Who was that?' asked Danyal.

'Some boy with a letter,' said Baatar. He handed the envelope to Danyal, who hurriedly opened it.

'It's from Elder Chuluun!' exclaimed Danyal. 'He is arriving today on the outskirts of the city. He says that with Chinggis's help they have raised a considerable force. We are to sneak out of the city to meet them this afternoon.'

'Can we trust the letter?' asked Millie. 'We know the sorts of tricks Tengis is capable of.'

'It is signed "Lily",' said Danyal. 'That is good enough proof for me.' They all concurred.

That afternoon Drudger readied horses for them to ride out of town. So as to avoid suspicion they ventured forth in pairs: Danyal and Bolorerdene; Millie and Sukh; Drudger and Baatar. Tsara flew overhead keeping watch for anything untoward. If Tengis had suspected there was any opposition to his reign, then he was keeping it very quiet. As Danyal rode through the streets, he felt that there were fewer intimidating Leggy members hanging around on street corners demanding to see your papers than there had been for years.

On the outskirts of the city they all met up again and Danyal used the map that was crudely scribbled on the bottom of the page to lead them out into the borderlands that separated the city from the Steppe. The map directed them towards one of Millie's agricultural sites, and within half an hour they were out of immediate sight of the city. Following a rough track a few kilometres from Baatarulaan they began to round a broad rise in the landscape. As they did so they began to see troops massed, armed and ready for combat.

Danyal raised his hand in peace. The soldiers nearest him bowed slightly. Evidently they knew who he and his party were;

they were expected. The track wound around the bend a good deal further than they had expected. With each step hundreds more soldiers came into view, each on horseback and each carrying two bows and two sabres as well as a number of nasty-looking weapons Danyal didn't recognise. The party from Baatarulaan was awestruck

'My friends!' shouted Elder Chuluun. He rode through a mass of genuflecting bodies towards them. 'I am so glad you received my message. What do you think?'

'It is quite something,' replied Danyal.

'Bloomin' brilliant,' said Drudger.

'What about the young lady who made this all possible?' asked Elder Chuluun. Danyal and his company looked skyward. Elder Chuluun looked bemused. He was expecting to see a glamorous lady riding side-saddle. 'Where is she?'

'We're looking,' replied Drudger. 'She ain't always easy to spot.'

'Why on earth are you looking up there?' asked Elder Chuluun.

'What with her being a falcon and everything,' said Drudger. 'I'm guessing she likes to fly high; puts perspective on things, I'll wager.'

'A falcon?' said Elder Chuluun. 'Wh—what on earth are you talking about man? Chinggis! Chinggis? Come over here, will you? This fellow is saying that you are wed to a falcon. Shall I scold him for you or would you like the pleasure?'

'As a matter of fact I am,' said Chinggis. 'Tsara is a spirit; she takes the form most suited to her needs while she is in the physical world.'

Elder Chuluun rode away, slowly mumbling to himself about what he had heard being incredulous.

Chinggis turned to the new arrivals. 'You must be the friends of Lily that Tsara has told me about. I am indebted to you. My name is Chinggis Khaan and I am here to assist my friends in any way I can.'

'It looks like you've done a pretty good job corralling the troops,' said Danyal.

'He who wants to build high must dig deep,' said Chinggis.

'Who are they?' Danyal pointed towards a group of horsemen wrapped in black from head to toe. They carried no bows or sabres but had a multitude of the more interesting weaponry which Danyal had noticed on his way into camp.

'Ah them,' said Chinggis – he immediately knew to whom Danyal was referring – 'They're the Ninja Nomads. Fearsome fighters and fearless frighters. I had no idea they still existed. They were my elite squad back in the day. It took some effort to track them down but here they are. Five hundred of the scariest men you will ever meet.'

This appealed greatly to Danyal, who was yet to recover from the loss of the Hairy Hordes. 'Can I meet them?'

Chinggis beckoned over their leader and Danyal was readily taken up into their throng; they had heard all about the Hairy Hordes and had many questions to ask about urban warfare.

'How are preparations coming along?' asked Millie.

Chinggis informed them that they had arrived the previous day, over nine thousand of them. During the night their numbers had been swelled by over a thousand as people fled the city to join them. Tengis was not nearly as popular, or even feared, as he liked to believe.

'They are bringing stories about Outsiders,' said Chinggis.

'We knew that,' replied Tsara. She swooped out of the sky and landed on Chinggis's shoulder.

'Yes,' replied Chinggis, 'but we didn't expect them to be here so soon or there to be so many of them. From what we have heard there are five thousand Outsiders marching towards Baatarulaan as we speak. Tengis seems to be planning a complete coup of a country he already controls. He wants to replace his own security and Leggy with hired thugs. That shimmering substance has a lot to answer for.'

'What should we do?' asked Millie.

'We must ready ourselves,' said Chinggis. 'We must all be prepared to be as brave as Lily and willing to lay down our lives in the name of justice and peace if so required. For now, though, we rest. We can talk of violence tomorrow. For now I want to meet my descendants.'

Chinggis jumped down from his horse. He was deceptively agile given his muscular frame. He walked towards Sukh and Bolorerdene with his arms wide open. A broad grin filled his face. 'You must be my great great great great great great great great great great-grandchildren!'

31

It had been many years since Chinggis Khaan had last ridden into the city he had created. He did so proudly, leading from the front at the head of his army. Ten thousand troops rode behind him. Every one of them was intent on destroying Tengis and Khad. Not a single person stirred at this early hour. The streets lay deserted. Trashy neon lights offering videos, fun and shows that were apparently 'three times more exciting' than any other flickered in the dawn.

'*Morindoo!*' shouted Chinggis.

The ancient call inspired them all. Each soldier pulled tight their helmet and readied their bows. Aged between fifteen and sixty, each and every able man living on the Steppe had answered to Chinggis's call. More importantly, their numbers were bolstered by every woman skilled in hunting, fighting and killing. There were many such women on the Steppe. The army rode slowly onwards, deeper into the city.

Using the signalling banners, Chinggis orchestrated his troops. He knew if he could choose the time and place of engagement he could best configure his attacks to suit his army. If he kept a tight rein over proceedings, he could relocate and reassign troops to the areas where most damage could be done and save them from futile or potentially costly skirmishes. Before the divisions split off into their pre-designated positions, Chinggis gathered his key generals close to him. Once when Chinggis had led his hordes into Italy he had met a fearsome warrior with an amazing life story and now, remembering his friend, he knew exactly what to say:

'Three weeks from now, I will be harvesting my loins. Imagine where you will be, and it will be so. Hold the time! Stay with me! If you find yourself alone, riding in the vast Steppe with the cold sun on your face, do not be troubled. For you are in the spirit world, and you're already dead!'

The generals raised their bows in the air, and their action rippled throughout the entire army. Ten thousand armoured arms held aloft their weapon of choice. The battle was upon them.

In the centre of Baatarulaan things were less ordered. Tengis lay in wait. The central square was overflowing with Leggy and hired thugs – more than twelve thousand of them. Tengis would see his victory marked in the city square that Chinggis had first built. It would be a fitting end to the one man whose reputation remained above his own. He had constructed a platform in the middle of the square from where he would watch the proceedings. The prospect thrilled him. He hoped his enemy would put up a better show than their previous encounter. After all he had cleared his diary especially for the whole day.

Khad whispered constantly in his ear, stirring up Tengis's mounting fury. Almost all of Tengis's remaining Ongolian troops took up ranks as foot soldiers and wielded large curved sabres. The remainder formed a cavalry which remained hidden out of sight in adjacent side streets. The Outsiders were to be used as archers. Tengis had worked with Oldortar to devise a wide variety of arrows for them, many with special purposes including some that could pierce armour, others that could stun foes and others still, dipped in poison.

'Why do they not simply give up?' asked Tengis.

'Because they are Mongols,' replied the voice in his head.

'Two bears in one cave will not end up well. So you must destroy Chinggis once and for all.'

'That's the plan,' said Tengis.

Tsara soared overhead unseen by Tengis. She swooped back to Chinggis now and then to tell him what Tengis and his troops were doing, where they were stationed and what routes looked most advantageous. As Baatar and Sukh led the cavalry down the main road leading to the square, Tsara kept a close watch on what Tengis's reaction would be. He did nothing but wait. Chinggis had insisted on trying to draw some of the troops out of the square. They had told him that this tactic had failed on the Steppe but he was adamant he would try again. As the cavalry neared the square, Tsara noticed that Tengis's cavalry had moved position to side streets leading towards where her allies were headed. *Blong!* The sound ripped through Tsara and she struggled not to plummet from the sky. She had forgotten the sound of terror that had tormented her last moment in the real world. *Blong!* Fighting against her fears, she raced back to Chinggis to tell him about the trap. Just in time.

A banner was waved and Chinggis's cavalry stopped just short of the ambush. Another banner waved and the Ninja Nomads slunk off their horses, climbed the sides of the adjacent buildings and set off across the rooftops leading to Tengis's cavalry. Beneath their black face masks they wore broad smiles. They simply loved killing people. Danyal had taken a crash course in their particular brand of warfare and Drudger watched as his friend sprang from perilous window sill to dizzying ledge with the nimblest of ease. Danyal had learned all about the strange implements with which the Ninja Nomads fought. Strapped to his belt were throwing stars, poisoned darts and knives for hand-to-hand combat. In his pockets were secreted a number of compounds of varying use. Some caused smoke, others blindness, while others caused small explosions. Strapped to his

back was a light double-edged sabre. As he sprang from building to building, he felt like the cat who'd got the cream.

The Ninja Nomads readily arrived upon the buildings
surrounding Tengis's hidden cavalry. Half of them dropped
invisibly into their midst. Throwing exploding compound all
around, the Ninja Nomads publicised their arrival. They sowed
chaos in the middle of the enemy and ran away. The cavalry
horses were so startled their masters could not control them
and they chased after the men in black. Tsara relayed this to
Chinggis, who ordered his own cavalry to charge towards the
square, retreat and draw the enemy away from the square into
the road.

As Tengis's army chased down the men in black, the Ninja
Nomads turned, stood their ground and ruthlessly cut through
the horsemen using their throwing weapons. By the time the
last horse arrived, its rider could see that every horseman ahead
of him had been executed. A gentle swishing of metal flying
through the air announced his own imminent demise. The men
in black sprang away from the scene of the crime and returned
to Chinggis.

Baatar's charge worked. A number of Tengis foot soldiers
could not resist chasing after the fleeing horsemen. As they ran
after them, they walked straight into the path of the remaining
Ninja Nomads who had stealthily positioned themselves to
cause maximum carnage. From their positions on either side
of the road and using blowpipes and knives, they slaughtered
at will.

By the time Baatar's horsemen had returned to Chinggis both
Ninja Nomad groups had wiped out over a thousand men.
The streets ran red with the blood of Tengis's men. The psycho-
logical terror that spread through the square could not be
controlled. Tengis's troops screamed like infants. In contrast,
Chinggis remained silent. He had not lost a single soldier,

although two of the Ninja Nomads had sprained an ankle as they tried to do a combined triple somersault with double twist and spangly fleckles.

Blong! Tsara sped into the sky to see what Tengis was planning. She saw his foot soldiers forming ranks facing towards Chinggis. Those who refused to stop screaming were slain where they stood by their officers. Over three hundred men lost their lives on this account. *Blong!* Behind the lines of foot soldiers Tsara could see the Outsiders lining up ready to fire. In their midst they wheeled a dozen carts. She swooped lower to investigate and was almost sliced in half by an over-exuberant foot soldier. The carts each held an enormous crossbow. The bolts she saw being loaded into them were the length of two horses. Horrified, she shot back to her lover. Chinggis hastily ordered a banner to be waved and his entire army split into the streets that ran off the spine of the main road. When Tengis ordered the Outsiders to fire, the bolts flew past Chinggis and came to rest at the city limits. The volleys of specially crafted arrows snapped and bent as they hit the pebbled road. He couldn't allow himself a moment to relax but Chinggis was pleased with the way things were going so far. *Blong!* Once more Tsara flew into the sky to investigate.

Tengis began to move his foot soldiers down the road towards Chinggis's troops. Their movement was aided by regular volleys from the Outsider archers who covered their progress. Chinggis ordered Baatar to lead the cavalry to circle the square. Sukh was told to position himself behind the square ready to rush upon his great- (times ten) grandfather's command. The Ninja Nomads were ordered to move between his cavalry and the advancing foot soldiers, and carry out opportunistic hit-and-run operations.

As the main body of Tengis's men approached, the banner signalling attack was raised. Chinggis's archers acted as one and sent a vast cloud of arrows soaring through the smog. The advancing foot soldiers began to fall. None of them wore any armour. Khad had advised Tengis that it was a better use of the budget to pay for more Outsiders than to protect their own men. He argued that they had such numerical supremacy that such protection would be a moot point. As the clouds burst upon his foot soldiers, Tengis watched in horror as Khad was proved irrefutably wrong. Tengis was about to chastise the voice in his head when he heard the Outsiders starting to shout and run about wildly. From behind his elevated position he watched as Sukh and his horsemen bore a hole straight into the heart of the square. Simultaneously, Baatar attacked from both sides, squeezing the Outsiders closer towards Tengis and his Council and separating them from the foot soldiers they were supposed to be protecting. Ninja Nomads assaulted the foot soldiers from all around as soon as their own and their enemy's arrows stopped raining on to Tengis's parade.

Chinggis called Tsara to report back. She flew into the sky above the bloodshed and watched in dismay as more and more people fell. They may have been enemies but she knew that most of them had been coerced by fear. Those who had joined of their own free will were only there for the shimmering substance; they didn't have any real loyalty towards Tengis or Khad. Other than those in power she had never heard of anyone who did.

'They have lost over one-third of their troops,' said Tsara. 'It is horrific; it's worse than the Steppe. Tengis has as good as sacrificed his men, so poorly trained and protected are they. Please show mercy.'

'We shall see,' said Chinggis.

He ordered banners to be waved, ordering an immediate halt to their attack, if only momentarily. Chinggis rode forward accompanied by his private guard. As he neared the foot soldiers that had previously been advancing up the road towards him, they parted to allow him to pass. Many fell to the floor, fearful of the legendary emperor. When Chinggis arrived at the square, he could see the wooden plinth on which Tengis and his close friends stood. Around its perimeter stood the Outsiders fanning out thirty men deep. An eerie silence pervaded Baatarulaan. As Chinggis rode into the square, he noted that the Outsiders held captured soldiers or even their own foot soldiers as a barrier around the front of them. Chinggis had never witnessed a human shield before and it sickened him; *kharash* had only ever been a dreadful legend but here Tengis had made horror reality.

'I wish to speak to your leader,' shouted Chinggis. All around him there was hush.

Those closer to the plinth looked up at Tengis, who remained still. Even the voice in his head was afraid to speak. If ever Tengis needed Khad's help, it was now but with everything going wrong Khad had seemingly decided to remain hidden within Tengis's cranium.

'Tengis. Khad. I know you can hear me. Come forward. If you are man enough, let us decide this as men; otherwise, I will kill your family and then I will kill your friends until there is no one left alive you know and then I will slowly rip your rotting heart from your chest.

'To you, fine soldiers of fortune, I am aware that your leader has promised you wealth. If you will willingly put down your weapons, I will show clemency. I will let those that live here return home. I will let those who are from outside this country return home. That is the wealth I offer you. It is better than anything your leader may have promised. Do you really think he is a man of his word? Do you trust that he would fulfil his promise to you? He is a despotic maniac, nothing more. If you wish to keep fighting, I will personally make sure that each of you gets to see your spleen as it is torn from your cadaver and fed to the dogs. Your call.'

With that Chinggis turned and began to ride back to his troops.

All around the city the clatter of falling sabres, spears, arrows, bows and knives resounded. The Ongolian soldiers fell prostrate upon the ground as one. The Outsiders turned to one another, sought approval and subsequently dropped their weapons. Only Oldortar remained defiant and aimed an arrow at Chinggis's back. From above Tengis's leader of the Leggy was rent asunder. Tengis turned just in time to see a falcon speed downwards and straight through the helmet of his general. The lifeless corpse of Oldortar slid to the floor, still clutching his bow. Tengis watched as the bird flew across the square, its face bloodied by the life of his comrade, and settled on the shoulder of his nemesis.

'Chinggis!' cried Tengis. 'Who are you that you control the hearts of men? Who are you that you can hold power over the wild beasts of our country?'

'I am merely a man,' said Chinggis, 'but I am a man all the same. I am a man who cannot sleep while his people suffer; who cannot rest while his nation hurts; who will not stop until justice prevails. That is who I am.'

With that Tengis fell to his knees and sobbed. Opportunist Outsiders ran up the steps to the plinth and arrested their former leader and his Council. Across the square an old woman let out a sigh of relief as she looked out from a window up on high. She was happy to at least see her son alive. Chinggis turned to look into Tengis's eyes. Once satisfied that Tengis had indeed surrendered, he turned and rode back to his men. Operation Falling Star was a success.

32

Although gaining victory had helped Chinggis feel like he had once felt long ago, his feelings for Tsara were stronger. So long as he remained in the real world he could not be with her. He could be with a falcon that spoke like her but it wasn't the same.

'Why did you write that riddle?' asked Tsara. 'It really confused Lily.'

'You mean it confused you!' said Chinggis. 'Have you worked it out yet?'

'I think so,' replied Tsara. 'The tiger was Tengis?'

'That was obvious,' replied Chinggis.

'His bell was terrible,' said Tsara. 'It brought about Lily's death but also starved Tengis of power because of his blind belief in its power. The cats were the fattened, lazy rich of Baatarulaan who willingly pledged allegiance to whoever wielded the most power at a given moment while making sure they never once endangered themselves.'

'Indeed,' said Chinggis, 'what about Heaven and Earth?'

'That puzzled me for a while,' said Tsara, 'well, at least until I realised that I was both Lily and Tsara. I should have known sooner from all my voyages into the spirit world. Some shawoman I am! So, that was your riddle? Why did you write it?'

'I needed to remind you of me,' said Chinggis. 'I needed to help you remember that I still existed.'

After a brief discussion Tsara and Chinggis joined their friends and announced that they would be returning to the spirit world. Sukh, Bolorerdene, Danyal, Millie, Elder Chuluun and Baatar were dismayed.

'What about Tengis?' asked Sukh. 'What do you want us to do about him?'

'I'm not a vengeful man,' replied Chinggis, 'but I think there is a little bit of Khad in Tengis. It would only be fair that he faced the same fate as I suffered. Here take this.' He tossed his great- (times ten) grandson a parchment. 'Follow this map. You will find two caves there. One of them is an icy grotto that well befits the heart of Tengis. Encase him there in a coffin of ice. If Odval insists, which I am sure she will, place her in a similar sarcophagus alongside. Then block the grotto. There can be no escape. Let them both enjoy watching one another perish without being able to comfort the other.' His friends looked on in silence. Although this was a horrific fate to befall anybody each of them knew that it was deserved. 'To his Council, show mercy but keep them close.'

'What about the other cave?' asked Sukh.

'I'll leave that as a surprise,' answered Chinggis. 'Consider it a parting gift.'

'Who shall run Ongolium?' asked Baatar. 'What shall we do with Baatarulaan?'

'First and foremost,' said Chinggis, 'it is Mongolia. This city is Ulaanbaatar. Never let anyone speak otherwise. Our hearts and instincts have brought us far. Now that I know my bloodline still flows I am confident that my empire can again be as great as it once was. No one man or woman should run a country. Accordingly, Bolorerdene, you shall be empress; Sukh, you shall be emperor. However, things change and you can't put two saddles on the same horse. From this day on Mongolia shall lead the way as a shining democracy. My descendants shall be emperors in name and title only. The real power will be formed by the people for the people. I task you, my friends, who have helped rescue our nation, to form the first coalition. Just assure me that you will allow the people to reassess your position every few years. Working together will forge a path to the future but remember, we are but one nation. I have seen what else exists; look beyond our border – there is a whole world out there. Rest assured that I will return here from time to time.'

With those final words Chinggis walked away with Tsara on his shoulder. Some distance away her form changed into that of her former self. Holding Chinggis' hand they walked on. Nobody was sure where they were going and nobody ever found out.